THE INVISIBLE HAND

BENJAMIN SOBIECK

NEW PULP PRESS

Published by New Pulp Press, LLC, 926 Truman Avenue, Key West, Florida 33040, USA.

The Invisible Hand copyright © 2014, 2015 Benjamin Sobieck. Electronic compilation/ paperback edition copyright © 2015 by New Pulp Press LLC.

For information contact:
Publisher@NewPulpPress.com

ISBN-13: 978-0692565278 (New Pulp Press)
ISBN-10: 0692565272

"*Every individual...neither intends to promote the public interest, nor knows how much he is promoting it. By preferring the support of domestic to that of foreign industry he intends only his own security; and by directing that industry in such a manner as its produce may be of the greatest value, he intends only his own gain, and he is in this, as in many other cases, led by an invisible hand to promote an end which was no part of his intention.*"

~ Adam Smith, *The Wealth of Nations*

"*The government, which was designed for the people, has got into the hands of the bosses and their employers, the special interests. An invisible empire has been set up above the forms of democracy.*"

~ Woodrow Wilson, 28th president of the United States

PART ONE: DOWSE

On June 17, 2014, after decades of development, oil production in North Dakota surpassed 1 million barrels per day, earning the state the nickname "Saudi Dakota." Wide use of hydraulic fracturing (a/k/a "fracking") methods ignited an oil boom in 2006 that continues to this day.

The following takes place in the fall of 2012.

Chapter 1

*T*wo beers later, the bartender in front of the Confederate flag decides I've been silent long enough.

"Got somewhere to be, Wil? Don't seem interested in being here," he says. Checks his watch.

He's no rebel. A Yankee through and through. Just a businessman. The other bar on the far side of town, it's called the Union. That's what passes for clever around here.

"Yeah, I'll have another one. Just thinking about … stuff," I say. Such as getting off the dot of a barstool seat in a pin of a central North Dakota prairie town, Betrug. And killing my neighbor's sick wife.

"I didn't offer another one," the bartender says.

"You are now," I say.

A wet mug materializes next to my parched hands.

"Plenty to think about these days," the bartender says. Nods to the radio.

The news report says something about a murder in the Bakken. No surprises there.

Bakken. That's the name for the oil patch. It's where hydraulic fracturing – "fracking" – sparked the NoDak oil boom a few years back. Suicide with a paycheck.

"Good to know the trouble is staying out there," I say. I hate competition.

Betrug, nestled inside Sheridan County, is still an hour or so from the boom. Close enough to inherit its problems. Too far away to reap any benefits.

"Hard to keep it that way," the bartender says. Calls out to the man in jeans behind me. He's been watching me drink from the far side of the bar. "Ain't that right, sheriff?"

The sheriff sighs. Nods. Goes back to his sandwich and

newspaper. Working on hour three of lunch.

"You're young enough," the bartender says. "Still got a strong back. Go and make your oil money. It's a wonder why you sit in here all day."

"Who says I'm not making money?" I say. Pay for the drinks.

The bartender looks over the $100 bill.

"I guess you are. You want change?" he says.

"Keep it."

"You been back at your family's farm? Started working again?" the bartender says.

"Nope. Not since the accident," I say.

The sheriff clears his throat behind me. I keep staring straight ahead.

"Think you'll get back into farming?" the bartender says.

"Nope."

The bartender hesitates before putting the $100 bill in the register. Thumbs a corner like he's testing for a fake.

"OK. I won't ask again," he says. Not the first time he's seen a $100.

Don't give me this bleeding heart bullshit about the "poor farmers" out here. There aren't any. Every one of them is a millionaire times 10. Even more so now that the oil boom hit.

They don't clear a couple million in a year, the feds give it to them for nothing. But they still dress like prairie dogs. Flannel shirts. Shitty trucks. Dirty hair.

It ain't like it used to be. Now you've got GPS tractors. Remote-controlled everythings. Crops that do the thinking for you. Insurance, subsidies, trade protection and shit-knows-what-else ag programs. All greased with PR straight out of the Dustbowl.

Means there's plenty of time to sit and think out here. Sort of like what I'm doing now in this bar. That's all there is to do. Think too long, you come up with solutions to problems that don't exist.

Good thing. Keeps me employed.

Farmers, they want to keep a certain image. Like the smiling cows on the milk cartons. Or the elves on cereal boxes full of what they grow here.

Bullshit. They move more money in a day than a drug lord. Got the temper to match. I'm just the part of the equation that's honest about it.

Things get dirty. Fifty-foot manure pile dirty. So they turn to me. Shovel their shit. Bust some noses. Break some laws. Get it together.

Which is about what my dad said the day before he died in that grain bin. The "accident."

"Get yourself together," he had said. "For the sake of your mother. You're 22. Been kicking around the prairie since you graduated high school. Find something you're good at. Then do it every day."

Yeah, I found something. She's sitting right next to me. With long hair of amber bubbles. She's always in the mood. Goes down real nice. Especially with one of those fresh-off-the-farm burgers they serve here. Shit, even in this prairie dog bar, you can't get off the fucking farm.

But that's just how it goes. I was too fucked up to work hay and heads. Never went east to Minneapolis like anyone with a brain. Never went west to the oil boom a county over like anyone with muscle.

Nope. Just slid right into this seat and took my dad's advice. "Find something you're good at. Then do it every day."

Sure thing, pa. Cheers. Drink up. Oh, and fuck your self-righteous work ethic. As if everyone will fit into one of three options out here. Farm, frack or get the fuck out. But I'm stuck like everyone else in this jar of flies.

Oh, and rest in peace, pa. Which is damn near impossible considering the way you died in that bin. Crushed to death under a frozen chunk of grain.

Anyway, it ain't a thing no more. It's done. I'm here. Got some money. Got some drink. And, in about 30 seconds, a job.

I know what's coming. What I'll be asked to do. A bubble of panic crawls into my chest.

I pull an eyelash out. Stoke the pain with the sharp edge of a fingernail against my eyelid. A quick jolt runs from my eyelid into my chest. Pops the panic bubble. The feeling of it dissipating is worth it, even if my eyelids are going bald.

I'd normally check to see if the lash has a gooey root at the end. Maybe even eat it. But my appointment just walked through the door.

"You Wil?" the big guy says.

"If you say so," I say.

The parts of his face not coated in two fat inches of whisker bramble show the scars of the wind. It finds a crease when you're young. Pulls hard on it the rest of your life. Slices away until your face looks like the Badlands.

"How about I call you Buy Me a Drink?" the big guy says.

"How about not. Beer's cheap here. Buy it yourself," I say between a sip.

"Don't look like you got anything better to do," the big guy says. Uses a tone I don't appreciate.

"I'm doing exactly what I need to do," I say.

"Come on. Just one," the big guy says.

"Fine. You owe me two," I say.

I motion the bartender over. He pours a mug of glorified piss water. I get a buck poorer.

We drink in silence. He takes the beer down like it's medicine.

Then he says, "Sorry to be a bother just then. You know how we Gideons are. Can't be seen buying alcohol."

Oh, yeah. I know the Gideons. Those motel nightstand

missionaries.   Bible-thumping,   prairie-humping hypocrites. Take Exhibit A, for example.

"So why'd you want to meet with me, Joe?" I say. Order another round. Forget to ask if he wants one.

"Ah, so you remember me," Joe says. "When we talked on the phone yesterday, I couldn't tell if you did."

"You taught my math class in grade school. Up until they shut the district down. Not enough kids. Not even after the consolidation. Wound up being home-schooled. Maybe that's why I'm getting shit-faced in a bar right now. What's your excuse?" I say.

"It's a shame things went the way they did. You learned how to count to 10. Then they sent you home," he says.

I down my beer. Order another one.

"Counting to 10 is all I needed. This beer is number nine. Two more to go before I'm back at one. Then I'm good to drive again. I'm pretty busy. What do you want from me?" I say.

I already know the answer. This is just part of the dance. An attempt at looking like two regular people having a conversation.

Joe scoots closer to me. I smell the earth in his skin. The wind paints it into you. Never washes out.

"I need a set of hands," he says.

"I don't do fences," I say.

"You know what I mean," Joe says in a whisper. His eyes dart to the sheriff behind me.

I get up from the stool.

"Outside. Give me five minutes," I say. Head to the bathroom. Too much beer too fast on too empty of a stomach.

In my mind, I hear, "Find something you're good at. Then do it every day." Fuck me if I can't even drink right.

I try not to look at the reflection in the toilet water as I hurl.

Chapter 2

J oe's truck. Still parked outside the bar. Windows rolled up. Wind presses against the glass like it's trying to peek inside.

"I need you to grant someone the mercy of ending her life," he says, plain as the miles-wide prairie view.

"Who is it?" I say.

Joe shakes his head. "People always said you were a screw up. But I didn't think it was this bad. You didn't even blink at what I said. Not even for a second."

It's not like I didn't know he wants his wife dead. Joe is a terrible secret-keeper. Always has been. Word got around on the prairie.

"Joe, the correct term is 'fuck up.' You can drop the Gideon church-mouth. If you think this is the first time I've been asked to kill someone, you're wrong," I say.

That's a lie. He doesn't need to know that.

I mainly do collections. Farmer-to-farmer stuff. Someone's cattle got into someone else's grain. Someone's chemicals went missing and showed up somewhere else. Someone trespassed and broke a farming implement.

Plenty of work in that line. People stay sore for years. They don't want to settle up in court. Too much open space around here to piss around with formalities.

"Fine. Yes, you're an f-up," Joe says. I grin at his self-censorship. "And I need you to ki...end someone's life. With compassion."

"You're being pretty blunt about this, too. If I was a cop, I could bring you in right now," I say.

Joe shrugs. In his best teacher voice, he says, "But you're not a cop."

Condescending prick.

I say, "Nope. I'm no one. Which is why you came to me in the first place. I take it our murder victim is your sick wife?"

Joe fires up the truck. He says, "Yes. And don't call it murder. It's an act of mercy."

"We'll compromise. Let's call it homicide. How's that, Gideon?"

Joe's eyes never leave the road the rest of drive.

Chapter 3

J oe is a big guy even by prairie standards. Thick. The kind that infuriates the wind's religious zeal to make everything lean east. Joe, he just leans right back.

So it only makes sense his wife, Elma, is also on the solid side. Not fat. Solid. Like the bison that used to live here.

But even I'm surprised by her condition once we get to the house. She's spilling out from a love seat in the living room. They've become one.

The room smells of warm skin. Salty and fried by wind burn. Like the ocean I'll never see.

Joe folds his hands. Looks me in the eye.

He says, "She's napping. It's all she does any more. Her body can't keep up. We found out about the diabetes last month. Turns out she's had it for a year."

I get where he's going.

A squirt of panic flutters in my chest again. I pinch out an eyelash when Joe's not looking.

I've put down sick livestock before. Simple as a bullet and a tractor ride. Maybe a mercy killing for a person isn't all that different.

But here's the thing. Elma doesn't look *that* sick. I thought she was near death.

It's one thing if someone needs that extra push to stop the misery. This is a little different. Not what I was expecting.

"You can't be serious," I say. "She's in rough shape, sure. But this isn't a mercy kill. This is just a kill."

Joe nods. He taps a Gideon Bible on the table next to us.

"Compassion for others, that's what the Bible says.

9

She's done living. It's time to bring her home. Seriously," he says.

For a second, I swear Elma slips an open eye to me. Like she was saying, "Seriously? What the hell do you think you're doing?"

Could be it was part of her sleeping. But I've seen that look before. Walking up to a lame cow. That nervous glance as I approached.

I saw it in my father's eyes, too. Or *eye*, rather. Right as the truck-sized chunk of frozen grain at the top of the bin came down on him. Maybe he saw the same in my eyes as I tried to tug him out.

One thing I know for sure, though. His last expression. It was a mix of shock and something you can't understand unless you actually watch a person die. Up close. Near enough to feel the heat of the body dissipating into the air.

The wind picked up the moment he died. I prayed it would take me with it. Off to join the herd of rushing bison shapes that curl over the tall grass as the wind blows. Shadows of the prairie that used to be.

Yet there I stood. No one disappears on the prairie.

I scrape a fingernail over the bald spot in my eyelashes. Breathe out a shiver of pain.

"Anything in that Bible tell you to get her to a doctor?" I say to Joe. One last attempt at salvaging humanity.

"We'd have to go several times a week. That's a lot of time away from the farm. We'd go broke. Work won't get itself done," Joe says.

"Seriously? This is a financial decision? You can't hire help?" I say. "Take her to the fucking doctor already."

"No. It's time to give her the mercy she deserves," Joe says.

The second he says it, the look on his face takes it back. He gets a little wet in the eyes. Lip starts shaking.

"You're not making any sense," I say.

"I know what this looks like," Joe says. "I don't know how else to say it. She's in so much pain every day. This is the right thing to do. You have to believe me."

Elma lets out a wheeze. Tries to shuffle onto her side. Doesn't work. Her eyes stay shut.

I swear I hear something in that wheeze. Can't make it out.

"Did you ask if that's what she wants?" I say.

"I can tell that's what she wants. I promise," Joe says.

"Doesn't look like Elma does a lot of talking," I say. Back away from Joe. "Are you sure there isn't another option?"

"It only looks like there are options. I've agonized, *agonized*, over this," Joe says. Takes a step toward me. "If you can't do this, I'll find someone who will."

"And risk me ratting you out? Even you're not that dumb," I say.

"You're the low-life here. You trying to tell me you're above this?" Joe says.

I want to say I am. But I ignore that bit of sense. Maybe in another life I was above it. Not anymore. There's no sense in anything out here. People die for stupid reasons all the time. Crushed under frozen grain. Sucked into an implement. Torn in half by a tractor. The least you can do is make a little scratch along the way.

"Let's talk about the money. I get half of the life insurance payout," I say to Joe. "Deal?"

I'm sure Elma has life insurance. Farmers have insurance for everything.

Joe nods. "Deal. Do it."

"How are you going to deal with the body?" I say.

"Bury her in the backyard. Like pioneer times. No need to get anyone else involved," Joe says.

It's not entirely unheard of these days. Tradition still matters. The nearest funeral parlor is 100 miles away. No one disappears on the prairie, not even in death. They just become it.

We stand there for a few awkward seconds.

"Uh, Joe, how do you intend on me killing her?" I say. "I'm not really about strangulation."

Joe shakes out of a deep stare at the floor.

"Oh, yeah, of course. Let me go get the gun," he says.

I watch him walk downstairs to the basement. Take the opportunity to stroll into the kitchen from the living room.

There's a row of coffee mugs hooked to the wall. Each one sports "Seriously!?" printed in big black letters on it. Word is they won them from a TV game show of the same name. Some sort of mail-in sweepstakes.

Joe comes back with a clunky 12-gauge Mossberg 500 pump-action shotgun. Produces a box of 6 shot. I stare at him like he's holding two shrunken skulls.

"Are we hunting pheasants?" I say. Sixes are for birds. Not people. How compassionate.

"I threw away all my bigger loads. I didn't want to let myself do...it...to her," Joe says.

"Way to think this through," I say.

It doesn't matter anyway. At such close range, the blast will be lethal. I'm trying to stall him out. Still having a hard time with this one.

I could take the shotgun and leave right there. But then what? Joe reports me to the sheriff? Says I stole a shotgun? I don't need the sheriff asking me why I was at Joe's place.

Joe shakes his head. "Just do it before I change my mind."

I take the shotgun. Feed the magazine full. Cycle the pump to chamber a shell.

Joe leaves the living room. Walks to the kitchen. Takes the "Seriously!?" mug off the wall. Fills it with coffee from a hot machine. I tell myself Elma didn't brew it before we got here.

I swallow and say, "Aren't you going to stand next to me for the big event?"

"I'll be OK from here," he says.

His back turns to me as he looks out the window. I hear a sniffle. Doesn't make him any more a saint than I am.

Elma stirs on the couch. That one eye rolls over me. Then the shotgun. Slips back under the crinkled blanket of her meaty eyelid. Long lashes on those lids. Not like the short bristles on mine.

I bring the shotgun to my shoulder. Aim for her face. Makes it look like she has a silver bead for a nose. Like a clown. Gives me a little grin.

People make all sorts of funny faces before they die. My father's left eye popped out as the frozen grain chunk hit him. He palmed it back in crooked. Fell right back out.

Dumb bastard. Should've spent that time trying to get free. He didn't know how dead he was until a few seconds later. Then he really started making faces.

I made some weird ones that day, too. Ones I'm glad he couldn't tell people about. Like when I realized I should have said something about the cracking sounds as he entered the bin. How something seemed off.

I lower the shotgun. Dig for an eyelash. Grab a clump of five or six with my nails. Give it a tug. Pop the gooey, hairy cluster into my mouth. Split the hairs with my front teeth. Swallow.

"Can you hurry this up, Wil?" Joe says from the other room.

I think of the moment my father died. When the wind picked up. Prairie wind, make me go away. Take me with you. Away from here.

I raise the shotgun. Pulling the eyelashes didn't work

this time. The knotted up panic in my gut comes back again. Overwhelming.

"Please, Wil. Do it. I can't take it anymore," Joe says. Starts toward me.

Neither can I.

Joe is five steps away when I spin on my heel to face him. I line the bead of the shotgun up with his left eye. The same one that popped out of my father's head just before he made that face. Like the one Joe is making now.

There's no more room in my guts for another gallon of guilt. Especially when it's Joe laundering his own through me. Thought the beers would convince me otherwise. Failed. I need justice. An equilibrium. Not guilt.

So I do the only thing I can think of in the moment. I pull the trigger. Send the BBs spiraling down the long tunnel of my vision.

Joe's face sauces the wall behind him. I stay in position until his body stops moving. It grinds against the wall before folding onto the floor.

Elma convulses in the love seat. She's mumbling something with both eyes open. Her legs shuffle in place. I can hear her now.

"Waaaa ... aaannnn ... want," she says.

No sense in leaving her to wait to die. *Now* it's a mercy kill.

I pump the shotgun. Plant the bead over her mouth. Squeeze the trigger slow. It's a surprise when the shotgun fires.

The whole thing takes as long as a chunk of frozen grain falling to the ground.

I pocket the spent shotgun shells. Find Joe's keys. Head to the truck.

The setting sun casts shadows over the prairie. They look like people. Stretching their hands toward me. Shadow people. Pushing me away. Or pulling me in.

I fire up Joe's truck. Let the grooves of the scarred prairie point me in a direction. Any direction. Just get me the hell out of here.

I tug out an eyelash and I'm gone.

Chapter 4

"It's Wil Reynolds. I'm sure of it," Sheriff Red Smith says.

He tucks in his shirt for the third time that day. He's crouched down thrice now. Head soup sticks to his boots.

So much for an undisturbed crime scene. Red doesn't particularly care, though.

"Very philosophical, Red. I'm sure he'll come running back to us then," Gus says. Cracks a smile. Lights a cigarette.

"Put that out," Red says. Paces to Joe and Elma's kitchen. Grabs a mug off the wall. "Seriously!?" is printed on the side.

Game show coffee mugs. That's Joe for you. No gimmick he wouldn't pass up. Used to say it summed up his take on life.

Used to.

Red pours himself a coffee. Been scalding in the ancient machine for about a day now. Extra black. Like drinking a cigarette.

"Elma smoked like a prescribed burn when Joe wasn't around," Gus says.

Gus is what the county calls a "reserve deputy." A sort of on-call citizen backup. That's not what Red calls him.

"Shit for brains," Red says. "Show some respect."

Red enjoys saying "shit." It's the highest acceptable cuss on the prairie for a respectable person like him.

"Fuck" is out of the question. Any curses involving "God" are also frowned upon. "Ass" or "asshole" is a gray area.

The unwritten rules weed out the people who don't belong on the prairie. Makes Red's job easier. Especially since the oil boom hit.

"You're right. Respect the dead and all," Gus says. Grinds the cigarette into the carpet. "So are we gonna play 'Smokey and the Bandit' today or what?"

"No. We're going to play, 'Where Did Joe's Truck Go?'" Red says. "Don't overthink the math. Joe is here. The truck is gone."

Gus checks the window. "Yup. That truck is gone. Gone-gone. Not here anymore, I can tell you that," he says.

"Wil and Joe drove off together from the bar in town. I was eating lunch inside. Watched them leave," Red says. "Find Joe's truck, I bet we find Wil."

"Tell me, Mr. Ace Detective. How do know so much about this? You swung by this house on a whim earlier today. Found Joe and Elma in a mess like this. And you also know Wil is our killer," Gus says. Cracks his knuckles. "You're the greatest, luckiest detective this planet has ever known. Or you know something I don't."

"It's him. It was Wil," Red says.

"But how do you know? Probably one of those freaks passing through."

Red fingers the badge in his pocket. It's never had a matching uniform. He's only flashed it once before. People around town know him well enough.

"Because I caught him in the act," Red says.

Chapter 5

"*H*oly fuck. Seriously?" Gus says.

They're out on the porch now. Roast beef sandwiches from the fridge commute between their hands and mouths.

"Don't talk like that. People'll think you're one of those oil boom out-staters. They'd steal the wig off a corpse," Red says.

"Run into any of them out-staters lately?" Gus says. Wipes his mouth with his shirt.

"Not since last month. Had one trying to thumb a ride at the gas station," Red says.

"Where was that one from?"

"South California. I don't want to know what he had to do to get there. Lots of lonely, over-the-road truckers out there."

"Ever met someone from California before that?" Gus says.

Red leaves out that the out-stater was black. Only the fourth or fifth man of such heritage he'd ever met.

"Nope. But he needed a map. He overshot. The Bakken oil patch is north and west of us," Red says. "Hitchhiking isn't a taxi service. These truckers stop where they stop. Then they're my problem."

"With what they pay just to pour coffee in Williston, I don't blame them for trying. Incredible money," Gus says. "These sandwiches are pretty incredible, too. Elma was one hell of a great cook."

"Elma hasn't cooked anything in years. Too sick. That's all Joe," Red says.

They head inside after finishing. Red picks up the rotary phone on the wall. Dials a number. Mumbles something to the person on the other end. Hangs up.

"Body baggers will be here in a few hours," Red says. "Need to finish up in the Bakken first. Had another eventful night."

Gus picks at his teeth with a dirty fingernail.

"You say you caught Wil in the act. Why didn't you stop him? And why did you wait a day to call me over?" Gus says.

"The reasons are why you're still a reserve deputy," Red says. "First, I didn't wait a day. I started the investigation. Took a look around the property. Made some phone calls. That took me the whole day. Then I called you over.

"Second, I didn't stop Wil because he was in Joe's truck doing about 90 outside of town. I let him go. Moving violations are for out-staters, not neighbors. Made me curious, though. Followed the skid marks in the dirt back to this place. Found the bodies. Doesn't take the world's greatest detective to figure out."

Gus nods. Then looks confused.

"So why aren't we on the road right now?" he says. "Aren't we going to chase Wil down?"

Red pours another cup of coffee. Finishes it in two gulps. "No."

Chapter 6

"So we're letting a murderer go free? What?" Gus says. Stands next to the door.

Red turns on the faucet in the kitchen. Gives the "Seriously!?" mug a light rinse. Hangs it back on the wall.

"We are. But that doesn't mean he's going free," Red says.

"And that means what?"

"It means we're not the folks who are going to wrap this up. We need to be there for Betrug and the rest of the county. Officially, the state and the feds will take over," Red says.

Gus lights another cigarette. "Officially? So there's an unofficial plan, too?" he says.

Red's glare almost puts out the cigarette on its own. "I told you to stop with that shit."

Gus shrugs, takes another drag.

"You're proving my point," Red says. "You want to play cops and robbers. You don't know shit about shit."

"Fine, Red. I don't know shit about shit," Gus says.

Red plucks the cigarette away. Takes two drags before tossing it in the sink.

"Wil hasn't been right in the head since his dad died. Grain bin accident. You hear about that?" Red says.

"Yeah. Nasty stuff," Gus says.

"Now he's out killing people. We're just two prairie dogs with badges and a phone book," Red says. "Loose cows in crop fields, sure. Meth heads stealing anhydrous, sure. Double homicide with a runner? No. Not even close."

"Maybe the other agencies will let us ride along," Gus says. "They could probably use the help, right?"

"I called them. They're taking over the whole thing.

We'll be pushed to the side. Off the radar," Red says.

"Oh, I see. So you want to go rogue. Is that it?" Gus says. He grins.

"You need to stop watching so many movies. No. I just told you. We're not the people to do it," Red says. "But I still want skin in this game. This is my community. These are my people. We need to be there for them. We need an extra hand we can work from a distance. An invisible hand. Someone only we know about."

Gus looks over into the living room. One of Joe's eyeballs glued to the wall looks back.

"Your people are starting to stink," Gus says.

"I know someone who can help us. And only us. Not the state or feds. She does good work," Red says.

Gus's face drops like a curtain.

"She? As in *her*?" Gus says. "Didn't you swear her off after last time?"

Red nods. "I don't have a choice."

Now it's Gus's turn to be the voice of reason.

"You can say I don't know shit, fine. But I know this much. After last time, you told me to stop you from calling her," he says.

"This is different. She's the only one who can find him before anyone else," Red says.

"Why bother? Let the big wigs take care of it. It's their problem," Gus says. Relights the cigarette in his mouth.

Red crosses his arms. Leans on the counter. Stares upward. Watches the smoke curl up and flatten against the ceiling.

"People will have a hard time processing these murders. They don't want the story from the feds or the state. They want it from me. There won't be any closure otherwise," Red says.

"Seems like you're making this a bigger deal than it is," Gus says.

"No. Been into Betrug lately? Everyone's nervous. Too many horror stories coming out of the oil patch. Folks are worried the troubles are coming here," Red says. Steps to the phone on the wall. Dials nine numbers. Pauses before punching in the 10th. "I'm calling her. Now keep your mouth shut."

Chapter 7

S id knows the equations well.
Booze plus mouth equals stupid. Stupid plus car equals going too fast for the shitty engine to handle.

Put that mess on Interstate 35, the main north-south route in eastern Minnesota. What do you have? A drunk, stupid fugitive in a piece-of-shit stolen car broke down at a rest stop off Interstate 35 south of Duluth.

So why did Sid start his morning with booze? It only served to solve the algebra of the day in the worst way possible.

"You stupid, stupid, stupid fuck," Sid says to himself.

His fingers wrap tight around the steering wheel. He squeezes until his knuckles turn translucent.

The car is parked where it died. The right side is triple parked by the rest stop building. The rest hangs out into the lot. The place is empty except for Sid.

And a single highway patrol car. It pulls up behind him. No lights. No sirens.

Two uniformed officers get out. One man. One woman.

The man carries a stack of hazard cones. He places them at the rest stop entrance. That way no one from the interstate will drive up.

"Shit, shit, shit," Sid says. Watches in the rear view mirror. Checks the locks.

He bites a nail until it bleeds. Reminds him of the cut on his arm. Mugged in north Minneapolis earlier that day. Fucker took his gun.

The female officer waits until the cones are placed. Heads toward Sid. Then the male officer does something odd.

He gets back into the squad car.

Sid thinks how he should've gone with a different equation that day. When sticking up a bank, do it alone. The money is only split one way.

He had trouble with the splitting part after the heist. Couldn't do the math to divide the haul by three. So he simplified things. Cut down the split to just one person. Math doesn't have to be hard.

Sid rips at another fingernail. Blood runs down onto his palm. He discovers it after wiping sweat from his forehead. It smears red on his face like Maybelline grease.

He sucks his finger clean. The female officer is here.

A gloved hand knocks on the window. Sid rolls it down.

"Having car trouble?" the female officer says.

She leans her face close to his. Breathes in deep. Like she's scenting him.

Sid talks out of the side of his mouth. Tries to keep the booze on his breath from leaking out.

"Yup. Car died," he says.

"Why are you talking like that?" the female officer says.

"Like what?" Sid says.

"Like you're trying not to open your mouth," she says.

Sid shifts in his seat. Checks the mirrors. Why is that other officer still in the squad car? Don't they usually get out in pairs?

"That's just how I talk," he says.

"Don't lie to me. I can smell it on you," she says.

Sid stares at her. Which F comes after fight and flight if neither is an option? Freeze? Fib?

"I have a disability," Sid says.

A quick smile punches through the corner of the officer's mouth. She stuffs in back down.

"OK. Is your disability that you're drunk?" she says.

Sid relaxes his mouth and lets out a breath. No use in hiding it. At least he can breathe again.

He checks the mirrors. That male officer in the squad car isn't even paying attention.

"Do you want my driver's license?" Sid says.

"Sure. I'll return it to whomever you stole it from," the officer says.

The comment throws Sid off. He's never met an officer like this before.

He flips the license to her. She slips it into her pocket without checking the photo.

"You're not going to look at it?" Sid says.

"No. I know who you are," the officer says.

Sid chews a fresh fingernail. Shreds it until he tastes blood. Wonders why the male officer in the car appears to be reading a newspaper. What the hell is going on?

Chapter 8

"Your ugly name is Sid Burt Dot. You robbed a bank in north Minneapolis earlier today. We've got you on camera with your two buddies. Remember them?" the female officer says.

Sid gets the feeling she knows the rest already.

"Yeah, I remember them," he says.

"Where'd they go, Sid? Are they inside the rest stop using the bathroom?"

Sid rubs his neck. "You know they're not. You want me to get out of the car now?"

The officer looks back at the squad car. The male officer inside lowers the newspaper. Gives a nod. She nods back.

Sid watches them. Chews another fingernail.

"Two questions for you," the officer says. "Are you armed?"

"No. Some hood stuck me up. Took my gun," Sid says.

"Oh, that's too bad. You get a good look at him?" the officer says.

"It was a guy in a hoodie. That's all I know," Sid says.

The officer pulls a plastic baggie from her pocket. It's a Colt Detective Special, a snub-nosed .38 revolver. There's a certain irony in that name.

"This look familiar?" she says.

The shock damn near melts Sid. The officer allows herself a smile.

"How did you...you got the guy who did it?" Sid says. "I swear that was a guy. It wasn't no female. Not you."

"Not me? Lay off the sauce, Sid. It helps with clarity," the officer says. "Me, I saw everything. Your face when I got the upper hand on you. Took your gun. Hit you a few times before you ran off. You looked like you knew you were going to die. Shocked. Desperate. Priceless. You're a joke."

"But...you're a cop. You can't do those things," Sid says. Unless she's not a cop? He's shaking now.

"You would've stood a better chance against me if your buddies were still alive. Maybe you shouldn't have killed them after you robbed that bank," the officer says. "And then maybe you should've walked instead of stealing a shitty car. Then you wouldn't be broken down at this rest stop. Or is it easier for you to steal shitty cars from poor northsiders who can't afford working locks? Lazy ass."

Now she's swearing? Sid's adrenaline has nowhere to go. It bottlenecks in his temples. Floods his head with pressure. Makes his jaw pulsate with the nervous rattle of bone on bone.

"But...but..." Sid says.

"But is right. *But* it's your gun. I stole it from you. Stealing is wrong," the officer says. She opens the bag. Holds the revolver by the barrel so the grips face Sid. "Here. Take it back."

Sid starts for the revolver. Hesitates.

"Go on. Take it," the officer says.

Sid's pink hand wraps around the revolver's grip. He follows his first instinct. Pulls the trigger.

Snap.

The officer's body doesn't flinch. Of course the revolver isn't loaded.

"Uh oh. You just committed a big no-no. You can't go around trying to shoot peace officers," she says. "And here I thought I'd give you a break. Give you your gun back. I tried, Sid. Remember that."

"I ... uh ..." Sid says. He can't help but start to cry.

The officer lets go of the revolver. Allows Sid to keep it between his bloody fingers.

"Oh, shut up," the officer says. "I have to arrest you now. Stay seated, please. I need to see how drunk you are first."

Sid closes his eyes. Tries to hide the tears. Puts on a brave face.

"I take it you've used a Breathalyzer before," the officer says. "You know what to do."

Sid feels a cold tube press against his lips. He keeps his eyes closed. Gives it a blow. No use in fighting it.

Funny. This one tastes like...

Metal?

Sid's head pops like a Coke can in a microwave.

Chapter 9

*T*he male officer finally puts down his magazine. Exits the squad car. Stretches. Saunters over to the female officer.

"He's still got the gun in his hand," the female officer says.

"Good job. I'll take care of the rest," the male officer says. "You're free to go after we finish up here."

"Go for it. I'm going inside. Change out of this uniform. Doesn't fit right," she says.

"Yeah, sorry about the uniform. We had to use a spare. Couldn't exactly ask for a new one. You know how it is working with you, Jane," the male officer says.

"I get it. At least Sid's little secret won't ever get out now. Tell your wife I say hi," Jane says.

The male officer pretends the words don't cut him.

"I will," he says.

"It'll be easier to sleep next to her tonight, don't you think? You won't be tempted with another fag blowjob between the bars. You liked locking up Sid. Didn't mind at all," Jane says. Smiles. "It's a funny thing about working with me. You hire me to solve problems stuck Bill of Rights bullshit. I do it with all the resources of government, none of the oversight and the lust of the private sector. But I don't solve problems. I absorb them. Sid's secret is now my secret. Don't ever forget that."

The male officer steels his vision onto Sid and away from Jane. "Your money's in your account," he says.

Jane cracks her knuckles. Admires the mess that used to be Sid.

"Keep it," she says. "I enjoyed this."

Chapter 10

R ed looks up from his newspaper, the *St. Cloud Times*. His eyes bring the Lincoln Depot into focus. An odd mix of college kids and truckers.

Jane agreed to meet Red halfway between Betrug and Minneapolis. She chose St. Cloud. It's more of a drive for Red than her. Way more.

Doesn't matter. The only distance that matters is money. Close that gap between his wallet and hers. Then on to solving Red's problem.

"Looks like your friend is a no show," the waitress says.

The watering hole sits a few feet from the railroad tracks. People cheer when the train shakes it. "That's how you mix a drink," they say.

"Give her another 10 minutes," Red says to the waitress. Pokes a steak knife at his napkin. "I'll order lunch if she doesn't show. Promise."

He watches the waitress walk back to the bar. Her shirt reads "Free Beer Tomorrow" on the back. It's a cliché at bars. Perfect for a place like this. Not interested in cleverness. Just biding its time until the train derails and comes through the wall.

Ten minutes come and go. Red's still alone. Jane's a no show after all.

Damn.

Red doesn't order lunch like promised. Just tips the waitress for her time. Leaves.

Red's fuming by the time he makes it to his truck. Jane was so particular on the phone. What time will you be there? What license plate is on your truck? Who else knows about the meeting? Makes him commit to St. Cloud instead of somewhere closer to him.

Then she bails on it.

Red starts up his truck. Rolls down the window. Feels the crisp sigh of autumn. That's when the waitress comes running out.

"You forgot this," she says. Got the newspaper in her hand. Minnesota Nice in action.

Red waves his hand. "It's yours," he says.

"Your damn right it's mine," the waitress says. She opens the passenger door. Gets inside.

"What the hell are you doing?" Red says.

His first instinct is to draw his revolver, a .357 Colt Python. It's in a hip holster concealed beneath his flannel shirt. What she says next changes his mind.

"Don't talk. Drive to Riverside Park," the waitress says.

It must be Jane. This is how she worked the last time. Nice disguise. Never saw it coming. Doesn't even look like the same person. Maybe it isn't.

Red parks under a bridge near the Mississippi. Faces the truck toward the water. Turns the ignition off. Pockets the keys.

Red sees a flash. The woman reveals a steak knife from inside the rolled up newspaper. Presses the tip against Red's side. Reaches for the revolver under his flannel. How she knew it was there is beyond Red.

"What the hell...?" Red says.

"Just give me the revolver. Now," she says.

Red obliges. No use in resisting. She's the one in control. Made that clear the last time they worked together.

Jane keeps the revolver aimed at Red with her left hand. Her right brings the point of the knife down on her thigh. The truck seat turns the color of Red's name.

"Hold this," Jane says. Offers the knife handle.

Red's in no position to refuse. He grips the handle for a second before Jane takes it back.

They sit in silence while she lets blood seep into the seat. Then she tosses the knife out the window.

"What are you doing?" Red says.

"Security. For me," the woman says. "If you can follow directions, you won't have to find out why."

"Seems a little excessive. I'm the one who wanted this meeting. Why would I want to rat you out? I would've the last time I worked with you, Jane," Red says.

Jane ignores his comment. Changes the subject.

"My name is Jane. The people I work with, we all go by Jane. That's all you need to know," she says. Cracks her neck. It gurgles before it pops. "You don't want to know my real name. It gives you plausible deniability."

Her hand with the revolver hasn't moved a micron. It's still on Red like a nail ready to be pounded.

"Plausible deniability. Don't recall asking for a lawyer," Red says.

"You have no way of identifying me. No name. No reliable physical description. You don't know me," Jane says.

Red nods. "Yeah, well, I sure appreciate..."

"What is it you want this time, prairie dog?" Jane says.

Red hates that nickname. Easy to overlook with how she works, though. Or how *they* work.

He pulls out a folder from under the seat. Jane grabs it without waiting.

"The guy's name is Wil Reynolds. Killed two people, then ran. There's a big investigation on. Feds. State. The whole works. I want you to find him first. Bring him to me. It matters that I get the final word," Red says.

"Done," Jane says. "This will cost extra. You still owe me from last time."

"Everything is deposited according to your

instructions."

"Good," Jane says.

Without another word, Jane starts changing out of her waitressing uniform. The clothes snap off her body. She pulls out a dress hidden inside her pockets. Pulls it on.

There's a flash of bare skin near the knife wound. Red spots something that looks like a penis. Happened so fast, he can't be sure. There are scars all up and down her legs. Could've been a bit of healing meat near her groin.

"I'll call you with an update," Jane says. Exits the truck. "Thanks for the gun."

Red shakes his head. Starts the truck up. Jane keeps the revolver trained on him.

"Remember. You do exactly as I say," Jane says.

"I know," Red says through the open window.

He doesn't wait to hit the gas. The truck fishtails as he guns it out of the park.

Chapter 11

I get up and flush the toilet. Feels like I've been crouching over the water for days. My sleeve wipes the vomit from my mouth.

Dry. No vomit.

What the hell? I know I puked.

I'm not in the bar any more. The bar doesn't have stalls. It's just a shitter in a room with wood floors. This floor is tile. And I'm between stall doors.

What?

I turn around in the stall, albeit still on the floor. Spot a sign taped to it. "Mall employees must wash hands before returning to work."

Mall?

I check my watch. It's 9:30 p.m. two days from today. Is my watch broke? What happened to all that time? Where's Joe?

I hoist myself up. Wipe at my eyes. Open the stall door.

"Are you OK?" a voice says from next to the sink.

Only it's not big, burly Joe. It's a young woman. About my age. Half my size. Twice as much hair. Blonde dreadlocks down her back. Olive surplus military shirt and pants. German flag on the shoulder. The good Germany. Not bad Germany.

"Am I in the wrong bathroom? Sorry," I say.

"No. I am," she says. "I heard shouting, like someone needed help. Are you OK?"

No. I'm not OK. How the hell did I get from the bar in Betrug to a mall? There isn't a mall in Betrug. Where is there a mall? Think.

Jamestown. Couple-few hours from Betrug.

"Am I in the Jamestown mall?" I say.

"Of course, stupid. And it closes in a half hour," the woman says.

She turns on the faucet. Cups the water. Brings it up to her face. It's smooth. Blank. Almost featureless. Not like the definition the wind whittled into mine.

I pat my pockets. Wallet? Check.

I feel two sets of keys, though. I pull both out. One of them doesn't belong to me. There's a tag that says "Seriously?" hanging from a ring. Another tag sports a picture of Joe and Elma.

Joe's keys.

I stare at the picture. Where's Joe? One minute we're talking at the bar. Something about a job. The next minute I'm here.

"Oh, is that your parents? That's sweet," the woman says. Dabs her face with a paper towel. Watches me staring at the keys.

"No. They're not my ..." I start to say.

She cuts me off. "Where are you headed?"

"I think I'm ..." I say.

"You must be going to the oil fields, right?" the woman says. "That's you, right?"

Too many questions. I can't make sense of anything.

"You asking for a ride?" I say.

"Yeah, to Williston. Or Minot. Somewhere in there. You're headed that way, right?" the woman says.

She's eager. Like hitchhiker eager. Must be one of those oil boom out-staters. Seen them around town before. Dirty drifters. I can smell it on her.

Yeah, they just want a "job" like anyone else. But they don't drive. They hitchhike. That's how you can tell the trouble from everyone else. The ones who drive trucks to the oil patch, they're in it for the long haul. Might even move their families up here.

People like her? They're ticks on the economy. Show up wherever things start to grow. Bum around. Stir up trouble. Maybe they work, maybe they don't. Take what they can. Leave after the locals wisen up.

Seems obvious now that I think of it. Dreadlocks? Practically illegal in North Dakota.

"Sorry. Not headed that way. Going east. To Fargo," I say. It's a lie, but I'm not a taxi. How's she gonna know? I need to get back to Betrug. Find Joe.

"Fargo? What's out there? A job?" she says.

Did I mention these out-staters don't take "no" for an answer?

"Sure. A job. What's it matter to you?" I say.

"Can I come with you?"

My head's too foggy for this shit. Feels like my brain's turned to soup.

"No. Bye," I say. Head out the door.

She's probably a hooker anyway. With a knife. Or a penis.

Turns out I'm right about one of them.

Chapter 12

"Guess my lucky raccoon penis isn't so lucky today," the woman says.

What? I turn before opening the door.

"Raccoon penis?" I say.

She flips a necklace out from her shirt. Oh, a *raccoon penis*. It's a penis bone. Trappers make them into jewelry. Shit's gross, but it looks cool. Like a stretched out S.

Her penis – that's a weird thing to say – is wrapped in gold leaf. People say these gold dicks bring luck.

Know what I say? You'll need a whole lot more than a raccoon penis out here. Not when you're asking people for rides. And you're a woman. In North Dakota. Headed to the oil patch. Where there are entire counties without a female in sight. That's as unlucky as it gets.

She can't possibly be that naïve. But what do I know? I don't even know what day it is, for fuck's sake.

"The way that thing's got gold on it, your luck might change," I say.

"It's solid gold. Not gold leaf," she says. Twirls the jewelry in her fingers. "The maker used a raccoon penis bone for a mold."

"Someone out there wasted gold on a penis mold?" I say.

"Gold is gold. Doesn't matter what it looks like. It's mine. That's what counts. It's very valuable," she says. Tucks the jewelry back into her shirt. "Maybe it's worth a ride to the Bakken?"

Oh, so she's one of these *rich* out-staters. The kind living broke just for the "worldly experience." Probably from one of the coasts. Old money.

I can't stand that shit. With all the poverty in the

43

world, you *choose* to live like a bum?

Forget Joe for the moment. It's clear whatever shit that was isn't going to happen now. I feel a need to accept this woman's offer just to prove a point.

You want to give me your solid gold jewelry *and* ship your out-stater ass to the Bakken? My pleasure. Welcome to reality for the first time in your life, you over privileged snot.

"What's your name?" I say.

"Sam. What's yours?" Sam says.

"Wil. With one L."

"Wil? Oh. You look more like a Rex. Something manlier," she says.

"Yeah, well Sam's a boy's name. Guess I was expecting something else, too," I say.

"Fuck you," Sam says.

"Fuck you, too. You want a ride or not?" I say.

Chapter 13

My head isn't cut out for I-94. We wind our way through Jamestown headed northwest on 52. Lots of stoplights. Not something I'm used to seeing. Hit the brakes a little too late.

Sam doesn't seem bothered. Just turns the cab light on and reads a book. *Three Cups of Tea*. Never heard of it.

"What are you reading?" I say.

Not that I need to ask. Need to make conversation, though. Silence on the prairie is one thing. Silence with a hitchhiker in a truck you have no idea how you got to be driving is another.

"Nothing," Sam says. Stuffs the book into her backpack.

"I guess so. Kind of dark out for a book," I say.

Sam flicks off the cab light. My eyes adjust to the road outside. We're outside Jamestown now. The pavement dangles beyond the headlights like a gray thread in a pool of black water. The night is bigger on the prairie. It circles everything in 360 degrees of darkness. Above and below the road.

Sam leans her head against the window. Fakes sleep. Relaxed as a pile of lumber against the glass.

I watch the keychain dangling in the ignition. It dances to the rhythm of the engine. I can still make out that word, "Seriously?" It's right next to the picture of Joe and Elma.

"Seriously," I mouth. "Seriously."

Chapter 14

"The flood of 2011. That was God trying to wipe Minot away," the preacher says.

He sits across from me and Sam. His long fingers peck at our fries.

We're in a booth at a 24/7 restaurant. The mediocre kind at the bottom of hotels. Outside the sign says, "No vacancy." Inside the restaurant is bare. Typical.

I figure we'll spend the night in Minot. Feel way too tired to keep driving. I'll collect my dick from Sam in the morning, then ditch her. Drive back to Betrug. Find out what the hell is going on.

"Didn't God say he wouldn't flood the world again?" Sam says. Seems to be having fun egging the preacher on.

She tugs the fry basket closer. It's her grub anyway. She paid for it.

The preacher gives her a look. Pulls it back.

"That's right. But Minot isn't the world. It's an exception because of the sin here," the preacher says. Eats another fry.

He'd spotted us five minutes before. Honed in like a crow on corn muffins. Started talking and eating our food. No introduction. Just a grin and a clerical collar.

I want to slap the grease off his face. This isn't the place for it, though. Security cameras everywhere.

"You really think that?" Sam says.

"Can you think of another reason?" the preacher says.

"Yes. The Souris River flooded," Sam says.

I remember reading about the flood. The Souris cuts through downtown Minot. They said it was a 500-year flood. Thousands left town for dry ground. You can still see rings around the houses that mark the water line. Glad

I was in Betrug at the time.

The preacher wipes his hands on a napkin. "You've never been to Minot before. You don't know what it's like here. Or why God would want to flood it," he says.

I scoot the basket near me. Stuff down a load of potatoes.

"I was here a few years back. Didn't seem so bad," I say.

"That was then. This is now. Once the oil boom hit, it brought in people. All sorts of ... *people*. Devils for the oil. Whores for the devils. Liquor for them all. Name a sin. It's here," the preacher says.

"Then why's it still here? If God wanted to wash Minot away, why are all these sinners still here?" Sam says.

I pass her the basket back.

"The water wasn't deeper than the sin. Couldn't wash it away. This fracking, it's like they're building thousands of inverted Towers of Babylon. Monuments to scoff at the Almighty while they pump oil and whores," the preacher says.

"So what are you doing out here?" Sam says. "Doesn't seem like the place for a man of the cloth."

"You're wrong. I came out here after the flood. Wanted to ease suffering of flood victims. Go through their houses. Help them salvage valuables, whether they knew they needed my help or not," the preacher says. "One place, it was a preacher's house. Abandoned. Found a box with his preacher stuff in it. Books, pamphlets, clerical collars. Like a preacher starter kit.

"I stayed many nights in the preacher's house, waiting. Never came back. So there's a gap in the ministry out here. I figured God sent me to that preacher's house knowing I'd fill it. Been spreading the good word ever since. Directing oil workers' money to my ministry instead of liquor and whores. Keep them from fracking straight through into

48

hell. I was a wanderer before. But I'm staying put now that the Lord found me. His flock needs me too much out here."

Sam laughs.

"And I suppose these fries are considered an offering?" she says.

"The way the money is out here, it's surprising these aren't free anyway. But yes, it's an offering in exchange for my little sermon. Wherever you're going, be careful. Don't lose your soul in the process of making that money," the preacher says.

The preacher takes one final fry. Gets up to leave. Sam rockets to her feet.

"You might want to pay me for what you ate," she says.

"Oh, I forgot," the preacher says. Reaches into his pocket. Comes out with a business card. Flips it onto the table. "Keep this somewhere safe. It's better than money."

"Oh, I forgot something, too," Sam says. "Fuck you."

"Read the card," the preacher says. Then he's gone.

I pick up the card. One side is a phone number next to the words "For Spiritual Help on the Bakken, Call Reverend Jim for a Talkin'."

I flip the card over. The word "Seriously" is printed large. Underneath it are the words, "God made the entire universe. No problem is too big for Him."

Seriously.

Seriously.

Sparks something in my mind. Not sure what. I stuff the feeling away.

I pocket the card. Sam raises an eyebrow.

"You planning on making right with the Lord?" she says.

"Just a little superstitious," I say.

"Or stupid," Sam says.

She might be right. I don't feel like jinxing myself. Eat

the last fry.

"I'm not the one with a lucky raccoon penis around my neck," I say.

We sip water until the waitress comes over. Asks if we need anything else. I say we do, a recommendation for somewhere to stay. She's got nothing. Everything is booked up. A lot of people sleep in their trucks, she says. I guess that'll include us.

I spot Sam slipping a steak knife into her backpack as we leave.

That's OK. I took one, too.

Chapter 15

The waitress didn't lie. We check every hotel in town. No vacancy anywhere. There won't be for weeks, the night desk clerks tell us. The oil workers rented it all.

Some stay in company houses. Others squat in skeletons of houses still wrecked from the floods. We spot a few storage containers with trucks parked outside them, too. Hell of a way to live.

The city government never knows what to do with them. I remember hearing a "good, hard frost" being proposed a bit back. The boys from the Minot Air Force base have their own plan, too. Crank the shit out of anyone with an out-state license plate.

We drive in circles. Even in the midnight streetlights, I see evidence of the Souris River on everything. A reminder that the flood never really receded. Water is history's paintbrush.

"You know where you're going?" Sam says.

"No," I say.

"Maybe try the NoDak fairgrounds. I see some people on benches. No one will care," Sam says.

She's right. Even in the autumn chill, out-staters sleep on sidewalk benches. Or try to sleep. Pile up their gear to use as pillows.

I cruise toward the North Dakota State Fairgrounds. Lots of picnic shelters. Well-lit. We could sleep with our backs to the river. Looks as good as any place so long as the gate is unlocked. For her, anyway. I'm staying in the truck.

One bit of business to address first.

"I saw you grab that knife," I say.

"I saw you, too," she says.

We leave it at that.

I park the truck on a side street next to the fairgrounds. The gate is locked. There's a gap in the fence wide enough for a person to slip through.

"You coming?" Sam says.

"Nope," I say. "How about my toll? Wouldn't mind collecting that now."

"Nope," Sam says as she gets out. Mimics how I said the word. "In the morning."

Hard to argue with the out-stater logic there. And I don't feel like wrestling with that knife. Doesn't matter anyway. I'll sleep, then leave. Head back to Betrug. Figure shit out.

"Fine," I say. Lock the doors.

"You better be here in the morning," she says. It's muffled through the window.

I nod to Sam, then work on nodding off. Close my eyes for what feels like a second. When I half-open them again, I have a hard time believing what I'm seeing.

Chapter 16

*I*t starts as a shadow. Something blacker than the night. Like a hole in the darkness. It wiggles at first. About 100 feet away. Across the street.

I'm not awake. I'm not asleep. But I'm here. Looking at this thing. The wiggles turn into shakes. The shakes turn into tremors. Then it blooms into the shape of a human.

It shuffles in place. Dragging its frame nowhere. Avoiding the glow of streetlights.

It's moving away from me. No. Toward me. Hard to tell. This must be a dream. Right?

I reach for the knife. It's not there. I go for the Mossberg 500 behind the seat. Not there, either.

I don't fear this thing, this shadow person. It's just there. A fact in front of me. No more terrifying than the moon. But still unsettling.

It's getting closer. I can tell that now. It's walking backward. I think. There's no face. No features. Just a shadow without a home. No light or objects playing tricks on me nearby.

It's closing in on 20 feet now. Should be easier to make out, but it isn't. I have to look to the side to see it. Definitely walking backward, though.

"Hello?" I want to say. I don't. Maybe it's an animal. I don't want to scare it. Just see it.

The air around me turns to static. Like I'm trapped in a TV screen trying to find a signal. Then I hear it say something. Like speaking through cotton. "Seriously."

Turn around. I want it to turn around. To see its face. Its eyes. Who is this? What is this?

It moves a shoulder. Its frame gets thinner. It's turning. Like it read my mind. Or is a part of my mind.

The Invisible Hand

There's a knock on the passenger window. A real knock. The sound propels the shadow person away.

I look to the window and spot a smear of blood.

Chapter 17

*T*he world turns from night to morning the second I focus in on the smear. Red, yellow and feathers. Must've been a bird.

I check for the knife I hid under the seat. It's there. The Mossberg behind the seat. That's there, too.

About that. I knew there was a shotgun behind the seat. No idea how I know that, though.

I could use a drink before I hit the road. Head back to Betrug. Yeah, it's only morning. Not that I ever gave a shit about that before.

I spot a gas station across the street. They probably sell the watered down can beer. It'll do.

I lock up the truck and walk to the station. Spot a tall, black garbage can in the parking lot. The shadow person came from this direction. Maybe I dreamt the can coming alive?

That's when I hear it. Coming from the fairgrounds. Sounds like people arguing. Not in a nice way. I'm curious at first. Then alarmed.

"Fuck you," I hear a voice say.

It's Sam's.

I don't know why I start heading for the fairgrounds. Most of me wants to turn around. Get in the truck. Drive off. Forget this out-stater.

But like most good advice in my life, I ignore it. Pick up my pace. Sure, Sam's an out-stater like any other. I'm not an evil person, though. I think. Mainly, this is the shit I live for, the action. Just like shit shoveling back home.

I spot three big guys huddled around a bench. I hear Sam from inside their semi-circle.

"Get away from me," she says.

I clear the fairgrounds fence in a blink. I'm at the bench in another two. Out of breath, but just in time. Spot Sam beating the hell out of all three guys. Straight knuckles to noses.

The guys look confused. Like they're not sure if they're supposed to hit a female back. More concerned with taking Sam's punches like a man. Doesn't look like it's working. She's already busted two noses under her knuckles. Working on the third.

Not sure whether to help her or just stand there. Seems to have things handled.

"Don't just stand there. Help me," Sam says.

Well, that answers that. I paid plenty of prairie penance as a dull church boy growing up. This'll even things out.

I bury a fist into one of the guys' kidneys. Shoulder him to the ground. Put a boot on his throat. Hold it there while Sam hunkers down and finishes her third nose job. The skin over her knuckles splits open. Reveals a sliver of bone underneath.

The expression on her face is welded in rage. A far cry from the fun she poked at Reverend Jim last night. Maybe she's not that over privileged snot after all. Able to switch between disarming naiveté to get a ride and extreme violence to protect herself. That's classic hitchhiker. Can't learn that stuff in the fancy schools.

I let the guy get to his feet. Recuperate next to the other two. Everyone is exhausted. Sam and the guys from fighting. Me from running. It's odd, but we all stand there for a minute. Catch our breath. Let the last bit of fight drain onto the ground.

"What happened?" I say to Sam. Not that I need to justify anything in my mind.

"Woke up this morning. Saw these guys going through

my backpack," Sam says. "Told them to go away. They didn't. So I broke in their fucking noses. Warned them I would." Looks at the sorry trio. "I told you not to touch my stuff, you stupid sons of bitches."

A voice interrupts before I can respond.

"And what do we have here?" says an older guy in a wheelchair. Didn't spot him before. Guess he was just a few yards away. Watching the whole time.

The way he says it, it's like he owned that park bench. He holds court with a long, steel cane. Arms ripped like tractor wheels. Handlebar mustache. Blue ball cap that says, "Navy Vet." Probably bald underneath.

Two other guys flank him. Thick and round. Like meaty hay bales.

Sam is prone on the bench. One hand in her pocket. Probably got that knife close.

"Ya'll making a mess of my bench, are you?" Navy Vet says. Smooth, Southern accent. Out-stater.

Sam doesn't hesitate to reply.

"Your bench? This is a public park," she says. "I was sleeping. These three guys snuck up. Tried going through my backpack."

Navy Vet laughs.

"Sure, sure, it's public. These guys are with me. They were just checking you out," Navy Vet says. Wheels over to one of the nose bleeders. Slaps the guy's jaw with the steel cane. Hard. Guy just takes it. "They needed a good ass kickin' anyway."

Navy Vet wipes the blood off the cane. Turns to me. "And you. You were sleeping in that truck over there, weren't you?" he says.

Had that been him? The shadow person?

"You were watching me?" I say.

"Sure, I watch everyone. See who comes. Who goes. Someone has to keep tabs on the out-staters. Lord knows the cops can't do it anymore. Outnumbered 1,000 to one," Navy Vet says.

"Creep," Sam says.

"Nothing creepy about it. Just playing my part in the boom," Navy Vet says. "There's too much money and time around here. Nowhere to spend either. People bring their oil money into town. They're bored, so they get drunk. Start feeling invincible.

"The police can't control them. The oil companies can't control them. The churches can't control them. If someone didn't bring some order to the situation, the whole damn thing would explode. And that's where I come in."

An out-stater that regulates out-staters? Now this is something new.

Sam crosses her arms. I spot a flash of the knife obscured by her sleeve.

"So you harass people sleeping on benches?" she says.

"Harass? No. Just check them out. For drugs. For weapons. For trouble. Get a head start. It's the newbies who sleep on benches after all," Navy Vet says. Points his cane at Sam's arm. "I hope you know what you're doing with that knife."

Yeah, I do, too. Fists are fine. You can heal up. Knives are all-in. Best used to convince someone they don't want a knife fight. Speaking from experience.

"Can we go now?" Sam says.

"Where are you headed? Maybe I can help," Navy Vet says. He looks at me. Then back to Sam.

"She's looking for work. And I ...," I say. Not sure how to fill in that blank. "... I just gave her a ride."

"Have a job lined up?" Navy Vet says to Sam.

Sam shows two empty hands. Must've slipped the knife back up her sleeve.

"Not yet," she says.

"Then allow me to introduce myself. My name is Les," Navy Vet says. "And I want both of you to watch very closely."

Les grins. Reaches into his leather vest. Produces a roll of cash bigger than his hand. More money in one spot than I've seen my entire life.

He peels off a few hundreds like they're toilet paper. Crinkles them up in his hand. Throws the ball at my chest. Does the same again for Sam.

My first instinct is to give it back. No such thing as free money. On the other hand, I wouldn't mind hearing what Les has to say. Can't hurt. Anyone shitting money like that isn't growing sunflowers and beehives for a living.

I need action. And it looks like this guy can give it to me.

Chapter 18

"What's your name?" Les says to me.

"Wil. With one L," I say.

"Wil, huh? OK," Les says. He points his cane at Sam. "And what's your name?"

"Sam," she says.

"Great. You two been in town here long?" Les says. Pulls out a silver flask. Takes a hit. Shakes it at Sam and me. "Little breakfast in a bottle?"

The flask catches the sun. It's like the Star of Bethlehem. Could go for an eye-opener.

Les passes it to me. I take a swig or three. Give it to Sam. She shakes her head.

"Never touch the stuff," she says.

"I suppose you like weed. Is that right, Dreadilocks? That's illegal here," Les says. Grins.

"So is drinking in a public park," Sam says.

"My park. My rules," Les says.

I wag the flask at Sam. She refuses. I pass it back to Les. His expression changes. More serious. More direct.

"It's not too early for math, is it?" Les says. "Let's see. You slept on my bench. You beat the shit out of three of my guys. You drank my booze. And you're holding my money. What do you suppose that equals?"

Then he says something about us owing him. I don't hear much. The booze goes straight to my head.

Something pops. I physically hear it inside my head. Like a knot pulling tight that explodes.

I hear my father. "Find something you're good at. Then do it every day."

I hear Joe. "Seriously."

Only I know he didn't say that. His coffee mug says

that. His keychain says that. When did he say that? Did he ever?

Doesn't matter. My body burns off the short buzz. And there's a cane in my ribs.

"You still with us?" Les says.

"Yeah, yeah. What were you saying?" I say.

"Before I can offer you a job, a really good one, you need to make things right with me. You and your girlfriend owe me. But I'll make it easy for you two, show you I'm a good guy. Go around the fairgrounds. Pick up trash. Anyone asks, say you're with a church," Les says.

I study the two hay bales flanking Les. They're on edge. Ready to tackle us.

"You're hiring us to pick up trash?" I say.

"Not really. You're paying off a debt now," Les says. Laughs. "Lesson number one. Never, ever take a handout from a stranger. That's how they get you. Rope you in. Everyone knows that."

"Aren't there park people for that?" Sam says.

"You really think they keep a full-time grounds crew? Not when a person could be printing money on the Bakken. Just like every other shitty service job out here," Les says. "Someone's gotta fill in the gaps. People come from all across North America just to clean my park. Imagine that."

Sam gets up from the bench. Jerky when she does it. Like she's ready to run. Shoots me a look. Like I should join her.

The hay bales grab me. One clamps my right arm. The other takes my left. Les wheels over. Reaches into my pocket. Pulls out my truck keys.

"What the fuck?" Sam says.

She pulls the knife from her sleeve. Les is already on her. There's a crack as the cane meets her hand. It goes invisible as her hand retreats up her sleeve.

The knife drops to the ground. One of the hay bales picks it up.

"Look, I'm trying to be a good guy here. You're making it hard with that knife," Les says. He pockets the keys. "I'll give them back when you're done cleaning the park. Then you're free to go."

The hay bales toss me to the ground. Les places the tip of the cane on my throat.

"See to it you do a good job," Les says.

Sam helps me up after Les relents. Uses her good hand. The bad one slips out from her sleeve. Looks plump and purple. Like a beet.

"We'll be back later," Les says. Starts wheeling off with the others. "Oh, and you might want to stay out of sight. People around here don't like *trash* in their parks."

Chapter 19

"Come in. Mary's not home. She left a note saying we could look around," Red says. Opens the door for Gus. "Maybe we'll find something helpful."

They walk into the kitchen of Berug's most well-read resident, Mary Reynolds. Married only in spirit to Jon Reynolds, Wil's father, following the grain bin accident.

Bruises on the walls mark where pictures used to hang. Mary's impressive book collection, once the unofficial Betrug library, cascades off shelves in the living room. Paper and leather spill into the kitchen. Trace a line where Mary must've walked.

"Keep your hands in your pockets," Red says. "Don't touch anything."

"Why not? My hands are clean," Gus says. Wipes his palms on his shirt.

"Aren't you superstitious?" Red says. "You're going to pick up Mary's bad luck. Husband dead. Son a murderer twice over. Just her on this farm now."

Red wants to say "spiritual" or "religious" instead of "superstitious." It doesn't fit, though. Murders are like that. Hard to invoke God or religion in the same breath as murder.

"Sure, I'm superstitious," Gus says. Plucks a coffee cup from the counter. Spits tobacco juice into it. "That's why I switched to chew. Have a look inside the cup. See, I'm not smoking."

"Good for you. Keep it up," Red says. "Mary doesn't allow tobacco in her house. Smokes or otherwise."

Gus cracks his knuckles. Thinks to himself. Odd Red would know that.

"Speaking of which, you think she still wants to live

here?" Gus says. "Personally, I'd sell the place. Move into town."

Red picks his way into the living room. Spots a portrait on the wall that didn't come down. Mary. Jon. Wil. All much younger. He only allows a quick glance. Hopes Gus doesn't notice how quick he is to look away.

"Mary'll probably stay. Too much wrapped up in the farm to leave," Red says.

Gus stays in the kitchen while Red browses the living room. A newspaper clipping hangs on the fridge. Details the farm accident that killed Jon Reynolds. Gus reads it.

"What do you make of this?" Gus says. Points at the clipping.

"Hard to say," Red says. "Jon dies in that grain bin accident. Then Wil kills Joe and Elma. If there's a connection there, I'm not seeing it."

Gus looks in the fridge. Nothing isn't expired. Closes the door.

"Maybe Jon dying wasn't an accident?" Gus says. "Is that why we're here?"

"Just having a look for good measure, that's all," Red says.

He grabs a pair of books from their shelf. One is about grief and loss. To be expected.

The other is different. It's titled, *Steps Forward: Finding Courage and Confidence to Make Big Changes.* Neither looks to have been read. Still out-of-the-box fresh.

"What did the feds say?" Gus says.

"About what?" Red says.

"This. All this. They went through it, right?"

Red puts the books back.

"They did. But we're just prairie dogs to them," Red says. "Wouldn't tell me much."

Gus cracks his knuckles agian. "So what did they say?"

"That Wil Reynolds grew up in Betrug," Red says.

"Lived here on and off from his teens through today. Never took to a career in anything. Not interested in farming, either. Then he killed two people and ran. The end."

"But they confirmed Wil is the guy they're looking for, right?"

"Yep."

Gus rubs his jaw. It's in a deliberate way. Like he rehearses it in front of a mirror.

"Seems like you got real lucky," Gus says. "Just happening upon Wil as he left."

Red looks out the window. The prairie is drying up. The tall grass knows to hide its water for winter. Turns paler by the minute, along with Red's face.

"Lucky break. Nothing more. Nothing less," Red says.

"I guess so," Gus says. Wipes his mouth on his sleeve. Turns it tobacco brown. "Without your lucky break, it wouldn't be clear who'd killed Joe and Elma. Or it would've taken longer. And you sure seemed eager to sic that help of yours on Wil, that Jane."

Red works hard to contain his voice.

"You suggesting something, Gus?" Red says. Each word is like a lid about to pop.

Gus spits into the coffee cup. Gives a wink.

"Like you always say, Red. I need to stop watching so many movies," Gus says.

That's when the house phone rings. It's the real reason they're there. Jane. She wanted to call at Mary's for whatever reason.

Red checks his watch. She's right on time.

Chapter 20

"What's your deal?" Sam says.

I've been staring at the trash can. The one Les assigned to us. Quiet. Thinking. Barely spoke a word to Sam.

"Huh?" I say.

"You're like a zombie. You know what those are, right?" Sam says. Unfolds a handful of cigarette butts. Only a few smokeable centimeters left. "Want one?"

"One of what?" I say.

Then I realize she means the butts. Didn't think she was serious. I shake my head.

What the hell am I doing here?

Not like I forget why. Les is paying us to clean this park. Not quite the action I had in mind. I just want my fucking truck back.

My truck. That's not quite right. It's Joe's. He probably wants it back. I need to find him once this is all done. That much I know.

I know something else, too. It's been too long since I've caught a respectable buzz. Maybe that's for the better. Need a clear head.

"What are you thinking about?" Sam says.

"I'm thinking about trash. Picking up trash," I say. An obvious lie. Still better than saying I zone out to the point of not knowing what's happening. Comes and goes.

"You're as boring as trash," Sam says. "Why don't you ask me about me? Aren't you curious?"

"I guess," I say. "So, what about you?"

Sam lights a butt. Takes quick sips as it burns. Passes it to me. Insists.

It's been a while since I lit up. Tastes as bad as I

69

remember, even more so since it's litter. Like over easy dog shit.

We sit down on a bench nearby. Sam lights, puffs, tosses, repeats.

"You really like those things," I say. "Why don't you just buy some?"

"Didn't have much cash until now," she says. "Just my lucky raccoon penis."

"Yeah, about that. It's not really solid gold, is it?" I say.

Sam flips the jewelry out from under her shirt. Plays with it as she smokes.

"It looks like solid gold. I tell people it's solid gold. They believe it's solid gold. So it's gold. Doesn't matter if it is or isn't. Perception is reality," Sam says. Lets out a deep chuckle.

I chuckle. No shit. And that's why I can't trust her yet. Hell, she could be a man for all I know. Wouldn't surprise me. Lots of out-stater freaks around here. Spot a few walking near park benches not far away. Punk rock patches on backpacks. Hair dyed crazy colors. Loose, hippie gait. All wearing shoes, too, not boots. Probably mining the trash for a fucking handout. Hope Les's guys got to them like they did Sam.

"How many times have you used that thing for a ride?" I say.

"For as long as the paint hasn't worn off," Sam says. Flashes me a smile. "You didn't think hitchhikers lie to get rides? Seriously?"

Seriously. There's that word again. And there's that jolt in my gut. Makes me pluck an eyelash out. Calms out that unsettled feeling.

"I figured as much," I say.

"It's only a half-lie. It's still a real raccoon penis bone," Sam says. "The paint is actually nail polish."

"Nice to know some out-staters are still honest.

Eventually," I say.

Sam picks up on the condescension in my voice. Races to the defense.

"You got a problem with out-staters?" she says. "You gave me a ride when you didn't have to. Now you're a few hundred bucks richer for picking up trash. What's your deal, asshole?"

Like that penis bone, she's only hit on half the truth. My head is the other half. I don't mention that part, though.

"Out-staters are the best and worst thing to happen to North Dakota," I say. "Kind of like you. My *deal* is that I shouldn't've gave you that ride. But for whatever reason, I did. Now we're here. Sometimes there isn't a real good explanation for things. Like there's an invisible hand pushing you into something. Doesn't mean out-staters aren't any more than a necessary evil. Maybe you'll be the exception."

Sam seems satisfied with that. Tucks the charm back into her shirt. Uses her good hand.

"You sure you're not an out-stater? I don't hear a lot of locals talking like you do," Sam says.

She's got a point there. It's why I never fit in on the prairie in the first place.

"My mother, she has quite the book collection. Guess I liked to read," I say.

"Surprising. You don't quite match the illiterate hick stereotype. Might make a person reconsider some of their own," Sam says. Lets that soak in, then switches back to her other mode. In-the-moment curiosity tossed with road-weary sarcasm. "So what part of North Dakota are you from, oh holy literate in-stater?"

I think back to meeting Joe in the bar. Crimps the wires in my brain.

I try again. And again. And again. Nothing. A hand

shoves me back to the present each time I try to access the past.

"I'm from Betrug. If you put a pin on a map where you thought the middle of North Dakota was, you'd probably hit Betrug," I say.

Sam waits for more. Nothing comes.

"That's it? You're from Betrug? No more to that story?" Sam says.

"I do odd jobs for farmers. Like a hired hand. I was at a bar in town the other day. Met a guy named Joe there. He had a job for me. But we drank too much. Then you found me in that bathroom in Jamestown," I say.

Not sure why I let Sam in on that. Feels good to talk about it. Lubricate my memory a bit.

"What a fascinating life you've led. Really, really interesting," Sam says. "You sound like the town fuck up. All that reading did you no good."

That stings. Screws into the truth.

"Enough about me. I let you in on something. Now you let me in," I say. "Is Sam really your name?"

Sam cuts loose a deep laugh. Like she can't believe I would ask that. I don't think it's out of line. Only safe question I can think of anyway.

"Yes. That's my real name. It's short for Samantha," she says. "But no one calls me that. Not for a long time."

"Why not?" I say.

"You really want to know?" she says.

"Sure."

Sam leans over. Brings her mouth to my ear.

"No, you don't, farm boy," she says.

Chapter 21

"You going to pick that thing up?" Gus says. Nods to the ringing phone.

Red walks over and brings the receiver to his ear. Doesn't speak. Just listens.

Gus does the same. Leans against the wall.

The call ends a few seconds later.

"That Jane?" Gus says.

"That was Jane," Red says. Runs a hand over his head. Swallows hard.

Gus looks out the window. "Jane is coming here?" he says.

"No. She found Joe's truck," Red says.

Chapter 22

The two hay bales have names. Solid, Christian prairie names. Doesn't matter now.

Les calls them Tor and Abe for whatever reason. Has since the meaty brothers washed up at a truck stop in Williston.

The three ride in Joe's truck. Abe at the wheel. Tor riding shotgun. Literally. He holds Wil's – Joe's, actually – pump-action spray stick in his lap.

Les sits in his wheelchair perched in the bed of the truck. Hangs onto railings on the roof. Talks to Tor and Abe through an open window into the cab.

"Drop me off at the hospital. I need to check on something," Les says. "Bring this truck to the shop. Fix it. Like how you normally fix trucks. Got it?"

Abe drives the truck to the expressway. Pulls over at the Minot hospital.

Les hoists himself out the open tailgate. Wheels around to the cab. Wags a finger at Abe.

"Make sure you and your brother do a good job. No pissing around this time," Les says.

Abe grunts in response. He's the smarter of the brothers. Not that that means much.

Abe drives off after Les scoots through the hospital doors. Pulls around to a side street. Stops in front of a large, metal shipping container. The kind trains haul across the prairie. It lays crooked in a vacant yard. Carried there by the flood. Forgotten.

The shop.

It doesn't look like much from the outside. That's the point.

"Go inside. Get the tool belts and a box cutter. The

ones we used last time," Abe says. Strokes his curly, red beard. "I'll work on the cab. You start under the hood."

Tor hops out. Unlocks the chain securing the shipping container doors. Hits a switch on an extension cord. Grabs a box cutter and two tool belts hanging on the wall. Brings them to Abe.

Abe cuts along the seams of the bench seat. Makes taping it back together easier. He pulls out a wad of stuffing first. Then dips his hand inside. Feels around.

"Anything?" Tor says.

"Nothing," Abe says. "Get under that hood."

They spend an hour going through every detail of the truck. Tool through anything not welded shut.

"Nothing?" Abe says from the cab.

"Nothing," Tor says. Hits his head on the open hood as he says it. "Ouch."

"Out-staters are almost always holding something," Abe says. "Meth. Speed. Weed."

"Yeah, but this truck has NoDak plates. So probably the guy was telling the truth. Only the one was an out-stater," Tor says. "So maybe there's no dope."

"Les will be happy either way. Doesn't like competition drifting in," Abe says. "Let's put everything back together. Get the new plates on. Give it a quick coat of paint, too."

Abe and Tor have the process memorized. The shop keeps a set of license plates handy. Rotate them out with each truck they "fix." Only takes one set of stolen plates to start the cycle.

They have the entire process down to a science. Abe primes the paint gun while Tor swaps the plates.

Abe moves the truck away from the container. Starts the paint job. It's the same color each time. Tan. Like prairie camouflage. Makes the truck look like a hay bale from a distance.

Abe's paint gun is too quick. Too sloppy. It's good

enough, though.

"There. It's fixed," Abe says when he finishes. "Time for lunch?"

No response.

Abe walks around the truck. "You there?"

"Don't move," comes a reply from behind him. Voice is unfamiliar. Genderless. Almost metallic.

Abe spins around. Fists clenched. No one there.

"Paint fumes got me hearing things," Abe says under his breath.

He heads back into the shipping container. Opens the door. Lights are out.

Abe reaches for the switch attached to an extension cord. Stops.

Something's squeezing his ankle.

Abe's first thought is it's a raccoon. They're known to hole up in shipping containers. But raccoons can't squeeze like this. Like it's trying to cut off his circulation.

Abe hits the switch. The lights flicker on. He looks down. Sees a hand on the floor.

At first it looks like it has paint on it. Only it's not tan. It's bright red. He follows it to an arm. It wears a coat of red. Then to a face. Tor's face.

Tor tries to say something. Voice won't work.

That's when Abe feels another hand. This time around his neck. It's coming from behind.

He watches as a second hand reaches up. Hits the switch. The lights go out.

"I told you not to move," a voice in the darkness says.

Chapter 23

I return from the gas station across the street. Small ice pack for Sam's hand. She's saying it hurts real bad.

"Thanks for grabbing that. Wish I could just chop this thing off. Have an invisible hand instead," Sam says. Rubs her swollen hand.

I give Sam the ice. She struggles to balance it on her bad hand. I help her hold it in place.

"Better?" I say.

"A little bit."

"Got you this, too," I say. Pull out a pack of cheap cigarettes.

"Thanks again," Sam says.

I pluck out a peg. Help her light it. Yeah, she's an out-stater. But with Les's cash, I have more than enough on me to pretend to be a gentleman.

I wanted a little liquor anyway. Pull out a short bottle of cheap coffin varnish. It scorches my throat sweet.

"Your hand getting numb yet?" I say.

"Yeah. The cig helps, too," Sam says. "Thanks."

We sit on the bench in silence. Drink. Smoke. Drink and smoke some more. Watch the sun ooze into the horizon.

I feel the air temperature falling. Wonder where Les went. No surprise he took off, I guess.

Wouldn't be any use to call the police. To explain what happened. They'd peg us both as out-staters. There's only one policy for those situations. Drive and dump. We'd be just as stuck somewhere else.

The truck, though. That pisses me off. Yeah, it's not mine. But still.

Les makes his appearance a few minutes later. Wheels

79

up the sidewalk. Face red as Sam's hand. Nostrils wide open. Wheel rails bent and abused. Each thrust a rapid shot forward. Doesn't give his wheelchair time to coast.

Les hooks through an opening in the gate. Skids to a stop in front of us.

"Where are they?" Les says. "They're here, aren't they?"

"Who?" Sam says.

"Those two fucker pigshits. Where are they?" Les says. Spit runs off his chin.

I take it he means the two hay bales.

"Haven't seen 'em since this morning," I say.

A damp shirtsleeve dulls the shine on Les's face.

"You're kidding me, right?" Les says. "They were supposed to come back with the truck. Your truck. Pick me up from the hospital."

Joe's going to be mad as hell.

"Sorry. Haven't seen them," Sam says. Lights another cigarette.

"Damn it," Les says. Takes his Navy Vet hat off. No hair underneath. Just sweat.

"They're probably just late," I say. Holding out hope I'm right. "Let's wait. I'm sure they'll show up."

Les shakes his bald head.

"No time for that. Help me find them," Les says. "We find them, we find your truck."

I don't feel like getting off this bench. Sitting and drinking are two things I've become somewhat of an expert at doing. I look at Sam. She shrugs.

"Might as well," Sam says. Turns to Les. "Where do even start?"

Les unsheaths his steel cane from the side of the wheelchair. Points to a street in the distance. "Over there. Let's go. Hurry," he says.

Sam and I start out, cigarettes and liquor in hand.

Les doesn't move.

"One of you sorry bastards needs to push me. I'm tired," Les says.

Fine. I volunteer myself. No sense in Sam pushing with that bad hand.

We head out down the street. Sam follows behind Les and me. It's a quiet walk.

Les points with his cane. "See that alley? Go there," he says.

It takes a couple minutes to cross the street. It's near downtown and busy as hell. Wasn't like this growing up. You could play baseball in the street. Oil boom changed that.

Lots more buildings now, too. I didn't notice them before. Chain restaurants especially. Sandwich joints. Coffee shops. Bakeries. I'm used to seeing those things served in the same place. Made by one person, not 20.

We head down the alley. It opens up into a patch of grass. A metal shipping container sits in the middle. Tools are scattered on the ground. A tan truck is parked outside it.

"Abe? Tor?" Les says.

No response.

Sam laughs.

"What's funny?" Les says.

"That's their names? Abe and Tor?" Sam says. "Did they walk out of a *Little House on the Prairie* book?"

"It suits them," Les says. Points to the side of the container. "There's your truck."

I look at the tan truck again. Montana plates. Only vaguely looks like the truck I slept in last night.

"I see *a* truck. Not *the* truck," I say.

"Nope. That's the one. Take me to it," Les says.

I review the scratches, dings and other beauty marks on the truck. They line up. Yep. That's the truck. New plates. Paint job. Wonderful. Why is any of that necessary?

Les's accent is all I need to know. He's a fucking out-stater and he's up to no good. Which also means he can keep my interest. That's the thing with these out-staters. You can only ever really half like them.

I push Les toward the truck. Stop about halfway there. Spot something.

Sam stops walking when she sees it, too.

"What's the problem?" Les says.

I point the wheelchair at what I'm seeing.

"That," I say and point.

"Holy shit," Les says.

Chapter 24

R ed wipes a sheet of dust from the chair in his basement. Been a long time since he's sat in it. Used to come down here a lot. Not so much anymore. Something about being upstairs. Near windows.

He scoots the chair to a metal desk. Switches on a light bulb above his head. It pops to life. Illuminates the tributaries of metal winding through the mess on the desk.

Even in the dryness of early fall, the basement is damp. Muggy. The whole house has its own climate.

His right hand searches a drawer. Pushes through papers. Finds a yellow highlighter.

His left hand simultaneously places a book onto the desk. Leans against book. The Bible. The Gideons gifted it to him when Red became sheriff.

Red doesn't reference that one. Not tonight. He's read the bookmarked pages enough. Needs something else this time.

"*Steps Forward: Finding Courage and Confidence to Make Big Changes*," Red says. Reads the title of the book out loud.

He'd pocketed it from Mary's living room. Not that she'd notice. The book is still fresh. The virgin spine clamps the crisp pages together.

Red looks at the Bible.

"Don't worry. I didn't steal this," he says to the holy book. "I was the one who bought it."

Red picks a chapter in the middle. Doesn't start at the beginning. That's where he wrote the dedication to Mary.

He almost flips to it anyway. Perches his thumb between the pages, ready to crack them open. Curious. Can't quite remember what he wrote. Remembers what it says, though.

Too painful now. Can't look at it.

Chapter 25

A few miles away, Gus toils in his basement, too. It's late. The rest of his family is in bed.

Gus isn't reading a book, though. He's taking the rust off a single-shot shotgun, a Winchester 37.

It's the same one he's had since a kid. Nicknamed it "Safety" back in those years. Sort of a play on "safety first, safety last, safety always" from firearms training. Simple kid thinking.

Only Red, as sheriff, is issued a firearm by the county. Gus, being on reserve, is left to his own devices. Literally.

Gus never thought once about those devices. Better to let Red shoot first if it ever came to that. Different story now. He figures he has good reasons.

Foremost is that Jane person Red hired out to track down Wil. It's common now for the oil boom to overwhelm law enforcement. Contracting the work is one solution. But the last time Red hired this Jane person, things didn't go so well. More trouble than it's worth.

That Red would hire out again despite that history means something's up. Something that makes Gus scrub Safety hard. Especially since his wife and kids are sleeping upstairs.

"Safety" is the only firearm Red doesn't know about. Never seen it. Good. Red's got an overreaction to things. Might ask Gus for his guns. In the name of "safety," "just in case" or "for your own good."

Gus won't let those words happen. He'll write them his own way. For *his own good*, Safety won't stay *just in the case*. No. It's staying with him. Right next to a box of BB shotshells. Goose loads. Hard stuff. With stopping power.

And a box of slugs. For making windows inside people.

Just in case.

Chapter 26

*L*es lets out a "what the?" as he spots the plum-sized red lump. It's on the ground a few feet in front of us.

"What the hell is that?" Sam says. As if it needs to be said.

I push Les closer. The tip of his cane pokes it.

"Looks like something the coyotes dragged in," Les says. "What do you think?"

I lean in for a look. Seen stuff like this back home. Coyote is a good guess.

"Maybe it's part of a deer?" I say.

"This is why a proper trash service is important. There's so much garbage just laying around," Les says. Cracks his knuckles against the cane. "Brings in the coyotes, raccoons and other trash critters."

"Yeah, just like Ugly and Fugly," Sam says. Cracks herself up.

"That'd be Abc and Tor. Two of my best guys. Watch your mouth," Les says.

He scans the scene. Eyes fall on the shipping container. The doors are locked. I spot him slipping a key from his pocket.

"You two wait here," Les says.

I let go. The wheelchair creaks to the container doors. Les unlatches the lock. Rolls into the darkness inside.

Sam motions toward the truck. She's had enough of Les. So have I. Don't have to ask me twice. This guy's proving to be more trouble than it's worth. Let's get the hell out of here.

I sprint to the driver side door. Get in. Sam's right behind.

The truck looks more familiar from the inside. There's tape along the seams of the seat, though. As if it's been cut open and repaired.

I run my hands along the edges of the seat. No knife underneath. No shotgun behind. Damn.

"Keys. You see keys?" I say. We dig through the cab. No hiding spot misses our fingers.

"Check the ignition," Sam says.

Great idea. There they hang. Dangling like honey drops in the setting sun.

Figures. The best way to hide something is to put it right in front of the person looking for it.

I glance at Sam. Relief spreads across my face. It's mirrored in hers. I almost smile. Almost.

I fire up the truck. Stick it into reverse. The nose of the truck is too close to the container to whip around and leave.

Sam glances to the container. Checks for Les. I hear the rusty cough of the container door opening. He's coming out.

My foot responds by pressing hard on the gas. The truck churns turf from beneath it. We careen backward.

I think we're in the clear. But then Sam shouts, "Watch out." I check my side mirrors. Can't spot what she sees.

Then I realize why. There's another truck inches behind us. I'm a quarter-second too late to do anything about it.

The truck stops with a violent shake. Our getaway didn't last 12 feet. We're trapped. Like flies in a jar.

Chapter 27

*T*he truck behind us is painted tan. Montana plates.
I damn well could've been looking at myself in the
mirror. Even got a man and woman inside it. Only
difference is our truck has a smashed rear. Their truck is
messed up in the front bumper.

I shift out of reverse. Nudge the gas pedal to see if
we're connected in a metal knot. The trucks separate as I
pull forward a foot or so.

"You OK?" I say to Sam.

She tugs at her necklace chain. The one with the
raccoon penis jewelry.

"I'm lucky. Knocked the wind out of me more than
anything," Sam says. "You don't look so good."

I check my forehead in the mirror. Got a little goose
egg hatching under the skin.

I spot the man and woman from the other truck in the
mirror. They head our way. Look mad as hell.

"You must've been in one sweet hurry," the man says
between huffs of adrenaline.

He's shirtless beneath a pair of grease-stained overalls.
Coated in bristly hair from the head on down.

Les is outside my door now. Jerks it open. Shouts
incoherent obscenities with a red face. Jabs at me with the
cane.

Sam intervenes. Now she's pissed, too. Leans over,
grabs the cane. Pushes back at Les with it. The wheelchair
glides away.

"Knock it off, you old fuck," Sam says. "What are you
getting so mad about? It was an accident."

I shut and lock the door to block Les's cane. He's still
yelling something. I wait until he's calmed down enough to

talk. Roll the window down.

"You owe me a truck. You backed into two of my people. Do you have any idea how hard it is to get a truck out here? Way more demand than supply," Les says. Points the cane at me. "I saw you making like a 'coon out of a combine. You should've been more careful."

"It was an accident, Les. We cleaned up that trash. Now we're leaving," I say. "Tell your people to move their truck."

"You were going to just up and leave?" Les says. "But we haven't found Abe and Tor yet."

"Frankly, Les, I don't give a damn," I say.

A *Gone with the Wind* reference. Sam grins even though it's cliché.

"If they weren't in the container, maybe they went to work for someone else," Sam says.

Yeah, maybe Abe and Tor didn't enjoy working for an unstable asshole like Les.

"Yeah, they probably got bought out. Happens all the time out here. Employers poach hands any way they can. Just can't find enough bodies out here. It's too bad. They were good workers," Les says.

I check the mirrors. We're still trapped. Container in front. Truck behind. More or less at Les's mercy. I feign sincerity.

"That's too bad, Les. I feel for you. I wish me and Sam could help, but I think it's time we got going. Now how about you tell your people to move their truck?" I say.

Les slides the cane across the open window. Pokes my cheek with the tip. Twists it so the flesh inside my cheek screws against my teeth.

I roll the window up so it's open just a crack. Getting real tired of that cane.

"You're not leaving," Les says. "You owe me for fucking up my truck."

Sam nudges my arm. Nods for me to check the rear view mirror.

I see the man and woman in the truck behind us loading shotguns. Extended magazine tubes on each.

Les looks to them. Then to Sam and me. Takes off his blue Navy Vet hat. Scratches his bald head. Thinks for a minute.

I do, too. Think of ways to outrun those shotguns if we bail from the cab. Nothing comes to mind. They have us in one hell of a tight spot.

Les looks like he's thinking, too. His face relaxes after a sec.

"OK, you two. I suppose it was an accident after all. You don't owe me for the truck," Les says. Probably faking sincerity as much as I just did. "Do you have any place to stay tonight or are you planning on sleeping on benches again?"

"Why you asking?" I say.

"Ever heard of the Man Camps? I run one of them. Got a few spare campers. Could set you two up for the night," Les says. His gentle tone betrays the fact two loaded shotguns behind us are ready to put us down. "Then in the morning, you could come work for me. Give it a trial run. If you don't like the pay or the conditions, you can leave. Sound fair?"

I've heard of the Man Camps before. Housing is tight, so fields become permanent campgrounds. Scores of oil workers making cities on the prairie. All of the population of a city. None of the government or services.

Stories coming out of the Man Camps are why I don't like out-staters. These places would be called slums in other countries. Shanty towns. Collections of trucks, campers and makeshift houses. Open sewers. Prostitutes. Drugs. Booze. Murder. You name it.

Looking at Les, I can see the truth in those stories.

This guy could just as easily be a prairie pimp as a trash collector.

I exchange glances with Sam. She shrugs. Not like we have too many options.

"You better be paying something sweeter than what we can get around town," Sam says to Les.

"I promise. The pay is like nothing you'll find anywhere else," Les says. "All you'll have to do is pick up trash, too. I need reliable hands."

"I need some real numbers," I say. If I'm going to a Man Camp, I need to know it's worth it.

Les tells us the number. Sam mouths a "Wow."

"All that for picking up trash?" I say.

"That's right," Les says. "That's how shorthanded we are out here."

Now I understand the boom. Thought I did before, but I wasn't even close. The rush of money goes straight to your head. Or maybe straight away from it.

"I'll take that as a yes," Les says. "Right?"

"Right," I say.

"Right?" Les says to Sam.

"Yeah," Sam says.

"Good. Then give me and my people a ride to the on/off bar near the expressway," Les says. Thumbs in the direction. "It's a real shithole, but I need to sort out a problem before we go to the Man Camp."

Chapter 28

L es is right. This place is a shithole. Like walking into a smoldering cigarette. Everyone here looks burned out. A tap away from falling off the edge. From their ashy clothes to their cherry red faces.

I assume they're oil workers. Must be in town for a drink. This is the place to do it. Cash only. Drive-through window. No security cameras in the parking lot.

We cut through the off-sale part. A lady says "hi" to Les like they've met before. Ignores the rest of us. Good. Wouldn't want to be recognized in this place.

The shortcut brings us to the back of the bar. We take seats at a table. Les peels off a few big bills. Tells the man in overalls we came in with to buy a round.

A drink sounds perfect. I start to tell him my order. He shakes his head. Laughs. No special orders here. There's one kind of beer. One kind of liquor. One generic cola. Just different ways of serving the three.

The man in overalls comes back. Passes out the beers. Watery, see-through stuff. Like the bar is trying to stretch supply to meet demand. I drink better at the hole in the wall back in Betrug. That's saying something.

The rest of the bar drinks the stuff like water. Rightfully so. Chug hard to catch a buzz.

Sam and I feign interest in the drinks. Les chats with the man in the overalls. Points at a door across the bar.

"Enjoy your beers. I need to take care of that problem," Les says. Wheels away with the man .

Sam and I drink in silence for the next couple minutes. Try to make small talk with that other woman. She seems as uninterested in us as we are in her. Switch back to silence. It doesn't last long.

Someone is screaming from the other side of the bar.

Chapter 29

I don't have to fight the urge to get up. Too tired. Sam must be the same way. Along with the rest of the bar. No one reacts. Just keep rowing through the ocean of pale beers.

Maybe it's just me? Maybe there wasn't a scream after all?

I look to Sam. She's listening with a perked ear. Must've heard it, too.

Someone turns the background music up. Way up. Sounds like George Straight is singing from inside my head. If there's another scream, no one is going to hear it.

The music returns to normal volume. I spot Les and the man in overalls returning to the bar. Shut that door on the far side behind them. They look happy. Beaming.

"Cheers," Les says when he wheels back to our table. Hoists a beer. "Problem solved."

He clinks each one of our glasses with his. Even the ones Sam and I didn't raise.

"What was that about?" Sam says.

Les and the man in overalls grin to each other.

"This oil boom is shaping up to be more and more like a war. Reminds me of the good ol' days when I was in the service. Miss 'em," Les says. Adjusts his Navy Vet hat. "That's an ugly truth. Veterans miss the action. There's nothing like it. A lot of 'em came home from Iraq and Afghanistan. Rebooted their lives working oil. But they never left the desert, if you catch my drift."

"From oil field to oil field," Sam says.

I spot a little blood on the tip of Les's cane.

"They want to play war out here, fine. But I'm from the old school. Vietnam. I don't play," Les says. Wipes his gray handlebar mustache on his sleeve. "When there's a problem, I don't get mad about it. I don't complain. I fix it."

"They say the first casualty of war is the truth," Sam says.

Les grins. "Trust me. The truth died out here a long time ago," he says.

Chapter 30

"*T*alk."

Abe's heard stories about wounded guys in wartime. Wake up in the hospital. Come to realize they're blind. Horrifying. Must be as bad to watch.

Not sure if it's like that now. Abe's eyes are open. Can't see anything. Either blind or the lights are off.

The voice behind his ear blurts out again.

"Talk."

Abe squints. No use. Can't make anything out. Not even a figure against the blackness. Wherever he is, it's the darkest he's ever seen. Or not seen, if he's blind.

"Open your mouth and talk."

Abe tries to get up. Feels restraints around his wrists and ankles. Tied to something. A chair? It's soft. Like a waterbed.

"Say something."

Abe remembers not being able to talk. Got the wind knocked out of him. Near the truck. When was that? How much time had passed?

His nose comes back to life. Smells like ... paint? Is he in the shipping container?

That voice. Can't tell if it's male or female. Almost like it's being filtered through a mask.

A wet bead runs down his cheek. Worms its way over his lips. He tastes it. Disgusting. Not salty like sweat. More like licking a rock. Iron.

Another bead meets his lips. And another. And another. He feels it dripping onto his head. Must be paint. What else could it be?

"Talk."

Abe spits the paint out. Breathes deep.

"Talk about what?" Abe says. "Where am I?"

"Good. You can talk. Now tell me everything," the voice says.

"Everything about what?"

"About your job. About the people you work with. Everything."

"Can I go then?" Abe says.

"We'll see."

Whatever is dripping onto Abe is increasing its frequency. If talking is the only option, Abe decides to take it.

He gives in and lets out. About Les and his background on the Bakken. The shakedowns. The extortions. The violence. The things that go in and out of the Man Camp Les runs. And the things that never leave.

The voice paces the room. Abe still can't make anything out.

"Good," the voice says.

There's a pause. Abe isn't sure if he's supposed to reply. Does anyway.

"Turn on the lights. Let me go," Abe says.

"Yes," the voice says.

There's a crackle as light scalds a hole in the darkness.

Abe barely has time to examine his surroundings. He looks up. It isn't paint dripping onto him. It's blood from Tor's body. Hangs by a chain a few feet above Abe's head.

Abe's scream is loud enough to exorcise his soul into the room. A hard blow to the head from behind takes it the rest of the way.

Chapter 31

*I*t's a long, cramped drive in the truck. Les tosses his wheelchair in the back. Sits in the cab. Sam takes the middle.

The other man and woman crawl into sleeping bags in the bed of the truck. Still don't know their names. Won't matter anyway. It's fall on the prairie. Nighttime. And I'm driving 65. They'll probably freeze to death. Fine.

US Highway 2 is the main drag between Minot and Williston. It's a main artery of the oil boom. Where a person can almost feel the pulse of the fracking underground.

Traffic is heavy. Big city heavy. What should be empty prairie is dotted with security lights. They illuminate the shadows of the windmills, the other energy boom out here. Their arms claw at the blank stars like they're trying not to drown.

It's a funny thing about those windmills. All these other states want "green energy" from wind. None of them want windmills on their horizons. Say it kills birds. Uglies up the view.

So they build windmills in North Dakota instead. On the prairie. Out of view. Ask a bird if that makes one damn bit of difference.

Same with the fracking. Nobody wants it in their backyard. But they'll wring their hands for the poor when no one can afford heat in the winter. NoDak to the rescue again. The place where hypocrites go to launder their guilt.

I guess that's why I'm taking a liking to Sam. Cuts through the bullshit. Boils things down to the dirt.

The more Les talks, the more I see he's the same way. I drive. Listen to him and Sam. Learn a lot about Man

Camps. Les is more than willing to offer a lesson. Beats the radio.

Once the boom hit, Les tells us, workers showed up in masses. Didn't matter if they had jobs or not. Slept in their cars until they found work. Some still did after they got jobs.

Local governments weren't too happy to see a pile of unemployed problems show up. Started restricting certain areas they could squat. A lot of them hit the prairie instead.

Of course, landowners weren't too thrilled with squatters in their fields. But law enforcement couldn't do anything about it. They were overwhelmed.

The oil companies played catch up to relieve the problem. They shipped in dorms, hangers, trailers, campers and all manner of human sardine cans. That helped the housing situation for a little while.

Thing is, the company camps are only for workers actually doing work. They cycle workers in and out in months-long shifts. Anyone on an "off time" had to leave the camp. That usually meant trekking back home or trying to find a non-existent vacancy at a hotel for an extended stay.

Along comes a guy like Les. Organizes the squatters into proper Man Camps. Cuts deals with landowners to rent out fields. Makes himself a sort of mayor. Charges "taxes" that fund services. Stuff like diesel generators for electricity. A well with running water. Hot showers. Bathrooms. Trash service. All shoehorned into a random corner of the prairie.

Little of that is particularly legal. But the government and the oil companies look the other way so long as things are kept orderly. Makes sense that Les plays with a strong hand. Or a strong cane, more like.

With the success of his Man Camp, Les branched out

into other services. Filling in gaps here and there. Like picking up trash in Minot parks. And recruiting the out-staters to do it.

"What if things get out of control? Aren't you worried the government will ban any Man Camps not affiliated with a company?" Sam says.

"Last time that happened, I let the cops take out a couple drug mules living in the camp. I keep a few trouble makers on reserve just in case some government agency needs a newspaper headline," Les says. "Does the trick every time."

I spot a blob of light in the distance. It breaks into smaller orbs as we get closer. Like BBs out of a shotgun in slow motion.

"Is that it?" Sam says.

"No. We've got another 20 miles or so. That's just one of the company camps," Les says.

The light is joined by others. Then more. And more. Tiny cities on the prairie.

How to tell one from the other is beyond me. Roads aren't marked. Just two-track paths cutting through the ditches.

Twenty miles turns into 45 minutes. We're stuck behind a rattrap RV. Can't pass. Too much traffic coming the other way.

Finally, Les points to a neon blue light in the distance.

"That's it," he says. "All my yard lights are blue. Helps them stand out."

We pull onto a service road next to a power substation. Another turn to a matted grass road and we're there.

Hard to believe what I see.

Chapter 32

T he phone on the desk in the basement wakes Red. The book glued to his sweaty face rises with him. He peels it off. Tosses it back.

Red doesn't need to guess the caller. The phone is connected to an unlisted line. Had it set up for Internet access. No one is supposed to know it. Except for...

"Jane," Red says into the phone.

"I'm following up," Jane says back. Scrambled. Metallic. Like she's talking through a harmonica jacketed in steel wool. "Ready?"

Jane always talks in grunts. Like each word requires another step up a hill. Annoys Red.

"How did you know I was near this line? Are you tracking me?" Red says.

"Yes. Always," Jane says.

No surprise there. Jane tracked Red last time they worked together. Figures she must have access to satellite data or something. Red would rather not know.

"Why?" Red says.

"Protection. For me. And you."

Red rubs his jaw. Jane's as paranoid as he is sometimes.

"That why you sent a cross dresser to meet me back in St. Cloud?" he says.

"You've never actually met me. You never will. No one has," Jane says. "But you will meet my people. I am the cause. They are the effects. You met one of them in St. Cloud."

"Alright, enough with the cloak and dagger crap," Red says. Still groggy from being asleep 30 seconds ago. "Didn't you have a follow-up?"

"Yes," Jane says. There's a pause. Like she's away from the phone. "As you know, I found the truck. Didn't find the target."

Red's free hand works on untying the knot in his neck. "Where'd he go?"

"Questioned two others. They were with the truck. They're part of a larger operation. One I need to address. Many factors at play now, not just the target," Jane says.

"What about Wil, though?" Red says.

He won't refer to people as "targets." Seems inhuman. Targets are for shooting.

Red doesn't want Wil dead. Just back to Betrug for a quick chat. Then hand him over to the federal and state agencies heading the search.

Of course, Red has no plans to let them know about Jane's news. They'd cut him out of the investigation since the beginning. Now he's returning the favor.

"What about Wil?" Red says again.

"That's all, sheriff," Jane says.

The phone line goes dead.

Red sets the receiver down. Looks around the room. Checks the desk. Feels for bugs. Not that he even knows how they look or feel. Gives up after a minute or two.

Jane's not telling him something. That wasn't so much of a follow-up as a shutdown. She's distracted by something. Or not giving him the complete picture. Maybe she'd already found Wil, but for some reason won't tell him. Hard to say.

Gus had the sense to try to stop Red from hiring Jane. It's what Red told him to do after last time. Red had told himself the same thing, too.

Neither warning worked. Why?

Red picks up the book, *Steps Forward: Finding Courage and Confidence to Make Big Changes*. Turns to the first pages. Reads the dedication written in black pen.

Reminds himself why it's worth working with Jane to get Wil back to Betrug.

> *Mary,*
> *I can't wait for our new life together.*
> *Red*

Chapter 33

*I*t's what I don't see when I pull into the Man Camp that takes me by surprise.

I'm expecting something rough. Broken beer bottles. Bloody noses. Meth tweakers barreling frantic apeshit on each other.

Nope.

Horseshoes. That's what I see. A game of horseshoes. Two makeshift pits sit under a bluish yard light on a tall pole. It's on the edge of the camp. I ease the truck past them.

Looks like a fun time. Four men versus four women. The sight puts me at ease. Can't be that bad here. Sam perks up, too.

Les tells me to stop. Rolls down his window. The drone of diesel generators outside spills into the cab.

"Who's winning?" Les says. Leans his head out the window.

One of the women comes over.

"We are," the woman says. Looks at me and Sam. "Newbies?"

"Yeah. Lost Abe and Tor today. Ran off. But I got even better helpers," Les says. "This here is Wil and Sam."

"Hey," Sam and I say at the same time.

"Nice to meet you," the woman says. "Gotta get back. There's 500 bucks on this game."

Wow. One hell of a horseshoes game they've got going. Guess there really is some money to burn out here.

"Have fun. We'll talk soon," Les says. Turns to me. "Follow the two-track into the camp. Go slow."

I follow the directions. Guide the truck down the two-track path. We crest a hill. Our headlights fall onto the main camp.

Now this is more what I pictured.

The camp is a mix of shit, crap, junk, garbage, trash, litter and campers. Yeah, those words all mean the same thing. But one word won't do when there's so much of it.

No open sewer pits, nothing like that. Just messy. Debris everywhere. If shit weren't assembled into loose rows I'd think it's a dump.

And that's just what we can see in the headlights and lanterns scattered around. There's plenty the light doesn't touch.

"Yeah, it's pretty bad right now," Les says. "Been short of trash pickers for a while."

"They can't pick up after themselves?" I say.

I'm not the most orderly guy in the world. But even I have enough sense to not shit where I eat.

"They actually do. But where do you put it? The wind spreads it around," Les says. "These guys work their asses off on the rigs. They drink, sleep and fuck here. That's it. Trash is the last thing on their minds."

"Don't some of these workers have families with them?" Sam says.

"Just wives and girlfriends. No kids. They're forbidden," Les says. "Kids mean school. School means government people."

I check license plates as we putt along. Texas. Colorado. Georgia. California. Alaska. Manitoba. Ontario. On and on.

Crammed between the campers are piles of gear. Firewood. Portable storage lockers. Tools. ATVs. Gas cans. Space heaters. Air conditioners. Stoves. Propane tanks. Fishing rods. Laundry. Boots. Overalls. Helmets. File cabinets. Coffee pots. Tomato plants. Canvas bags overflowing with soup cans. All balled up in miles of electrical cords.

The campers and vehicles aren't in bad shape. Most look brand new. The workers probably bought them on the way here. It's just all the shit around them. A meteor could hit and no one would know the difference.

We pass row after row. I pay attention to the license plates. Looks like the workers grouped themselves by state.

"So where's all this great stuff you built?" Sam says. "This just looks like squatters."

"It is squatting. Glorified squatting," Les says. Points somewhere into the night. "Built a big bathroom over there. Another one just for showers. The third one is for laundry. Dug two wells to water the camp. All the waste water drains into ... well, it goes away. Plus, 24-hour diesel generators provide all the electricity a person could need. It's all included in the rent."

"What about food? You supply that, too?" Sam says.

"A couple RVs got stuck in the mud a while back. I bought 'em both. Converted them into camp stores. Don't have much, but it's got the essentials. Everything from toothpaste to cooking oil," Les says. Sounds proud of himself.

He's right to brag. This is one hell of a set up. Like its own city.

We near the end of the rows. Les tells me to take a left. It looks like we're headed out onto the prairie. Then I see the outline of a small cluster of RVs. It's separate from the main camp.

"Everyone who works directly for me lives here," Les says as we come to a stop.

Not bad. Not bad at all. Much cleaner over here. The campers are more spaced out, too.

We help Les into his wheelchair. He shows us to a big RV. Damn near the size of a city bus.

"This was Abe and Tor's place. Can't say what's inside.

They weren't in it much. Should be unlocked. Never lock your door here. It's against the rules," Les says. Nods to the RV. "It's yours now. If those two bastards come crawling back, let me know. There's a shotgun waiting for them."

Les wheels off. Talks with the man and woman from the truck bed. They're half frozen from the ride, but somehow alive.

Sam and I circle the RV. She seems unsure. Like maybe spending a night in an RV with me isn't the best idea.

I pick up on her apprehension.

"Look, you still got that knife, right?" I say. Keep my voice low. Les and the others are busy talking about something else.

"Yeah," Sam says.

"Well I don't have mine," I say. Empty my pockets to prove it. "So I'm not going to touch you."

"So you would if you did?" Sam says.

Good question. Shit. Real good question. Because I'm still not sure how much we trust each other. Guess we're about to find out.

"It wouldn't matter if I had a bazooka. I'm here to make a little money, then see what happens next," I say. "Besides, your penis thing has worked so far."

Sam gives a weak smile.

"Seriously?" she says.

"Seriously. That word's still like tinder in my brain."

"Yeah. Seriously," I say.

Sam's smile gets a little wider.

"OK. But we're not playing house. We're partners. Roommates. Whatever you want to call it. Nothing more than that. Got it?" Sam says.

"Got it. I'll even take the couch if it makes you feel better," I say. "Assuming there's a couch in there."

"It would," Sam says.

I open the RV side door. Take a look inside. It's a good thing one of us is armed.

Chapter 34

The RV is spotless. All except for one area. The kitchen table. There's a nest of shredded cardboard. Breakfast cereal. Granola bars. A silver hump mills about in the mess.

A raccoon.

"Oh, shit," I say.

The raccoon makes a face roughly the same as mine.

I look back to Sam.

"You should take out that raccoon penis. Wave it around. Maybe it'll get the hint," I say.

Sam's already opted for the knife. Clenches it in her good hand.

"I've got a better idea," she says.

The next 10 minutes are straight out of a *Three Stooges* skit. Corralling the raccoon out the door or into the knife is like trying to pick the salt off a basket of French fries.

The raccoon hisses like a pack-a-day demon. Sounds bloated. Must be eating well in the Man Camp. We corner it. It hisses. Tries to bite us. We back away. It runs off. Repeat.

We finally herd the varmint out the door. It bolts into the night toward the main camp. Off toward heaps of 'coon paradise.

Sam clears her throat when we're done. Says, "I see there's just one bedroom in the back. A bunk bed in the hall. But you're taking the couch in the kitchen, right?"

The bunk in the hall makes more sense than the couch. I get her point, though. Not going to fight her on it.

"Sure. I'll take the couch," I say.

We take turns hitting the RV's small shower. The

bathroom is fully stocked. Soap. Towels. Toothbrushes.

Oh, the hot shower. Never felt so good. Didn't realize how filthy I was until the drain backs up.

Abe and Tor kept quite the assortment of jeans and flannel shirts. They're baggy, but they come with belts.

I find a pile of blankets in a closet. Build a quick bed on the couch. Sleep hits quickly, but something wakes me only a few minutes later.

The shadow person is back.

Chapter 35

*T*he shadow person. It found me. It's outside the RV.

I don't have to look out the window to know it. It's a feeling at first. Hits me hard. A tightness in my muscles. Pulls me up like I'm chained to a gurney. An invisible hand tilts my head to look out the window.

There. Look. Coming from within the Man Camp. It starts as a wobbling dot. Then it sprouts arms. Legs. A head. No face.

The night blends in and out with its limbs. Blurs the edges of its shape. But I still know it's there. Coming toward me.

It controls my pulse with its steps. Each one churns my heart faster. Then slower. Then faster again. It's playing with me. Dribbling my heartbeat like a basketball.

I should panic. I *want* to panic. But I don't.

If I let fear take over, how fast will it run? Will it beat my heart out of my chest?

Or maybe it's not even real. This must be my head. There's no other way.

It moves out of view. I shuffle to the next window. Hope it won't be there. That it's just my imagination.

No. It's there. Still a good distance out. It's pacing now. As if it's making a decision. Then it stares right at me.

A feeling, a word, comes over me. I know it before I hear it. And the voice comes from just behind my right shoulder. It's clear. Crushes the air in my ear. This is not my imagination.

"Seriously," a voice says.

I hear footsteps from inside the RV. They're inches away.

I spin my weight around. There's a shadow against the wall.

What happens next tosses me back to reality.

Chapter 36

"Seriously?" Sam says. Flicks on the light.

"What were...you were...?" I say.

I can't tell what I'm saying. Adrenaline cools in my veins. Feels like I just picked myself up after jumping out an airplane.

"The hell are you doing?" Sam says. "I heard all this noise."

"Looking ... uh ... out the window?" I say. Just as puzzled as Sam.

She reaches over to my hand. Jerks away something. The knife.

A knife? I had the knife?

"Thought you said I could trust you," Sam says.

I got her knife? When did that happen?

"Really, I don't know," I say.

"Uh huh. You're just another creeper fuck," Sam says. Grabs the truck keys from the counter.

The last thing I want is for her to leave. Whatever twisted shit is going on in my mind, I can't be alone. And I don't want Sam to not trust me. She's all I've got out here.

"It's just...I've been having these nightmares. Real weird ones," I say.

My faces creases in a way it hasn't in years. Desperation. It's always been there. The husk of my skin kept it hidden.

Not anymore. Something is wrong with me. My insides feel like a balled up knot of worms. Constantly writhing. Nervous. Anxious.

Sam scans my eyes for bullshit. Finds none. At least I think she doesn't.

"Fine. But I don't care if you're sleepwalking or having

nightmares or what. You come near me at night, I will hurt you," Sam says. Keeps the knife in her hand. "What were you dreaming about anyway?"

I stand up. Put myself between her and the door. Check the windows.

"For two nights now, I've had dreams about seeing this shadow person. I wake up. Look out the window. Watch this...thing...walk around," I say. "Scares the hell out of me."

"That's fucked up," Sam says.

"Yeah, I know. It's the truth, though. Keep the knife. Keep the truck keys. I'm not trying to hurt you. Just been having a brainfuck," I say.

I watch Sam put the keys back on the counter. The knife rotates in her palm.

"I'm going back to bed. But I'm not here to fix you. I'm not your shrink," Sam says.

I can handle that. Don't blame her. The money is why we're here. *Damn good* money. It's why anyone is here. Friendship is cheap.

I'm about to wish Sam a good night's sleep. Something cuts me off.

Three heavy knocks on the door.

Chapter 37

My first thought is the shadow person is at the door. It's a stupid thought. It's what I feel before my better sense takes over.

Sam backs into the hallway. Watches me answer.

I open the RV's side door. I do it slow. Like a coyote creeping up on a covey of sharpies. The right way.

Learned that after shaking down an out-stater farm hand. Stole a year's supply of tractor hydraulic fluid. Expensive shit. But that's what you get for hiring out-staters.

The fucker knew I was coming. Had a hatchet ready to go on the other side of a door. Only he didn't count on one thing. You can see a whole helluva lot through a quarter-inch crack. I got the drop on him.

I do the same thing now. Only I don't see a hatchet. I see a scrawny bastard with a body that looks like the shotgun in his hands. He's leaning on the gun. Like a construction worker on the side of the road with a shovel. Idiot will get himself killed that way.

I open the door the rest of the way. Nice and slow. No surprises.

"What?" I say.

The scrawny guy shoulders the shotgun.

"Heard some noise. There a problem here?" he says.

"Who the hell are you?" I say.

Was he the shadow person?

"I'm the night watch. Make sure everyone's safe," the scrawny guy says. Cranes his neck inside. The bulbs in his eye sockets light up when he spots Sam. He calls to her. "You OK?"

"I'm fine," she says.

"Oh, yeah? What's the knife for then?" the scrawny guy says. His shoulder leads his way into the RV. "Maybe I should come in."

I stick a hand up. Stop his advance.

Here's another thing I learned as a shit shoveler back home. No one who shows up with a gun in hand and says, "I'm here to help," ever does. Not cops. Not neighbors. Not random guys with shotguns at a Man Camp in the Bakken.

Honest folk, they just help. They don't announce it. And they don't need guns to do it.

"We're fine," I say.

He backs off. That was easy.

"Well, if the lady ever needs it, I can be a helpful person," the scrawny guy says. Turns to leave. Looks over his shoulder before heading out. Gets another look at Sam.

"Bummer. That's twice now I didn't get to use this knife tonight," Sam says after he's gone.

"Then let's break the streak. You hungry?" I say.

"Always," Sam says.

I dig out a loaf of bread. Jar of peanut butter. Use the knife to glue a couple sandwiches together. Haven't eaten anything since lunch.

"So what makes your raccoon penis lucky?" I say. Just making conversation between bites.

"Funny story about that," Sam says.

What she tells me next is hard to hear.

Chapter 38

Sam unwinds the penis bone from its chain. Dips it into the peanut butter jar. Spreads a thin layer on another piece of bread.

"I'm from Ohio. A big town, but a one-business town. And it ain't there anymore. Found myself with two options: Military or motherhood. Guess which one I picked?" Sam says.

I buy some time with another sticky bite of sandwich. Not sure if this is a trick question. It's set up like one.

"So where's your kid?" I say.

"Nowhere. I signed up for the Ohio National Guard. Made it halfway through training. Then they made some changes. Closed a base. Would've had to move across the state," Sam says.

"And then you had a kid?" I say.

"Wise ass. I dropped out of training. Took my chances on the road instead. Thumbed my way to the oil boom," Sam says. Cleans the penis bone with a napkin. "Your turn. What about you?"

Was hoping she wouldn't stop talking. Still curious.

I say, "Not much more to say. Told you everything already."

"Everything?"

"I skipped the boring parts," I say.

Now it's Sam's turn to be a wise ass.

"So where's your kid?" she says.

"You're funny," I say. "Not too many opportunities in Betrug for that. Or in much else of North Dakota."

Sam looks out the window. Watches the scrawny guy pick his nose outside. Still hasn't left our view.

"Hopefully he's from Betrug, too," she says. Nods to

the scrawny guy.

"Never met him," I say.

We eat in silence for a minute or two.

"What about your family?" Sam says after the break in conversation.

I shake my head. "Not much to say there, either."

"You're a pretty boring person," Sam says. Grins.

"I come from a pretty boring place," I say. Return the grin. Helps ease into my next question. "So how'd you end up hitchhiking? Someone like you, seems like you'd at least have a car. You're not a total fuck up. Trying to keep a low profile or something?"

Sam leans over the table. Speaks in a whisper.

"I think I killed someone," she says.

Chapter 39

"Seriously?" I say.

"Seriously," Sam says.

There's a long pause. I can't work up a comeback. What do you say to that? Congratulations? How'd you do it?

"So ... you *think* you killed someone?" I say.

"Yes. I think I killed someone," Sam says.

She says it slow. One. Word. At. A. Time. Her eyes watch me process the confession.

It feels more like an accusation. Like *I* killed someone. Shouldn't feel that way, since obviously I haven't. But it does.

My mouth is smarter than my gut. This is about her, not me.

"What do you mean?" I say.

Sam's silent. Like she doesn't like me asking. Maybe she wanted me to say something else?

I'm ready to grab the keys and leave. Yeah, I've done plenty of illegal shit in my time. But murder? That's my line. That's everyone's line. Not hanging out with murderers.

Hell, even the farmers who hired me would ask if the shithead I roughed up was OK. Hit 'em. Cut 'em. Whatever. But never kill 'em. It's just money, after all. There's plenty of it. The farmers more or less wanted to get a point across. Not put people in the ground.

This is why you can't trust out-staters. They fuck with your head. Tell you all kinds of stories.

I reach for the knife. It's already gone. Sam's licking the peanut butter off it. Real nice and slow. Eyes on me the whole time.

"Do you think I did it?" Sam says.

"How am I supposed to know?" I say.

One of us is fucked up in the head. Or both, but I can't tell. Not with the adrenaline greasing my heart beat into overdrive. Not with the brainfuck of this entire night. Wouldn't be surprised if that shadow person walked through the door and made a sandwich.

"You must think I'm a murderer. You reached for the knife. Maybe you know something you're not telling me," Sam says.

"Like what? That I know something about a murder? I thought this was about you, not me," I say.

"It is about you. Not me. Because I thought I could trust you with a secret. Turns out you've got a killer streak yourself," Sam says. Points the tip of the knife at me. "What would you have done if you'd got to this knife before me?"

"Just being careful. A pretty forgivable offense. I didn't want you to *think* you'd killed me next," I say. "Isn't that what you would do if you thought I killed someone?"

"I just did," Sam says. Twirls the knife.

What the hell?

"Seriously? You think I killed someone?" I say.

"Maybe. You've been pretty shady so far. You don't carry yourself well. Something's bothering you. I can tell," Sam says.

No shit.

"Speak for yourself," I say. "Look, I'm a fuck up from a farm in North Dakota. I haven't talked to my folks in a long time. I do odd jobs as a hired hand for a living. This is one of them. That's it. The end. I'm no murderer. Now did you kill someone or what?"

The answer is not what I expect.

Chapter 40

Sam puts the knife back in the peanut butter jar. Looks me square in the eyes. Never blinks. Not once.

"At training camp. I'm in the shower by myself. A guy comes in. Outranks me by quite a bit. Puts his hands all over me. Doesn't go further than that. Leaves. Same thing happens again and again. Training went to hell from there," Sam says. Doesn't speak the words. Sheds them. "I knew he took three vitamins every day from the same bottle. Long, white pills. So I ordered some synthetic dope off the Internet. Long, white pills. Swapped them for the vitamins. Didn't stick around after that. Just hit the road. Heard on the news he died a couple days later. Heart attack."

No wonder she waited to tell me. Had to see if I would rat her out.

But that's not the first thing in my mind. It comes out my mouth. I immediately regret it.

"Why didn't you tell someone? Turn him in?" I say. "It's not worth losing your shot in the Guard, right?"

I must sound like an asshole. Blaming the victim.

Sam shakes her head.

"He was one of those lifers. Been there forever. Just pushed papers. Everyone loved him," she says. "Well, not *everyone*."

"You think you really killed him?" I say.

Sam shrugs.

"Maybe luck killed him. I took his lucky raccoon penis jewelry when I swapped the pills. It's lucky for me now. I can rest my conscious on that instead of the pill thing," she says. Flicks the grotesque gold totem on the chain around her neck.

I nod. Makes sense now. But I can't help but wonder one thing.

"OK, this isn't me being a dick. Honest question. Why'd you swap his pills? Why not just leave anyway?" I say.

Sam balls her hand into a fist. Squeezes tight. It shakes when she talks.

"If someone punches you, you punch back, right? That's fair?" she says.

"Yeah, that's fair," I say.

"This was worse than a punch. So I hit back. Right in his heart. That's fair," Sam says.

Can't argue with that.

"He deserved it then," I say.

Sam unclenches her fist. Nods.

"I tried to go back to a regular life after that. Nothing clicked. Lost faith in the rules. They're only there to protect the people who benefit from those breaking them," Sam says. "Figured I'd disappear into the oil boom up here instead. Make my own rules. My own life. Free from getting fucked over by the economy and the boss man. I won't ever let that happen again."

Sam leaves it at that. So do I.

We clean up and head back to bed. It's a good thing. We'll need the rest for tomorrow.

Chapter 41

"Joggers. It's always joggers. Forget bloodhounds. Forget search parties. Forget psychics. Just release the joggers."

FBI Special Agent Tom Roe always brings the humor. Says it lightens things up. Good PR for the Bureau. Shows the agents aren't stereotypical stoic robots with sunglasses.

The trench coats are the exception. They're true to form. A special shade of black. Like an undertaker.

The coats are fitting for a cool, fall morning in Minot. Tom stands near the Souris River in Oak Park. The fairgrounds sit half the town away to the east.

Yellow tape and squatting officers huddle near the water. The lazy churn of the Souris echoes off the bandshell behind them. Makes the river sound louder than normal. Crinkles the illusion of a benign, unassuming body of water. Two male bodies lay face down on the river bank. Look like meaty hay bales.

"That's an old joke," Special Agent Beth Haen says. She wears a matching trench coat.

"An oldie, but a goodie. Like the North Dakota radio stations. If you're into country gold," Tom says.

"Also an old joke. The radio is better than I thought it would be out here," Beth says.

She hates the hick stereotypes. Mainly because she used to live them. And they're not all bad.

The one about the ass-kicking country woman? It came to life one day at the bank. A guy came in with a shotgun. Beth handed over her deposit. Plus a shit-kicking heel to the son of a bitch's groin.

The stereotype died that day, too. The world opened up. Beth jumped right in. Decided to head to school.

Become an FBI agent.

"Fair enough. Do you want to check the bodies out? Or can you see what I see from here?" Tom says.

Another of Tom's pop quizzes. Beth is the junior of the two. Means there are no right answers.

"You mean that there's no blood?" Beth says. "And that there are restraint marks around all four ankles?"

"Nope. I see something else," Tom says.

Of course. Beth sips her coffee.

"Both their faces are shot up. Point blank," Tom says. "Know anyone violent with that kind of flair?"

"Wil Reynolds. Same person we've been chasing for a week," Beth says.

"Actually, it's been six days. Not quite a week," Tom says. Of course. "And, yep, looks like Wil isn't done killing."

Chapter 42

"How can you tell they don't have faces? We haven't flipped them over yet," Beth says.

She and Tom huddle near the face down bodies.

"Unless one of those rocks they're face down on is actually a pillow, I'd say there's no way their heads could've sunk down halfway," Tom says.

"Their fingers are still intact, though. Whoever did this wasn't worried about preventing identification," Beth says.

"Whoever? It's Wil. I'd bet my pension on it," Tom says. Winks.

Beth crosses her arms.

"The rookie thing is old and tired. Like your jokes," she says. "You planning on dropping it anytime soon?"

Tom shrugs.

"Sure, when you start making your own old, tired jokes," he says. "Then you're ready."

Beth keeps her arms crossed. Waits for the smart ass look to fade from Tom's face.

Tom's well on his way to retirement. It's why he's known in the Bureau as a top-notch asshole. A little bitter he's hit the point in his life when he's mentoring his replacement.

"Judging from the other injuries, it's pretty obvious they were tortured," Beth says.

She reviews the spaces of missing flesh in the two male bodies. The gaps are carved out. Scooped. Chunked. Shredded. Biology clearly exited the bodies in unnatural ways.

"You're missing the larger point here," Tom says. "Wil is escalating. He's becoming more dangerous. The other bodies in Betrug, they weren't mutilated like these two.

129

Just shot in the face with a shotgun."

Now it's Beth's turn to be a dick.

"Actually, you're the one missing something. There are no tire tracks in the wet dirt leading down here. So either they were dumped from a boat in the Souris River or they fell from the sky. Which means UFOs. Obviously," she says.

Tom coughs up a throaty chuckle.

"See? Now you're getting the hang of it," he says. "Tire tracks or not, they were still dumped in clear view. So for one, Wil wanted us to find them. Two, the exsanguinations happened somewhere else. In my professional opinion, he's fucking with us."

"Maybe that's the point. Maybe he's leading us to where the mutilations took place?" Beth says.

Tom cracks his neck. Scans the bodies a few more times. "It's fun to play *Da Vinci Code* with dead bodies. But a lot of times, the bad guys leave a back up, just in case the Bureau sends a couple knuckleheads who don't appreciate a well-executed rebus," he says.

"A rebus? That's a new one," Beth says.

Tom points to a folded piece of paper stuffed between two rocks a few yards from the bodies. "Just like I thought," he says. Retrieves the paper with a gloved hand.

"How'd you know?" Beth says.

"It's the oldest trick in the Bureau playbook," Tom says. Grins. "Let the local police tell you about it when you show up. Then take credit for the find."

Beth rolls her eyes. "What's it say?"

Tom unfolds the paper. It's clean of any blood or gore.

"That we need to go," he says. "Right now."

Chapter 43

"You sure about this?" Beth says.

The long, rectangle shipping container looks imposing. Isolated. Ominous. Just dumped in a vacant lot off an alleyway. East side of town. Not far from the fairgrounds.

Tan paint stains the ground outside the container. Tire tracks and miscellaneous car parts score the dirt. They look fresh. The container looks old. Rusty.

"Yep. This is the place the note said to go. Used our names specifically even. This job gets easier every day," Tom says.

"No. I mean about even doing this. We should get the local officers to help," Beth says. Sweat blurs her vision for a moment. She blinks. It stings. "This doesn't feel right."

"Wil wants to talk. We shouldn't spook him," Tom says. "Don't look a gift horse in the mouth. Words to live by."

Beth rests her hand on the semi-auto pistol, a Glock 23, holstered to her hip. It's compact but newer than Tom's full-sized Glock 22.

"You got any jokes for this? I could use one," she says.

"OK. Two FBI agents walk into a sketchy shipping container. Guy inside confesses to a pile of murders. The agents take vacation. The end," Tom says.

The pair trade smirks before heading to the container. There's a hesitation in Tom's dominant hand. Can't decide whether to knock or step aside to open the door.

He doesn't get the chance to make a choice. The door creaks open on its own.

The burning stench of bleach overcomes them. They cough and step back. Beth clicks on her flashlight.

Their eyes don't have time to adjust. A piercing light reflects back at them. Makes them look away.

"Wil? Turn your flashlight off," Tom says. "Wil? You in there?"

A metallic growl answers from inside the container. Almost like it's playing from a recording.

"Turn your flashlight off, agent. You're facing a mirror," the voice says.

Tom nods to Beth. She clicks the light off. The blinding light goes away.

As their eyes adjust, the mirror becomes clear. It partitions the dark cavern of the container about 10 feet away. Only the agents are reflected. Nothing but stinging air rests between them.

"Identify yourself," Tom says.

"Wil Reynolds isn't here," the voice says. Could be coming from behind the mirror. Or inside the agents' heads. Hard to tell.

"Then who are you?" Tom says.

"Call me Jane."

"Jane who?"

"Jane who knows something you'd be very interested in pursuing. You'll be working for me now," Jane says from inside the darkness.

"Come out of there and let's talk," Tom says.

"No. Now is the time for you to listen," Jane says.

Jane lists the names of the agents' supervisors. Phone numbers. Confirmation codes. Details only someone inside the Bureau could possibly know.

Now Tom produces his Glock 22. Beth follows suit.

"How would you know any of that?" Tom says. "You've got five seconds to come out of there."

The mirror falls to the ground in response. Tom and Beth dart away from the container opening. Inch their way back with flashlights on. The container is bare. Nothing but glass shards.

"What the hell?" Beth says as they peek inside. Her light falls on a tiny microphone at the top of a far corner.

"You'll be taking orders from me now. Call your superiors if you like. They will confirm," Jane says. "Your plans are changing."

Chapter 44

"This is getting bad. Real bad," Gus says.

A tremor in his hand mixes cream into coffee. No need for a spoon.

He sits at the table in Red's house. A cordless phone is next to him. The receiver is as warm as the coffee.

"You could say that. It's bad," Red says. Sits down across from Gus. "At least we know the feds are actually doing something other than take credit for our work."

"We should go to Minot. We can't just sit here. Drinking coffee like damn fools," Gus says.

Gus had come over earlier that morning. Good timing. Red took a call from the federals in charge of the investigation.

Turns out Wil killed another two people. Dumped their bodies on the banks of the Souris in Minot.

"We'd be damn fools to go up there," Red says.

"Why?" Gus says.

Red responds with a long sip of coffee. Then silence.

Gus breaks it with a slap on the table. "Getting kind of tired of your runaround. You hiding something?" he says.

"Hiding?" Red says.

"Yeah, Red, hiding," Gus says. "It's just too strange. You spot Wil driving off in Joe's truck just after the murders. Then you go hiring this crazy hand, Jane, to track him down. Two more murders, you don't lift a finger. We just wait with thumbs up our asses."

Red clears his throat. Shuffles his fingers. "It's best to let Jane work."

"You're a real son of a bitch. You know that?" Gus says.

Red doesn't bother to blink. Lets the coffee burn on his tongue as Gus stomps out.

Chapter 45

*P*icking up trash at a Man Camp is exciting. Thrilling. Interesting. More fun than I should be having.

Who am I shitting? I can't even pretend to enjoy it. But it's a job. Fast money.

Sam holds a big, black trash bag. I fill it up. We tie the top. Drop it on the ground. Repeat, repeat, repeat.

It's hard to separate trash from the "gear." Les had that scrawny guy stop by to define it.

"If it's stuff, it's gear. If it's shit, it's trash," the scrawny guy said.

To which I said, "If it's stuff stacked on top of other stuff, it's gear. If it's stuff just laying there, it's trash."

Made Sam laugh.

The scrawny guy laughed over the top of her. Sarcastic prick.

He's watching us now. Supervising. Not that trash collecting needs management. Maybe he's watching in case we trash "gear" instead of "shit."

Or maybe he's watching Sam.

I give him a wise-ass wave. He acts like he doesn't see my hand. Moves out of earshot.

"Nice to know they've got quality control around here," I say to Sam.

"He's got no one else to watch," Sam says. "All the workers left this morning to the rigs."

"Yeah, I heard some of them talking this morning," I say. "Sounds like about half are employed. The others head out to get temp work."

"I thought there weren't enough bodies to fill good jobs?" Sam says.

"So did I. Unless these are the, uh ..." I say.

"Unemployable?" Sam says.

"Yeah. Unemployable," I say. We come on a pile of beer cans. "Maybe there's a good reason."

"I wonder if the company Man Camps are like this. More beer around here than anything else," Sam says.

She opens a new trash bag. I practice my free throw with the cans.

"Beats me. But I know out-stater shitheads when I see them. If you blow into town and can't find a real job in this economy, you're it. This camp is full of them," I say.

Sam closes the bag. My free throw misses.

"That include me?" she says. Her face sours. "You're picking up trash, too."

I back pedal.

"You're not so bad. Make for a better hoop than a goalie, though," I say. Toss a couple more cans. Bounce them off her chest. Grin.

"Just watch how you say things, OK?" Sam says. Hurls a can back at me. "Don't be a dick."

Fine. It's settled. Or not. Damn, we're almost like a real couple.

The scrawny guy slithers up. He's leaning on that shotgun again. I hope he slips and shoots himself.

"There a problem here?" the scrawny guy says.

Sam fires back.

"Do you have any other catchphrases or just that one?" she says.

The scrawny guy spits in the dirt. How dramatic.

"Doesn't answer my question," the scrawny guy says.

His eyes don't meet mine. They just focus on Sam. Like he's challenging her. Give him a reason to put hands on her.

"No," I say. "We're just talking."

"Talking ain't picking up trash. Get to it," the scrawny

guy says.

I cross my arms.

"Yeah, we're on it. Maybe I tell Les you ain't done shit today other than bother us," I say.

"Les is in town today. Won't be back for a while. Same with the workers. Just me and you two. So figure it out," the scrawny guy says.

He shoulders the shotgun. Goes back to pretending we can't see him.

"Creepy," Sam says.

"Yeah. Real creepy," I say.

Creepy isn't the half of it. We hear a shout from the other side of the camp. Then another. That's when things get downright bizarre.

Chapter 46

The scrawny guy sprints toward the noise. Sam and I drop our trash and follow.

I hear a truck come to a stop a few rows away. Then a voice gushing agony. A couple other voices scramble the air with quick barks.

We turn a corner. Spot what's up. A worker is on his back in the bed of a pickup. A fleshy tear runs down his left arm. I spot flashes of white within his meat-red sleeve.

The rest of him is slopped in "mud." Not mud-mud. "Mud" is the lubricant for the big machines on the oil rigs. It gets everywhere. Paints his coveralls brownish-gray. Stinks.

A guy hovering over him yanks at a belt. It's wrapped around the worker's bicep. Must a tourniquet.

A short guy comes out from one of the campers. Didn't see it before, but the camper's got a red cross spray-painted on the outside. Must be the camp doctor. The other guys call him, "Doc."

"He got hurt tripping pipe on a rig, Doc. Real bad," one guy says.

I guess so. You could stick his shredded arm in a grocery store and sell it as beef.

Sam seems more curious than anything. Rolls onto her toes for a better look. We keep our distance until the scrawny guy spots us.

"What are you looking at? Help get him out of the truck," the scrawny guy says.

Seriously? There's nothing some quack Man Camp doctor can do for this guy. He needs to get to a real hospital. Fast. Unless, I suppose, there's a reason they don't want to go to a hospital.

We jump in and help anyway. Lower the worker onto a cot. I let the scrawny guy handle the bad arm. No way I'm getting on the hook for fucking it up even more.

We haul the cot into Doc's cramped camper. A sign on the side reads, "Infirmary." It's an old Bethany pop-up. A table sits between two collapsible bed wings.

"Put him there," Doc says. Points to the table.

The injured worker groans as we set him down. I secure a good position. Curious what crazy ditch medicine this Doc is packing.

The rest of the guys must feel the same way. We're all just standing there, waiting. One guy passes around a rag. We wipe the "mud" from our hands.

"Everyone just stay out of my way and be quiet," Doc says.

Sam and I take a seat next to the scrawny guy. He's still got that shotgun. It's tucked between his legs. The end of the barrel rests on his cheek.

Doc starts by clearing the wound best he can. Then he pulls out a bottle of blue liquid. Says "caine" on the side. I assume it's "Novocaine" until I see the whole label.

Cocaine. Liquid cocaine, at that.

Doc soaks a rag with it. Dabs the wound. The worker's moaning stops in a few seconds.

It's surprising until I remember the time I saw this done. I used to get bad nosebleeds as a kid. Like he's-going-to-bleed-out-and-die bad. When the clinic in town couldn't stop it with cotton, I remember getting a hit of liquid cocaine. Made the blood seize up.

The trick works now, too. Together with the tourniquet, the bleeding stops.

Just when Doc's looking legit, he pulls out another bottle. This one isn't marked.

Doc loads up a syringe, jabs it into the worker's arm. The worker's face glazes over. Like someone poured glue on it.

"Opium," Doc says. "Works every time."

"You gonna sew him up now?" the scrawny guy says.

Doc nods.

"But first, I need to clean the wound. Get the debris out. That's why I put him under," Doc says. Picks up a tweezers. "Need to do some digging."

Cocaine and heroin? Shit, what's next, meth?

As it turns out, yes. But not for the injured worker.

"Good work guys. Here's a little something to help make up for your lost work time," Doc says.

He passes each of us small bags. Yeah, that's meth. Been on the prairie long enough. I'd know that devil dust anywhere. No way I'm putting that inside me.

Sam and I don't refuse the bags, though. Better to fit in. We stuff them in our pockets. Leave the camper with everyone else.

The other guys pile into the pickup. Drive off. The scrawny guy stays behind. Takes to being a pain in the ass again.

"Back to work. Now you got no excuse to be lazy," the scrawny guy says.

I watch him slip a pinkie into the bag. Snorts the minute crystals like he's done it a million times.

Sam has her bag out, too. I'm hoping she doesn't do the same. Nope. She tosses her bag at the scrawny guy.

"There. Now you don't got an excuse, either," Sam says.

Chapter 47

With Gus gone, Red retreats to his basement. He's heard from the feds. Time to wait for the other call. Jane's call.

He plops down at the desk. Figures the phone should be ringing soon. Glances at the two books on the desk. *Steps Forward: Finding Courage and Confidence to Make Big Changes.* And the Gideon Bible.

Joe is a Gideon. Or was until Wil killed him. That Bible used to bring Joe and Red together. Gideons are a big thing here on the prairie. That and Islam.

Yeah, surprised, right?

Islam's a thorn in Red's side. Nothing to do with the religion on a personal level. A hunting lodge north of town went out of business. A couple bought it up. Muslims. White Muslims, but Muslims. Converted the lodge into a mosque to serve Islamic oil workers.

More signs of the times. Most people considered Catholics a novelty only a few years ago.

Sure, it's nice to talk about freedom of religion. Makes people feel good. Just so long as the right religions are free. That's the dirty little secret.

The mosque's neighbors are always calling Red. "I don't have a problem with Muslims, but I'm pretty sure they're up to something at that mosque," they'd usually say.

Red used to give a damn. A pretty big damn. There are enough out-staters polluting North Dakota. Why throw gas on the fire and build a mosque? Can't they live somewhere else? It's a free country, after all. Nothing stopping them from moving.

Used to give a damn. Then something happened.

Something inside him. Made him realize the subjectivity of morality. Of what's right and wrong. The standard "rules" of religion only work up to a certain point.

So prairie dogs worrying about a Christian NoDak turning Muslim, it's bullshit. Doesn't matter. Like paranoid unicorns.

Red still can't give up the Gideon Bible, though. Doesn't feel right. Not yet. It can sit there on the desk. But it won't be opened. If God does exist, He'll forgive Red for the doubt. Any reasonable, omnipotent being must be aware of its own unlikeliness.

That's the direction Red took. Agnosticism. Makes sense. Allows for a kind of weary indifference to perfume existence's frustrating incompleteness. They say after a tragedy, a person's faith gets that much stronger or weaker. He picked the latter. Or it picked him.

But Red can't think about that now. The phone is ringing. He picks it up.

"Yes?" Red says.

Nothing but static on the other end. Then a voice comes through. It's Jane.

"There's been a change of plans," Jane says.

Red listens to what Jane says next. Wants to disagree. But he can't. There's no choice.

The plans are changing. And Red isn't a part of them anymore.

Chapter 48

I smell it now. The meth. It's cooking in a trailer beyond the bathrooms. Way out on the prairie by itself. Painted a muddy tan. Just like Les's trucks.

The scrawny guy insists we "trash it." Meaning we pick up the piles of shit around it. Not knock it over.

Which I wouldn't mind. Farmers around here, they keep loads of anhydrous ammonia. It's a key ingredient for large-scale meth operations. Dopers used to knock 'em off left and right.

Volume labs aren't popular anymore. Now it's all about the small batches, the shake-and-bake method. Meth lab in a bottle.

I've seen it done before. A farmer paid me to check out a squatter. Just a car parked in his field with a guy inside. Turned out to be a mobile meth lab.

I watched the shithead make it. Forced him, actually. I was the one with the hatchet. He was the one missing brain cells. Had him explain the process to me.

It starts with a standard soda pop bottle. Then you throw in some crushed up cold medicine. Pieces of the metal strip inside an AA battery. The pellets from a cold pack. Drain cleaner. Lighter fluid. Some other crazy shit. Add a drop of water to kick off a chemical reaction. Give it a shake and let it bake.

Let the fumes out every now and then. The batch is done when the metal strips turn a copper color. Pour the mix through a coffee filter.

Bingo. Meth.

I asked him about his buyers. Told me oil workers. He considers himself an essential part of the boom. Helps the workers keep at it for long, hard rig shifts.

I busted the fucker's nose right then and there. Because no one needs to be doing meth.

"Can't snort your shit now, can you?" I said. Only later did I learn about the needles.

I left him in his underwear to freeze on the prairie. Drove his car to the bar in Betrug. Got loaded in the proper fashion. Then wrapped the car around a tree.

So I know a bit about Satan's snowflakes. This trailer here. The one we're picking up trash around. It's hot with ice. I can tell.

Dots are connecting in my head. About how Les makes his money in the Man Camp. And how the oil companies must be quietly benefitting from it.

But there's another dot I'm worried about. It's on the end of that scrawny guy's shotgun. So I keep quiet about the meth. Not that I need to say anything to Sam. She's sharp enough to know what's up here.

The trash we pick up is nasty shit. Piles of whatnot soaked in cat pee stench. Bottles of this. Containers of that. Filters. Hoses. Tanks. Tubes. And one teddy bear.

Seriously, how fucked up is that?

Not sure why they even care if it's picked up. Not like much effort went into proper disposal anyway. Maybe they ran out of room inside. Or want to keep up appearances.

We burn through dozens of black trash bags. And I mean *burn*. Some of the bags just melt. We pick the shit up again. Wear thick gloves. Face masks. Triple-bag it.

The scrawny guy watches all the while. Keeps sticking a pinkie in that baggie.

My hands start to tingle. The work gloves are thick. Doesn't matter. This trash is toxic. Sam starts to cough. The mess is getting to her, too.

We use up the last of the bags. There's still plenty of filth around the trailer. I don't plan on finishing.

I turn to the scrawny guy.

"Hey, we're done here," I say. "Outta trash bags."

Sam tosses her gloves into an overflowing bag. Good idea. I follow suit. Don't want to re-contaminate myself.

"Yeah? Well, so is the whole damn camp," the scrawny guy says. Digs in his pocket. Pulls out a roll of cash. Thrusts it out. "Go on. Take it. Get into town. Buy some more trash bags. Get a lot if you can."

I hesitate. Not used to money just being handed out.

I start walking to the scrawny guy. He shakes his head. Pulls the money back.

"Nah, boy. This is for the lady," the scrawny guy says. Wags the bills at her. "Come here, girl. Take it."

My eyes meet Sam's. She's stuck in place.

"Come on then," the scrawny guy says. "Keep the change for all I care."

"You trust us to go into town?" Sam says. "What if we take the money and don't come back?"

"There's so much money around here, it's damn near worthless. It's the goods, like trash bags, that matter. People, they're replaceable. Even you, honey," the scrawny guy says.

Sam walks to the scrawny guy. Plucks the money from his hand. Just as she pulls away, the scrawny guy grabs her wrist.

"You and me could have fun," the scrawny guy says. Releases her wrist before she can respond.

Sam pockets the money. Her expression cuts him in half.

"Give me the chance again," she says. "I'll show you fun."

Chapter 49

S am and I hit the road to Williston. The pavement aches like bedsprings in an hourly rate motel. Isn't designed for traffic. Not this kind.

Just ask the farmer a mile back. Stuck in his pickup. Trying to turn left out his driveway. He probably lived his whole life never even looking both ways. Now he's just in the way.

You'd expect that in Minneapolis. Or, shit, BisMan. But not out here. Nothing but horizon and trucks now.

It's mostly sand trucks. I can tell from the license plates. Minnesota and Wisconsin. The fracking kicked off a sand boom in those states. Big sand mines popped up on either side of the St. Croix and Mississippi.

Lots of money in sand over there. Farmers used to complain the stuff would tip tractors. Wouldn't grow shit, either. Guess they lucked out after all.

It's got a down side, too. Who wants to live next to a sand mine? I remember reading about how mad the locals got when those farmers sold. How they pressed for mining moratoriums. So much for Minnesota Nice.

I guess they use the sand for fracking. Not sure how. But I know one thing. All those jokes about dirt farmers? The ones who could only grow dirt? You can't tell them anymore.

"Holy shit, watch out," Sam says.

I hit the brakes. The tractor-trailer in front of us careens to the right. Slips on the loose shoulder. No surprise there. Half the roads are glorified goat paths.

The state tries to keep up with it. Upgrades the roads. Builds new shoulders and ditches. But it's a slow process. A lot of the state's money – and attention – is wrapped up in abortion legislation.

The tractor-trailer corrects and swings back onto the road. Then it brakes hard. I follow suit. Looks like a water truck slipped the ditch trying to turn off the road up ahead. Clogs traffic.

I spot an oil rig in the distance. The water truck was probably heading there. Takes a lot of liquid to run those things.

"We're going to run out of gas if traffic's this bad," Sam says.

She's right. I turn the truck off. It's going to be a while.

"They'll hire anyone to drive trucks out here. It shows," I say.

"This is a lot of hassle for fucking trash bags," Sam says.

"Yeah, well, meth labs won't clean themselves up," I say.

Sam cracks her neck.

"About that. We need to talk," she says.

Chapter 50

"Talk about meth labs? You think that's what it was, right?" I say.

"It couldn't be anything else," Sam says.

"Agreed," I say.

Sam brushes hair from her face. Sends a chill down my spine. There's something about when women do that. Hell, I shouldn't even notice right now. We're talking about a meth lab. But I can't help it.

The thought of us digging through more meth lab trash is disgusting. But there's a certain appeal to it.

"I suppose I could say we shouldn't fuck around with meth. That methies are beneath the cow shit on my shoe," I say. "I suppose I could say I wanted work, but not like this. That it's a perfect time to take off and never look back."

Sam stares out at the oil rig. It's flanked by windmills. Big ones. They're everywhere. Clawing at the horizon.

Funny thing about those windmills. States pass all these clean energy mandates. Then they don't want the windmills breaking up their view. So they build windmills in North Dakota. Then complain about birds dying from them. Funny how that works.

"You suppose you want to work on one of those instead?" she says. She points at the oil rig. Damn, I can smell it from here. Then she points at the water truck. "Or those?"

"Not really. You grow up in a state this flat, you need something with edges. With color. With action," I say. "I'm not sure I mind this one bit. Because I get the feeling we won't be trash pickers for long. What about you?"

Sam shrugs.

"I don't have a problem with it. Money's money. You think every company out here is legit? Les is just being honest about things," she says.

There's a swell of panic in my sternum. My fingers automatically pluck an eyelash out. The panic disappears. Better.

"What did you just do?" Sam says. "Are you pulling out your eyelashes?"

"What? No. I just, I don't know. I wasn't even thinking to do that," I say.

"Come here. Let me look at you," Sam says.

She cradles my face in her hands. Points it so it meets hers. There's that rushing feeling in my sternum again. Only this one isn't panic.

"There's a bald spot in your eyelashes," she says.

A quick glance in the mirror confirms it.

"Huh. I guess there is," I say.

"Stop doing that. It looks weird," Sam says. Releases my face.

It is weird. But it's also a habit.

I run a finger over the bald spot. The tender skin responds to my touch. Pulls at my finger with an electric tug. Like it craves to be scraped raw.

Holy shit. Where are these feelings coming from?

I run my nail quick across the skin. Just want to see what happens.

My gut squirms in place from the pain. Then it relaxes. The drop in tension brings a wave of relief. It feels good. Pleasurable.

I snap out of the experiment. Sam is giving me a look.

"OK, weirdo, you can play with your eyelashes later. Do you want to stay at the Man Camp or not?" she says.

"I think you do," I say.

"You think right. I've bounced around enough. I want to save up some money. Figure things out," Sam says. "The meth thing, I'll just find a way to avoid it."

Yeah. Figure things out. Save up some money. Cave in a few noses along the way. I could use that.

"Cool. But we need to keep our guard up. Be ready to leave if shit gets seriously," I say.

"You mean, if shit gets serious," Sam says.

Man, I'm losing it.

"Yeah. If shit gets serious," I say. "Seriously."

"Seriously?" Sam says. Laughs.

"Seriously," I say and smile.

Chapter 51

W illiston greets us with an out-stater vomiting in the Wal-Mart parking lot.

"You need help, buddy?" I say. Call out the window.

The out-stater replies with a wave. Resumes vomiting. We keep driving.

The parking lot is packed. Even the signs that say, "No overnight parking," aren't keeping the crowd down. Wal-Mart didn't always mind overnighters. Even encouraged it. Not anymore.

Despite that, we spot truck after parked truck with sleeping bags in the cab. Unrolled.

"Must be looking for work still," Sam says. Drives home her earlier point.

"This is probably their first stop on the prairie," I say.

That's better than a guess. Williston is ground zero for the boom. Even more so than Minot, which tries to keep the veneer of its former self alive.

"Watch out for the slow pokes," Sam says.

Sticking out from the masses is an older couple. They shuffle down the aisle of trucks. Not dressed like oil workers. Must be locals.

I skirt the truck around them. We hear the old guy say something as we pass.

"Takes twice as long to do anything," the old guy says. "Can't even cook a decent meal anymore."

The old lady nods her head. Gives us a look as we drive past.

"Yeah, well, screw you, too, bitch," Sam says out the window.

I can't blame the older couple. There's a shortage of everything. Especially in Williston.

It's not just food. It's everything. ATVs. Truck parts. Appliances. Repair services. Footwear. Fishing rods. Short supply is the norm now. Try waking up to that every day. It'd make anyone crabby.

"The oil boom is why North Dakota has all this money in the first place. They could show a little appreciation," Sam says.

"I think the honeymoon's over," I say. "You're from out-of-state. You don't remember how it was before the boom."

"Does that mean I don't get an opinion?" Sam says.

"No, I'm just saying. The boom changed a lot. For every good thing it brought, it brought a bad one," I say. Point a thumb behind us. "Like that out-stater in the parking lot. Public puking wasn't exactly a common thing."

Out-stater. I shouldn't have said it. I can tell Sam's still sore about that word.

"Fine. I'll just keep my opinions to myself," she says.

We drive in silence before finding a parking spot. It's next to a rusted out RV. There's a mangled tent tangled around its back bumper. A couple hundred yards of duct tape are webbed around the mess for no particular reason. Looks like the whole conundrum's been there for a few thousand miles.

A guy with a gut down to his knees leans on the van. Cigar in one hand. Burrito in the other. Sports a haircut that could charitably be called a skullet.

"Would that be an example of a bad thing the boom brought?" Sam says. Points and grins.

I return the smile. Break the ice.

"Oh, I'm pretty sure that's just Wal-Mart," I say. "Nothing to do with the boom."

Chapter 52

"Is there a hurricane coming or something?" Sam says as we enter Wal-Mart.

Bare spots break up the mess of products still clinging to the shelves. Workers run with their carts from aisle to aisle. Toss in anything within arm's reach.

A display of spatulas spills out onto the floor. Carts plow over them anyway.

Two burly men argue over a pack of batteries. A third one slips the pack into his cart when the others aren't looking.

The deli area is down to mustard packets, potato salad and napkins. Trays of scummy water mark where the sliced meats used to sit.

Lines at the checkout stretch 100-deep at each register. Security guards watch for anyone trying to budge.

And that's only what we see after the first 30 seconds. The whole place is earplugs loud. And dirty.

A streak of dried mud runs along the lower shelves. Probably from the ceaseless stream of work boots. A film of sticky something on the floor rips at my feet. I trace it back a pile of shattered glass.

There's a heat to the floor, too. Radiates up my leg. Makes me itch.

I'm doing that when we finally reach the trash bags. Or what used to be trash bags.

"You've got to be shitting me. They're out?" Sam says.

Two loose bags on the floor are all that remain. I inspect the other shelves. Nothing.

"We could ask if they have more in the back," I say.

"I guess it's worth a try," Sam says.

We find a clerk stocking shelves an aisle over. I try to

get his attention. He ignores me.

"Hey, we need some help here," I say.

The clerk just walks off.

"Asshole," Sam says. Loud.

That gets his attention. The clerk walks back to us and unloads.

"Don't talk to me like I owe you people anything," he says.

I'd normally cuss out someone talking to me that way. Can't help but feel for him, though. We just happened to catch his steam. I get that.

Sam, on the other hand, isn't one for sympathy.

"You people? What's that supposed to mean? Maybe you need a reminder," she says. Reaches into her pocket. Pulls out the fist-sized clump of cash. Shakes it. "See this? It means fuck you and get us some trash bags."

Sam crumples a few bills. Pitches them hard into the clerk's chest.

He tries to catch them. Misses. Stoops down to collect them.

"Now get us some trash bags from the back, asshole," Sam says.

"Trash bags. OK," the clerk says. Rushes off.

"Seriously, Sam? That was lame," I say. "The guy's stressed out. Give him a break."

"Good for him. But I'm not getting pushed around by some prick at Wal-Mart," Sam says. Looks me up and down.

I don't give an answer. Spare the whole out-stater-versus-locals thing. Probably the better choice.

The clerk comes back with a pallet of trash bags. I don't wait for him to unload it. Just grab the pallet jack from him. Head for the checkout.

"Hey, you can't do that. That's our entire stock," the clerk says.

"Don't talk to me like I owe you something," I say. Mimic what the guy said before. "Asshole."

Sam smiles.

Chapter 53

The pallet of trash bags uses up the rest of our cash. No problem. We make it right back before we reach the truck.

A couple workers spot us in the parking lot. They're followed by five more. Then a dozen more.

We price gouge the shit out of them. Sell bags for three times what we paid. They don't care. Buy it like insulin.

None of this looks out of place. The parking lot is covered in makeshift vendors. Hadn't noticed it before.

There's a lady selling burgers not far from where we parked. Runs a Coleman stove on her truck's tailgate. She's making a killing.

Another guy is hawking batteries. The line is long for that one.

Other people lean homemade signs against coolers. Barter away beer, pills and ammo.

Off to the side, I spot a Wal-Mart worker walking a woman back to her vehicle. Policy. It's after 8.

We sell off half the pallet before calling it quits. The workers cuss us out. Want to know why we'd need so many for ourselves.

Sam out-cusses them all by a mile. They go away.

The burger lady hollers to us as we reach the truck.

"Wanna trade? Burgers for bags?" she says.

May as well. I toss her a few boxes of bags. Sam retrieves the burgers. The lady even gooses them up with ketchup.

We eat them right then and there. Watch as she sells the bags for even more than what we were charging.

"You like 'em?" the lady says.

"Yeah. They're real good," I say.

"One of the last places to get a burger in Williston. Restaurants can't keep staff anymore. Keep leaving to make better money," she says. "Got me a nice business going."

Sam gives her the thumbs up between bites.

We gas up before heading back to the Man Camp. It's dark out, but the roads are lit like runways. The trucks take off and land on a glow along the rolling horizon.

Sam nods off. I turn the radio down. Think how good right now feels.

Chapter 54

"Any news?"

Gus sits down across from Red. The café in Betrug is busy. The crop is in. Not much else to do now.

"Got a call about some hunters trespassing," Red says. Points to a carafe of coffee on the table. "Help yourself."

It's been a couple days since their verbal scuffle. Time doesn't heal all wounds. But coffee does.

"Thanks, I will. Starting to get cold out," Gus says. Pours a cup. Leans back into the booth. "What about the hunters?"

"Neighbor spotted them. Turned out they had leased the property," Red says.

Betrug won't get the oil boom. Not in any proper sense. But it will get something else. Hunting.

It's still a new business around here. Some say recreation is the future. Others say you can't harvest what you don't plant.

The ones running hunting businesses are usually from out-of-state. Minnesota or Colorado. They come in, buy up a bunch of land. Talk crazy about prairie restoration. Plant native grasses. Fly in hunters from the East Coast.

Then the locals call Red about the hunters. And he has to tell them it's nothing. It's OK for them to be there. The look on their faces. It's like he's betraying them.

They're only betraying themselves. Crop subsidies are political chips. Could go away tomorrow. If they don't find oil in Betrug, if the young people move away, what's the future like?

A group of farmers walks by the booth. One of them tips a hat to Red. He returns the gesture.

"Off to the festival?" Red says.

"Yeah, got a pumpkin to enter," the farmer says. Heads out the door.

"See you there," Red says.

The Betrug Fall Festival is a big deal in town. Pumpkin competitions. Live musicians. Hot food. Games. It's less about those things, though. More about meeting up with neighbors before the serious harvesting starts.

Pumpkins are the centerpiece to it all. People don't usually put pumpkins and North Dakota in the same sentence. But they grow like orange tumors on the prairie.

"I wasn't talking about news on the hunter front. I was talking about the other thing. Where we left off," Gus says. Lowers his voice. "Wil Reyno ..."

Red cuts him off. "Don't even say that name in here."

Gus looks around. Someone in the back waves. Gus returns it.

"You mean people don't know yet?" Gus says.

"Not many. Didn't even make the paper," Red says. "The editor was happy to oblige my request."

Gus reaches over to a table. Grabs an abandoned newspaper. The latest edition of the *Betrug Bugle*. He thumbs through the pages. There's plenty about the Betrug Fall Festival. Some tax notices. Nothing about the murders. No obituaries.

"Not a peep," Gus says. "I haven't told anyone, either."

"Good," Red says. Takes a long draw from his coffee cup.

"Won't people notice two people are missing?" Gus says. "Joe and Elma?"

"Three, actually. You forgot to count Wil," Red says. "They'll figure it out when they're not at the festival."

"What about Wil's mother, Mary? Heard from her lately?" Gus says.

"Been stopping by her place. Quite a bit, actually. She's a mess," Red says. "First her husband dies in a grain bin accident. Then her only child murders two and runs. I'd be a mess, too."

"That'll be good for you to visit her. Get you out of that house. Living by yourself isn't healthy," Gus says. Pushes the newspaper back to Red.

"What's that supposed to mean?" Red says.

"It means you've been a crab ass lately," Gus says.

A waitress comes by. Takes a breakfast order from Gus. Ham, egg and cheese egg sandwich. To go.

"You're not sticking around?" Red says.

"I'm a pumpkin judge. I've got important work to do," Gus says. "You're coming to the festival, right?"

Red looks out the window. His last phone call with Jane did not go well. Plans changed. And not in the way he wanted.

"I don't feel like it," Red says.

Gus tells the waitress to put the sandwich on his tab. They'll settle up at the end of the month. Just like he always does.

"You want to talk about anything, Red?" Gus says.

"Nope," Red says. Shifts in the booth. The paper in his pocket makes a crinkling noise. Gus doesn't notice it. Red does. It's loud.

It's a folded sheet of printer paper. Wil Reynold's obituary. As written by Red.

He'd read it over last night. Again and again. Forgot to leave it at home.

"You still haven't answered my first question," Gus says. Plucks the sandwich from its bag. Takes a big bite. "What's new with Jane?"

"I thought you were judging pumpkins," Red says.

"I've got time," Gus says.

Red sips coffee. No use hiding it anymore.

"Jane dumped me," Red says.

"I didn't realize you two were dating," Gus says.

"Wise ass. I mean she's refusing to do what I hired her to do," Red says.

Gus swallows hard. Cracks his knuckles. "So don't pay her. Let the feds find Wil. What's the issue?"

"The issue is she said her focus changed. Something else caught her attention," Red says. "She told me there's no choice. The feds will bring Wil in."

"Well, thank goodness for that. Jane isn't worth the hassle," Gus says. "Why is it so important you get to him before the feds anyway?"

"I need to bring Wil in the right way. For the sake of Betrug. For these people. You don't just spring something like this on them," Red says.

Gus shrugs. "Why not? Murders happen. I still don't understand you on this."

"Locals trust locals. It's how it's always been. You know that. The feds get him, it's not the same," Red says.

Red shuffles in his seat again. The crinkled paper seems even louder. Scrapes against his eardrums.

"No, I think it's the same. We're not doing anyone any favors by keeping these murders under wraps," Gus says. Pauses. "Unless the favor is for you."

Red folds his arms. "Judging starts in 10 minutes. You better get to it."

"Then you've got 10 minutes to tell me what happened," Gus says. Doesn't budge.

"Or what?" Red says.

"Or I break some bad news at the festival. Let the cat out of the bag," Gus says.

Red thinks the options over. He'd rather keep the town quiet. That's always been the plan.

"Fine," Red says and pulls out the obituary.

Chapter 55

W il Reynolds, age 2_, of Betrug, North Dakota, passed away _____. Preceded in death by father Jon Reynolds. Survived by mother Mary Reynolds and Red Smith.

Gus's eyes do a dance as he reads the obituary. "This isn't right."

"I'll fill in Wil's age later," Red says.

"You know what I mean," Gus says. "Wil isn't dead. Or is he?"

Red drinks from his coffee cup. "He's not. That's why I haven't turned it in yet," he says.

Gus flips the paper over. Like he's expecting another version. There isn't one. Raps his fingers on the table.

"Why are you and Mary listed here? You're together now?" Gus says.

Red stays silent.

"What? No explanation? You just give me this and expect me to go away?" Gus says.

"You wanted to know, didn't you? Here it is. Put the pieces together. You wanted to play cops and robbers. Here's your chance," Red says.

"I don't feel like games. I'm done with your miles-long stare. Your little hints. Your clues. Just tell me," Gus says.

Red plucks the piece of paper away.

"That's all for today," Red says.

"So the plan was to let Jane kill him," Gus says. Remembers he's holding a breakfast sandwich. Takes another bite.

"No. The plan was to let Jane bring Wil to me," Red says.

Gus stops mid-chew. Swallows. "Holy shit, Red, what's

going on here?"

They pause as the waitress brings a fresh carafe. Red puts on his phoniest grin as she does it.

"This so fucked up," Gus says.

"Watch your mouth," Red says. Crosses his arms. Tries to stare Gus into silence. Doesn't work.

"You got nothing more to say to me?" Gus says.

"Maybe later. You're going to be late for the festival," Red says.

Gus looks at his watch.

"Yeah, let's do that, Red. Let's talk later," Gus says. Stomps toward the door. "Now if you'll excuse me, I'm going to meet with the community you try so hard to protect and avoid."

Red stuffs the obituary back into his pocket. Sips his coffee. Orders a second breakfast.

Chapter 56

"Quite the pumpkin you got here. Think you'll make the front page of the paper?" Tom says. Raps a knuckle on the side of a behemoth pumpkin.

The bloated fortress of fruit sits on a skid in Betrug City Park. Joins a few dozen other orange monstrosities.

The farmer barely visible from the other side of it shakes his head.

"No touching. Not before weigh-in, please," the farmer says. Face turns flush.

"Sorry about that. Just seeing if it was real," Tom says. Gives it another knock. "That's no fake."

Tom adjusts the shoulder strap on his overalls. The store in Minot didn't have the right size. Too big. But they work.

"This was a good year for pumpkins," the farmer says. "They like hot summers. Plenty of rain. You grow pumpkins at all?"

Tom glances at Beth. She shakes her head. Tugs at her shirt. Her outfit has the opposite problem. Too small.

"No, horticulture isn't our thing. We're more in the ag programs side of things," Beth says.

The farmer nods. The U.S. Department of Agriculture is always visiting.

"So you guys must be federals. With the crop insurance program, huh?" the farmer says.

"Yeah, crop insurance. Just in town for the festival. Catch up on some business," Tom says. Opens a copy of the *Betrug Beagle*. Flips to a feature on the festival. "Any chance you know the judge, Gus? Where'd he be?"

The farmer points. Aims at a man sitting at a table. "Yeah. That guy. That's ol' Gus."

"Thanks much," Beth says.

Tom takes a knee to roll up the cuffs of his overalls. Beth hunches down next to him.

"Why did we need disguises again?" she says.

"To fit in," Tom says.

"I think we were better off with the suits," Beth says.

"We don't need to get anybody worked up. That's the point. Not sure how many people even know about Wil or the investigation," Tom says.

"It wasn't in the paper. They must not know," Beth says.

"Yeah, but did you read the lead story? The Johnsons had the Andersons over for dinner last week. Had grilled pork chops and a quote, *nice salad*, unquote. Apple pie for dessert even," Tom says. "This place is crawling in intrigue."

Beth smirks.

"Maybe it wouldn't have been in the paper anyway," she says. "Doesn't seem like the *Bugle* is all that interested."

They rise and reach Gus. Introduce themselves as bean counters with the USDA. Need to talk to him about something important.

"Sorry, guys. I need to start the pumpkin judging," Gus says. Points to a large, flat scale on the other side of the park. "The weigh-ins are about to start."

"Maybe we can meet up afterward," Beth says.

"Nope. Busy. You might try calling ahead of time. I'm sure the USDA has my phone number," Gus says.

Tom reaches into his overalls. Pulls out a business card. Bears the seal of the U.S. Department of Justice, not the USDA. Hands it to Gus.

"Make some time. Tonight. After the festival," Tom says.

Gus looks at the card. Then at Tom and Beth. Now he

understands why they didn't call ahead of time. Why the agents' clothes don't fit.

Not that Gus tailors his clothes. But out here, the clothes wear the person, not the other way around. Happens when you work with your hands.

"You sure you don't want to talk to Red? He's the sheriff," Gus says.

"No," Tom says. "We want to talk to you."

Chapter 57

"Who won?" Tom says as Gus approaches a few hours later.

Tom leans against a rented pickup truck. It's parked behind the Betrug Café. One of the few spots in town out of view. Perfect for a nighttime meeting.

Beth grabs a briefcase from the cab. Places it on the tailgate of the truck.

"First winner was a cheat. Drilled some lead shot into the pumpkin. Second winner was clean. The Bauers. Third year in a row," Gus says. Shakes hands with Tom and Beth.

"A controversial win, I'm sure," Tom says.

"I just point to the scale. Numbers don't lie. Only people do," Gus says.

Beth leads the two to the tailgate. Taps on the briefcase.

"Let's talk," she says.

"I'm all ears," Gus says.

Beth opens up the bricfcase. Pulls out a red envelope. Sets it on the tailgate.

"We know Red has a personal stake in the William N. Reynolds case," Beth says. Throws in the middle initial on purpose. Sets a certain tone.

"I knew it," Gus says. Repeats it. Nods his head.

"Did you know he's no longer playing an active role in the investigation?" Beth says.

"That a recent development? Never seemed like he had a role to begin with," Gus says.

Tom raises a palm. "In a certain way, he did. Do you know what way we're talking about?"

Gus rubs his jaw. "Yeah. I think so. But you say it first. Then I'll tell you if I agree."

Beth exchanges a look with Tom.

"It'd be better if you just told us what you know," Tom says.

Gus shakes his head. "Don't talk to me like that. None of this country bumpkin bullshit."

Tom misses a beat for the first time in a long while. Beth takes out a pen. Writes something on a business card. Hands it to Gus.

Gus inspects the card. There's only a single letter written on it.

J.

"Jane," Gus says.

Chapter 58

"That's right," Beth says. Takes the business card back. Folds it into her pocket. "Jane."

Gus scrapes at the ground with his foot.

"So...you're Jane?" Gus says to Beth. Points to Tom. "Or is it you? And how do I know you're even feds? Anyone can make a business card."

Beth flips out her badge. Tom follows suit.

"Trust us," Beth says. "But we're not Jane. Jane isn't a federal."

"Then what is she?" Gus says.

Beth starts to say something. Tom stops her with a look.

"Jane made contact with us. We're cooperating with her in this investigation," Beth says.

"And?" Gus says.

"And that's it. Jane is helping us find Wil. She's not working with Red anymore. He was out of line to hire her," Tom says. "That's why we need your help."

Gus pulls a pack of cigarettes from his pocket. Pops out a filtered stick. Lights up. Offers one to Beth and Tom. They decline.

"Why do you need my help?" Gus says.

"Red needs to stay away from this case. Far away," Beth says. "If he starts acting irrationally, we need you to step in."

"What do you mean by step in?" Gus says.

Beth picks up the red envelope. It's coated in a plastic laminate. There are no folds or openings on it. Like a baby without a belly button, it looks willed into existence.

"Don't let him go looking for Wil," Beth says. Hands the envelope to Gus. "If he does, give him this."

Gus inspects the red envelope. "There anything in this thing? Or is it just a laminated piece of paper?" he says.

"Cut it if you need to open it. It'll only work in the next 30 days. The contents inside will dissolve at that point," Beth says.

Gus flips the envelope over and over. Holds it up. Tries to see what's inside.

"And what if I don't feel like helping you? What am I getting for my time?" Gus says.

Tom closes the briefcase. Nods to Beth.

"The one thing all this is really about," she says.

"What's that?" Gus says.

"Land," Beth says.

Chapter 59

"You two must be magicians," Les says. His wheelchair crowds the bonfire. It's a cold night at the Man Camp. Arctic winds came early.

"How's that?" I say. Shift in my seat at the fire.

Sam zips up her jacket. Sits next to me. A dozen or so oil workers huddle with us. One of them, Moe, tunes a guitar.

"Because my guys tell me you went for trash bags. Came back with plenty. Plus more money than when you left," Les says. "Good work."

We handed over the trash bags once we got back. The scrawny guy with the shotgun spotted our cash. Said he changed his mind about us keeping the change.

I didn't want to put up a fight. Not then and there. So we gave the money up.

"Yeah, we wound up with a pallet of trash bags. Sold half of them to workers," I say.

"You're thinking like me now," Les says.

The wind carries something like cat pee into the air. The meth lab.

Sam smells it, too. Wrinkles her nose.

I ignore it. So do the workers. They stare into the fire. Too tired to talk.

Les, on the other hand, announces its arrival with pride.

"I love the smell of money," he says. Leans back in his wheelchair. A grin fractures his leathery face.

"I still think it's gross," Sam says.

Moe's guitar goes silent. A relief. The tuning isn't going well in the cold.

Les straightens up in his seat.

"Aw, don't get all high and mighty on me now. You know who Wyatt Earp is, right?" Les says.

"Sure. Shootout at the OK Corral and all that," Sam says.

Les digs out a bottle of peppermint liquor. Takes a pull. Passes it to Moe. The bottle makes its way around the fire.

"Close, but no dice," Les says. Exhales. Burns the alcohol off his breath. "The shootout happened *behind* the OK Corral. And I suppose you think Earp was a lawman, too?"

"Yes. But you'll probably say I'm wrong about that, too," Sam says.

"Half wrong. He didn't start life as Mr. Law and Order. He was the Pimp of Peoria. Ran a whorehouse in Illinois," Les says.

I take a pull from the bottle. Too sweet. Pass it to Sam. She feigns a sip. Passes it on.

"Then he beat the shit out of some cowboys. He was headed to jail, but ol' Earp, he weaseled his way out of it. Told the sheriff he'd help handle cowboys getting out of line," Les says.

The bottle makes its way to back him. Empty. He tosses it into the night. Lands with a sharp *clink* on the cold ground. We'll be picking that up tomorrow.

Les says, "That got him a job as a lawman. He also ran shotgun for Wells Fargo. Kept their investments secure. After he retired, he met someone named Marion Morrison. Do you know who that is?"

Sam shakes her head. I know the answer.

"John Wayne," I say.

"Very good. John Wayne, the actor. Used Earp as a template," Les says.

"What's all this have to do with a meth lab?" Sam says.

Good question.

Les says, "The point is this. To organize chaos, you have to be bad before you can be good. The bedrock of any civilization is a bunch of bad people doing bad things. They're the invisible hands pulling the strings, making everything tick."

"So you're a bad guy?" Sam says.

"Yes. And I'm proud of it. This prairie needs a Wyatt Earp. Someone to do the dirty work until civilization is established. Same as it's been throughout history. Criminals become the lawmen, the government. Shouldn't be a surprise," Les says.

The scrawny guy appears at the edge of the fire. Holds a fresh bottle. Hands it to Les. Gives Sam a long look before leaving.

Les pops the bottle open. Takes a loud chug. Passes it to a worker.

"Go back to ancient times. Civilization was just a group of people sitting around a fire. Kind of how we are now," Les says. "Every now and then, raiders would come and steal their supplies.

"But it didn't make sense to rob these people blind. They couldn't produce as much to steal later on. So the raiders charged a protection fee. They'd fight off other raiders. In return, they got just enough food and shelter in return.

"Now you have a population that can produce things without fear of attack. Now you have a civilization with a chance. The more the civilization grew, the more these raiders expanded their power. Formalized things. Became governments and institutions. Until the original raiders basically became invisible. Doesn't mean they aren't there, though.

"And now history is repeating itself. Right here on the prairie. Starting with bad guys like me. Cheers to that."

The bottle makes its way to Sam. She polishes it off.

"Great story. I suppose this gives you a pass to feed meth to oil workers," Sam says.

Les laughs.

"I like you," he says. Looks at me. "You're a lucky guy."

I look at Sam. I certainly feel lucky. I just don't know if I am yet.

"Meth keeps these guys working. Too much money out here for morals," Les says. Points his cane at Moe. "You gonna play us a song? Or just tune that damn thing all night?"

Moe strums out a couple tunes. I think he makes them up as he goes. Don't recognize them. Might also be due to the fact he's missing two fingers on his fret hand.

The scrawny guy fetches more bottles for Les. We drink until the fire dies. Then it's off to bed.

I take the couch again in the RV. Sam gets the bed. I almost feel like asking if she needs company. It's cold.

Almost.

A soft wind rocks the RV. Sleep comes easy under warm blankets on the couch.

I'm halfway there. Get the feeling I'm being watched. Glance out the window.

I'm right.

Chapter 60

*I*f shadow people have eyes, I'm looking into them right now. The dark blob of a face peers back at me through the window.

I rub my face. This must be the alcohol.

Readjust my vision. It's still there. Looking right at me.

I follow it to another window. Trip on the kitchen table. Sam stays asleep.

The shadow person is joined by two others. Darker than dark. Like they're being projected into the night. All the same size. All the same manner. All moving in unison.

They all point to the same spot on the ground. I look. An outline of a grain bin appears. Towers high above the other shadow people. Not sure what that's supposed to mean.

The shadow people stop pointing. Start staring. Their heads stretch toward my window. Like they're being bent.

The heads warp into long threads of darkness. Slither across the ground. Head straight for me.

Words teleport into my head.

Death.

Grain bin.

Death.

Grain bin.

I feel a storm of panic bubble in my chest. The elongated heads are closing in on me. They merge into one as they reach the RV.

I want to pull away. Can't. I'm sucked toward the window. My eyes move without my command. Force me to stare into the encroaching darkness. To watch as the head snakes its way up the side of the RV.

Death.

Grain bin.

The panic reaches a boil. Hammers at my bones. Hugs my lungs. My mouth wants to cry for help. It's locked by a swollen tongue.

The merged heads form a hand. It makes a palm that presses against the window. My hand meets it. Fingers spread out.

Death.

Grain bin.

The shadow hand meets mine. Then, together, we pluck an eyelash.

Death.

Grain bin.

The sharp shot of pain kicks me back onto the couch. My whole face burns.

I look at my fingers. They clutch a nest of eyelashes. Juice from their soggy roots glues them together. I rest them on my tongue and swallow. Check the window.

The shadow people are gone. No grain bin, either. Blown away by the prairie wind.

Pain from my eyelid gives way to relief. It cools the rest of my body. Unravels the tension with a rush of blood.

I fetch a drink of water. Let my tongue soak before swallowing. Take a deep breath.

I'm asleep before I hit the pillow.

Chapter 61

"Disgusting," Sam says.

I can't help but agree. Kicking frozen trash out of the ground is disgusting. We exhume bits of chicken bones. Plastic. Laundry. Trash goo. Pop them into bags.

A shovel would be nice. Les denied that request. Said we weren't ready for shovels. Whatever that means.

The gelid prairie wind grinds into us. Keeps our faces red. Warm clothes from the RV help, but they're too big. Let the wind inside. Feels like dropping a knife down your shirt.

The workers at the camp seem especially haggard. Some go back home. Others, housed in leaky campers, move into their trucks. Anything to escape the wind.

Cold weather means a shift change at the rigs. Workers between shifts are told to beat it. Come back in a few weeks. Some take off. Others stick around. Hope to find housing. They usually end up in parking lots. Sleep in their trucks.

New workers cycle in at the same time. There's usually an overflow. Companies hire more workers than they can house.

Les is all too eager to solve both shortages. Offer up the Man Camp. Makes trips into town. Finds guys sleeping in trucks. Offers them up a spot in the Man Camp. Hot showers. Electricity. Toilets. How could they say no?

They don't. Les takes them in. Collects his rent. Identifies the ones who could help run his business.

Seems like he could use the help. Man Camps. Meth. Trash collection. Civilization building. There's not much Les doesn't do.

I think to what he said the other night. About raiders.

Civilizations. Wyatt Earp. If history repeats itself, is another Shootout at the OK Corral inevitable? Can there be progress without violence?

Thoughts too deep for a prairie dog like me. I get interrupted by a voice approaching anyway.

"Well, well. If ain't my favorite trash pickers," the voice says.

I look over to see the scrawny guy. Shotgun. Jeans. T-shirt. Fucker must be cranked on meth again. The wind chill is brutal.

He struts over to us. Walks with a certain slouch. I know it well. The bro walk. The cock walk. Whatever you want to call it.

Not that I ever walked that way. It's the out-staters. When they'd come into Betrug. At the bar. Strut like they just had their nuts drained.

"Ain't you going to say hi, girlie?" the scrawny guy says.

He's crowding Sam now. She ignores him. Keeps picking up trash. I do, too. Think back to that National Guard story Sam told me.

"Go away," Sam says.

"You liked my company just fine last night at the fire. Drank my liquor," the scrawny guy says. "You like liquor? I got more in my trailer. Give you all you want. I'm a nice guy. You'll see."

He drags the end of the shotgun barrel on the ground. Never a good idea. Debris gets inside. Plugs up the barrel. Can make the whole thing explode when the trigger is pulled.

That's what they say, anyway. I've never plowed a shotgun barrel through the dirt. Mostly because I've never been a meth head.

"Seriously, go away," Sam says.

The scrawny guy doesn't react. Stays trained on Sam.

"How about you put that trash bag down," he says to her.

"Come over to my place. We'll warm up together. Been so long since I've had company. You're the prettiest thing I've seen in a long, long time. I treat you right."

I watch the shotgun barrel poke at Sam's calf. It travels up her leg.

Motherfucker.

I drop the trash bag. Tear off my gloves. I won't give him the luxury of padding.

I get a running start on the prick. Sam beats me to the punch. Literally.

She works it in a single motion. Snatches up an apple-sized rock. Spins around. Smashes it into the scrawny guy's face. His nose explodes like roadkill on a freeway.

The scrawny guy stumbles backward. Mouth open. Lower jaw lagoons the crimson effluence from his nose.

Sam moves in for another strike. I shift my gait toward her when I spot the raising barrel of a shotgun. He's going to kill her.

I'm so close. The only option is to knock her away. I do it as gently as I can. It's still a rough landing. The frozen ground is hard as lumber.

The scrawny guy pulls the trigger a few feet away. We find out what happens when a shotgun barrel becomes obstructed.

An explosion turns the end of the barrel into metal feathers. The scrawny guy's face is lost in gore.

He collapses. Cries for help as the wind carries steam from his face. Mangled tissue freezes before it can bleed out.

We ignore him for the time being.

"You OK?" I say to Sam as we rise.

"I think I'm OK," she says.

We check each other for shrapnel. Lucky to have made it unscathed.

"What just happened?" Sam says.

I look at the rock still in her hand. Then at the shredded shotgun. Les will want to know the same thing.

"What happened is he got loaded on meth. Tripped. Fired his shotgun. Messed himself up with a dirty barrel," I say. Point to the rock. "Put that somewhere."

Sam stuffs the bloody rock into a trash bag. Dumps a few newspapers on top of it.

There's a rushing of feet in the distance. Trucks firing up. Doc will be here soon enough.

"You sure you're OK?" I say.

"I didn't kill him, right?" she says.

Her breathing comes in gasps. She's panicking.

The scrawny guy hollers again. It's beyond awful.

Sam stuffs her head in my chest. I hesitate to close my arms around her. But she's not going anywhere. So I do it.

It's hard to comfort her with all the pleading for help a few feet away. I tell the guy to keep it down. That gets Sam laughing through the tremors.

Then I hear a voice call to us.

"What in the unholy hell just happened?"

It's Les. And he doesn't look happy.

Chapter 62

"And to think I was just starting to like you two." Les is more mobile the colder is gets. His wheelchair gains traction on the frozen ground.

He's here now. Two guys with shoulders like bulls in tow. Mean looking sons of bitches. Got a couple shotguns of their own. A sneer that says they're disappointed the shooting's already stopped.

Les whips his cane out. Bends at it. Too furious to finish sentences.

"Someone want to tell me just what...what the hell...what...damn it," he says.

Les made it clear from the beginning. He owns the monopoly on violence. No fight goes unapproved. Even the little scuffles. It's where he gets his power. His authority.

I try to say something. Les cuts me off.

"There's no unapproved shooting inside the camp. Go out on the prairie if you want to shoot. It's for everyone's safety," Les says. Aims the cane at the scrawny guy. Doc is administering some unorthodox pain relief. "Because this is what happens. Now I'm down a guy. Someone explain to me what happened here."

I glance at the scrawny guy's arms. They still cradle the shotgun.

"It's pretty clear we weren't the ones shooting. Your boy here tripped and fired. The shotgun barrel was muddy. The clog blew up in his face. He's lucky to be alive," I say.

Or not. The scrawny guy wails as Doc helps him onto the tailgate of a pickup truck. Serves as the Man Camp ambulance.

Les shakes his head. Sighs.

"That shit-for-brains had it coming. Never was one to be careful," Les says.

He motions with the cane to Doc. Doc digs in the scrawny guy's pockets. Holds up a small baggie. Then another. And another. Until there's a whole pile on the ground.

"Just like I thought," Les says. "He's been buying up all my supply. Reselling it for a profit. It's fine to use, but not to sell in my Man Camp. I told him to quit it. That you'd have to be stupid to compete with me. Guess he just proved me right."

The "ambulance" drives off. It's a bumpy ride. The scrawny guy vocalizes each frozen rut.

I figure we're done here. Les doesn't agree.

"What were you two doing with him?" he says. Points his cane at us.

"Just picking up trash," I say.

"And then what? He comes over to say hi?" Les says.

"I guess so. One minute we're working. Next thing I know, the shotgun goes off," I say.

Les wheels in close.

"You weren't buying dope off him?" Les says. "Because buying dope from a reseller is as bad as crossing me to sell it. No difference."

"Never touched the stuff," I say.

Sam shakes her head.

Les aims his cane. It's pointing some place I wish it didn't.

"Prove it. Empty your pockets," he says.

"Come on, Les. We wouldn't buy meth anyway. We don't do hard drugs," I say.

Les jabs his cane at my jacket.

"Open up. Empty those pockets," he says.

Sam stays stoic as I show Les my pockets. Tug the contents out. I'm expecting him to be satisfied. But I see the opposite look on his face.

I follow his eyes to the ground. There's a small, square baggie at my feet.

Chapter 63

O h, shit. I remember now. Sam and me were back in Doc's camper. He gave everyone a bag. Sam tossed hers to the scrawny guy. And I completely blanked on mine. Never got rid of it.

Les pokes at the bag with his cane. Flips it over. There's a red cross marked on it.

I'm expecting the cane across my temple. Les surprises me with something else.

"This one came from Doc," Les says. Flips the bag back up to me. "Lucky you. He's approved to pass this stuff out for good behavior. You must've done right by him lately."

"Keep it," I say. Toss it back. "I don't want it."

Les hands the baggie off. Aims his cane at Sam.

"You, too. Let's see them," he says.

The two guys with Les close in around us. Watch Sam invert her pockets. Nothing.

"Well, well. You two are straight shooters after all. I like people I can count on," Les says.

I take the opportunity to kiss a little ass. Help cool Les down.

"We're here to work. Not to shoot guns or buy dope," I say.

"But you are here to fight, apparently," Les says. Points his cane at Sam's hand. "I see you got a little blood on you there. I don't suppose you took a swing at my guy, did you?"

Sam doesn't lie. Seems proud to tell Les that, yes, she planted a rock in the scrawny guy's face.

I suck in a cold gulp of prairie wind. Not sure how he's going to take that. Unapproved fighting is against the rules, too.

Les shrugs.

"Can't blame a woman for protecting herself. Especially out here. These guys don't see many females. Go a little loopy when they do," he says.

"Thanks, I guess," Sam says.

Les offers us a pull from a flask. We don't refuse. Warms us up.

"How did it feel when you hit him? Good?" Les says to Sam.

The drink puts the edge back in her. Me, too.

"Yeah. Real *fucking* good," Sam says.

"Good. Think you could do it again?" Les says.

"Yeah. I could do it," Sam says.

Les scoots his wheelchair around. Motions for us to follow him.

"I think you two might be a better fit for a different line of work," he says. "There's something I need you two to do for me."

I tie up the last trash bag. Let it sit. We won't be coming back.

PART TWO: DRILL

Chapter 64

*L*ou Larson is a pile of shit.
I tell myself that over and over. Makes every fist to his face feel softer. Easier on my hand.

Turns out Les had concerns about meth resellers before. The scrawny guy's firearm face plant confirmed them.

Les tells us about another guy in the Man Camp in on the racket. Name of Lou Larson. Says he drives dope out to the oil rigs. The "cool" rigs. Where the managers look the other way.

Lou buys it off the scrawny guy. Drives to cool rigs. Charges double. Skips giving Les a cut.

Not anymore.

Les sends Sam and me to Lou's rusted out RV. We're to explain with our fists how he's not welcome in the Man Camp anymore.

Now this is more like it.

A couple neighbors try to break it up. Can't blame them. They had no idea. Sam tells them Lou's dealing meth. Most of the camp still acts like it's taboo. As if they haven't noticed.

Sam tears through the RV. Les told her to find his stash. She drops in between punches. Asks Lou where he's hiding it.

May as well ask the wind. Lou can't talk anymore.

Sam hits him for good measure. I pick up the beating once she heads into the bedroom. Opposite end of the RV.

I hear a yell. Not a painful one. A surprised one.

I drop Lou and head over.

Sam leans over a woman on the bed. Checks her pulse.

"What the hell? She dead?" I say.

"No. She's plenty alive. Just having a nap," Sam says. Points to a nightstand. There's a bottle of pills. "What are those?"

I pick up the bottle. Oxycodone.

"Hillbilly heroin," I say. Toss the bottle to Sam. The blood on my hands makes my dry skin sting.

She stuffs the bottle in her pocket.

"What are you doing?" I say.

"I'll give it to Les," Sam says.

I raise an eyebrow. "Don't turn doper on me."

"You don't think I'd seriously do that?" she says.

Seriously.

There's something about the way Sam says that word. And the sight of that shotgun exploding. And Betrug.

Seriously.

I look at the blood on my hands.

Seriously.

Shotgun.

Betrug.

Grain bin.

Are these things connected?

I feel the urge to pluck eyelashes. Do it when Sam isn't looking. But I don't eat them. They're stuck in the mess coating my hands.

"What's her deal then?" I say.

Sam pushes aside some blankets. Reveals the woman's crusty nightgown. And a pair of handcuffs.

One cuff is around the woman's wrist. The other is to the bed frame.

"Looks like ol' Lou was delivering more than meth to those oil rigs," I say.

"Motherfucker," Sam says.

She clenches her fist. Heads back to Lou. I'm right behind her.

Except there's a problem.

Lou is gone.

Chapter 65

I search the rest of the RV. Nothing. No Lou. Not many places to hide anyway.

Sam double-checks the bedroom. Just that unconscious woman.

That's when we hear something outside. Sounds like a *thwap*.

Les's cane.

We hurry outside. Sure enough. Les has Lou on the ground. Issues a terrible beating with that cane.

Glad I'm not underneath it. Lou isn't going anywhere. Not now. Not for a long time.

Les doesn't let up. Just keeps bringing the cane down again and again.

There's a line in the sand with me. It's when the guy either stops fighting back or grasps the point being made.

There's no sand on Les's prairie. The only line is Les's cane.

We slip back inside the RV. Mill around for the dope. Nothing.

Les calls for us once he's finished.

"Good thing I was watching you two work," Les says. Wipes sweat from his forehead. Blood from his cane. "Fucker nearly got away. Not that he'd get far in this cold."

I toss a blanket from the RV over Lou. Not that I feel bad for him. But he's alive. And it's cold. Anyone raised on the prairie would understand.

Sam only offers a final kick in the side. Doubt Lou even feels it.

She gives me a puzzled look. Points to the blanket. I think how she's not from North Dakota, but I don't mention it.

"Can't learn your lesson if you're dead," I say.

I spit on Lou for good measure. Won't hurt him or me.

Les wipes his cane clean. Points it at the RV. "You find any dope?"

"Nope. Nothing," Sam says.

"Damn. How about money?" Les says.

Sam shakes her head. "No money. But we did find something else. A woman. Handcuffed to the bed."

"No shit, huh? I'll have my guys figure out where to send her. Same with Lou. Don't want either of them in the camp," Les says. Rubs his jaw. "So Lou was running pussy at the oil rig, too? Don't make much sense."

"How you figure?" I say.

"Guys are too busy on the rig. Not even for a quick fuck. It's dirty there, too. Muddy. Filthy. Smart whoring doesn't fit with that, not in my experience. But Lou wasn't so bright anyway," Les says. Thinks for a minute. "Way I see it, his business is now my business. Right?"

I agree. Not much room for any other argument.

"I know the rig Lou's been servicing. Would make sense if you two filled in. Get a feel for the market there. There could be a lot of money in it for you," Les says.

I'm not liking where this is headed. I can tell Sam isn't either.

"I'll run dope. But I didn't sign up to be a prostitute," Sam says.

Les cracks knuckles against the cane.

"And miss out on such an outstanding business opportunity? You'd have to be stupid. Wil will work dope. Sam, you'll work on your back," Les says. Points the cane at each of our faces. "You bring me the money, I give you your cut. It's that simple."

Sam takes a step backward. Looks down at Lou.

"You're kidding, right? No way I'm going to do that," she says.

"Yes, you will," Les says.

I interrupt. Fight the urge to pluck an eyelash. And to beat Les with his own cane.

"We'll pick up trash. We'll lay down your laws. But this isn't what we had in mind," I say.

"Living in my Man Camp isn't what you had in mind, either. But here you are," he says. Taps his cane on the ground. "It's like I always say. You can have either money or morals. But you can't have both. Especially not on the Bakken."

He looks Sam up and down.

"Tell you what. You two go out there a few times. Sam, you may not even have to get plugged by a worker for all I know. I just want a bead on the revenue potential. Then I'll find some replacements. Deal?" Les says. Extends a hand to Sam.

My eyes dart to hers. She raises the one Les hit with the cane back in the park.

I wonder why she's not putting up more of a fight. Then I remember the pills. The oxycodone. She never gave them to Les. Maybe she's planning on sedating herself? Or maybe we won't let the workers know she's there?

"Deal," Sam says. They shake.

Too late to go over it now.

"Good. I'll have someone bring you the dope and directions to the rig. Use Lou's RV, not yours. Be there before sunrise. Tell them you're filling in for Lou. Everyone's so short on manpower they won't question it," Les says.

I stick my hand out. Wait for a shake that never comes.

"We going to shake on this, too?" I say to Les. He starts wheeling off.

"Handshakes are for hard deals. You're going to work on a rig. You've got it easy," Les says. Picks up his pace.

I catch up to him. "What do you mean? I thought I was just running dope?"

"What did you think? Lou set up a meth lemonade stand? He worked on the rig. Pushed dope on the side," Les says. "Be sure to count your fingers and toes tonight. Then you'll know how many you lost tomorrow."

Chapter 66

"What the hell were you thinking?" I say.

A salty pot of canned soup steams between us. We huddle around the small kitchen table of our RV.

"Money. That's what," Sam says.

"It's just money. What about you being safe? Doesn't seem like you to volunteer like that. Is there something else going on here? Something that makes you want to work with Les like that?" I say.

"Nothing in particular. I just, I don't know," Sam says. Gnaws on a fingernail. "It seems like a way we could make a lot of money really fast."

The way she says "we" makes me shiver. My folks argued about money. A lot. Used "we" like it was standing in the next room. The detachment always made me nervous. Things felt so much more unpredictable.

My folks never had a great relationship in the first place. Seemed distant these past couple years. Mary, my mother, would leave for days at a time. Come back. They'd make up. Over and over again.

I'd moved out well before that last argument. It was so bad people in Betrug were talking about it. Might've even made the paper. Small towns are like that.

I heard about it at the bar in Betrug. Killing time and myself. Collecting odd jobs. The inevitable gossip that came with both.

The bar.

Joe.

Joe came into the bar. Had a job for me to do. What happened then?

Joe's dead.

The epiphany strangles my pulse. I'm not even sure

how I know it. But I do.

"Joe's dead," I say to Sam.

"What? We're not talking about Joe," she says.

"Joe's dead. He had a job for me. But he's dead now," I say. "I just remembered this now."

Sam stares at me through the ribbons of cooling soup. Her hand plays with the raccoon jewelry around her neck. Rubs it hard. Has been all night. Like she's trying to squeeze the luck out of it.

"OK. Great. Can we get back to talking seriously about this?" Sam says.

That word. Seriously.

Kind of like the way she says "we." It fuses something together in my mind.

Joe's dead. Seriously.

Seriously, Joe's dead.

Then I think back to those other words from today. Are they related, too? I add Joe to the list.

Seriously.

Shotgun.

Joe's dead.

Grain bin.

Oh, and shadow people, too. Although that could just be me losing my fucking mind.

"Hello? I'm talking to you," Sam says. Snaps her fingers.

"Yeah. The money," I say.

"That's what I'm saying. Make some fast cash. Move out before winter gets bad. The quicker the better," Sam says. "Seems like the fastest way to make money is us going to that rig."

"Is that why you didn't give Les those pills? To make tomorrow more bearable?" I say.

I can't blame her for doing that. It's no wonder why that woman in handcuffs had them.

"Exactly. Wake me up when this is all over," Sam says. "I'll lay low. Hopefully the workers won't even know I'm there."

I wonder if Sam will get hooked. Only happens to certain people. If she's one of them, we may never get out of this Man Camp.

"You sure about the pills?" I say.

"Do you not trust me with them?" Sam says.

"I'm sorry. I just ..." I say. Trail off.

"What?" Sam says.

Out with it already. Just put it on the table.

"I care about you," I say.

Been thinking that for some time now. Yeah, she's an out-stater. But she's also not full of shit. Not like the hypocrites in Betrug.

Sam's expression changes. Her eyes crease along the edges.

"I care about you, too," she says.

Her hand slips over mine. Rubs her thumb on my wrist.

Our moment is interrupted by a knock at the door. I open up to see a box on the ground. Bring it inside.

There's a map to the oil rig. Directions scribbled on notepaper. Several baggies of dope. A Smith & Wesson Model 60 revolver, a snubbie. A pocket holster. Two boxes of .38 Special ammunition. A five-round speed loader. A tight bundle of cash. One folded paper bag.

"What in the bag?" Sam says.

I tip it out onto the table.

Condoms.

Chapter 67

Tom picks up his cell phone after the first ring. Been waiting for it since 2 a.m. The coffee beside him is still hot.

Only it's not his cell phone ringing. It's the landline on the motel nightstand.

"Hello?" Tom says. Tired.

The reception at the Betrug Motel isn't the greatest. There's a voice on the other end. Can't make out if it's male or female.

"Which one is this?" the voice says.

"Is this Jane?" Tom says.

"I ask the questions. Is this Tom?" Jane says.

"Yeah," Tom says.

"You're the funny one, right?" Jane says.

Tom cups the receiver. Looks to Beth. She raises an eyebrow. He nods.

"People call me that, Jane," he says. Waves Beth over.

"I don't want to talk to you. Put the other one on," Jane says.

Tom rolls his eyes. Passes the receiver to Beth.

"Why are you calling on a land line? We instructed you to use our cell phones. They're more secure," Beth says.

"It doesn't matter. I call you how I want," Jane says. "And don't ask questions."

Tom cups his ear in his hand. Tries to listen in on the conversation.

"Understood. I'm listening," Beth says.

Jane pauses before continuing. There's a sound like water being poured into a glass. Or maybe a car coming and going.

"I will give you Wil soon enough. I will make it easy for

the prosecutors. Murder. Battery. Meth. Prostitution. Organized crime. I will give you everything you need to make it happen," Jane says.

Beth glances at Tom. He nods in agreement.

"We'll need all that for the warrant," Beth says.

"Don't worry about warrants. Warrants are pieces of paper. Formalities. Like tissues. What needs to happen will happen. Understand?" Jane says.

There's no life in Jane's voice. It's like the words floated into the phone from the ether.

Tom hands Beth a cup of coffee. She'll need it.

"Understood," Beth says.

"Listen closely. I need Wil to sign some paperwork. Before you take him anywhere, he needs to sign them with his own hand. It's one of the very few things I can't do myself for the sake of legitimacy. The appearance of legitimacy is very important. Then he's all yours," Jane says.

Beth takes a few seconds to think.

"You just told me paperwork isn't an issue for you," she says.

"That's correct. Paperwork isn't an issue for me. But everything must look like it happened on its own. That the sale of his family's land was all due to the invisible hand of the marketplace," Jane says.

Beth presses a knuckle into her temple.

"Understood. There's also the issue of Red, the sheriff. We made contact with Gus. Gave him the envelope you sent to us," Beth says.

"Good. And you told Gus about the land opportunities if he complied?" Jane says.

"Correct. He seemed very enthusiastic," Beth says.

"See to it Gus keeps his word. He needs to keep Red from going anywhere. I'll kill them both if not," Jane says. Hangs up before Beth can respond.

"Did you catch that last part?" Beth says to Tom.

Tom drinks from his coffee.

"Yeah. What do you think?" he says.

"This doesn't feel right," Beth says.

"Of course it doesn't. We find two bodies in Minot. Then we're propositioned by some anonymous entity calling itself Jane," Tom says. Rubs his neck. "She says she'll help us find Wil. Throws in the promise of a drug dealing eco-terrorist trying to blow up oil rigs as a pot sweetener. Establishes her credibility by being spot on about everything in the case so far. What could feel right about that?"

"We might be getting played despite all that. I'm just not sure," Beth says. "But I defer to you as the veteran here."

Tom cracks his neck. "When in doubt, call the Bureau. We did. They say Jane is in charge now. Weird way of going about a strategy shift, but fine. I have my reservations, but we should roll with this for now."

"I'll go along with it, but I'm double-checking. For the record. Final answer. Are you sure?" Beth says.

"Yes," Tom says. "Seriously."

Chapter 68

R ed wakes to a knock at the upstairs door. Looks at
the clock. 9 a.m. Overslept.

Not hard to do in the warm basement. Sitting at his
desk. Only comfortable spot in his empty house. The wind
tackles the upper floors. Frozen drafts wiggle through gaps
in the construction. Everything leans east.

Wil's obituary lay unfolded next to him. A small bottle
of corn whiskey rests beside it. Empty. The one revolver
Red still has, a .45 Colt Anaconda, leans against the bottle.
Loaded.

"Red? You home?" says a voice.

There's another knock. Red gets up. Climbs stairs too
narrow for a submarine. Answers it. It's Gus.

"You smell like you went to bed really early or really
late," Gus says.

Red looks at Gus's hands. A thermos of coffee and a
box of pastries from town.

"Yeah. Guess I do," Red says.

Gus motions to come inside. Red doesn't give him
space.

"Miind if I come in?" Gus says.

"Yeah, actually. Wasn't expecting visitors," Red says.

Gus holds up the box.

"This is saying I'm sorry. I shouldn't have pushed so
hard," Gus says. Gives the pastries a shake. "Truce?"

Red's expression softens. Glances at the box's see-
through lid. Crusty layers of glaze are the only things
keeping the fall-apart pastries from melting in their own
lard.

Forget chain bakeries. The kind exploding across the
state. The real North Dakota is inside that box.

"I suppose a couple truces can't hurt," Red says. Flips open the box. Grabs a bear claw.

"That's more like it," Gus says.

Red lets him through the door. They take a seat around the kitchen table. Red pours coffee from the thermos.

"So what do we do now?" Gus says. "I'm not prodding. I'm asking."

Red leans back. Looks at the ceiling. Feels the headache of last night's liquor circle the drain of his sinuses. Can't be doing that every night. Might as well hurry things up with the revolver.

"Wait for the feds or whomever to get Wil. Let them deal with it," Red says. "I'll tell you what I'll do right now, though."

"What's that?" Gus says.

"Get something off my chest," Red says.

Chapter 69

R ed brings up a book from the basement. *Steps Forward: Finding Courage and Confidence to Make Big Changes.* Shovels it to Gus.

"Is this for me or you?" Gus says.

"It's for Mary Reynolds. This was on her bookshelf when we were at her place. Remember that?" Red says.

"Not really. I was more concerned about the fridge," Gus says.

Red taps the cover of the book. "Open it. Read the dedication," he says.

Gus flips the book open. Finds the dedication. Reads it out loud. Red moves his lips with the words.

"Mary, I can't wait for our new life together. Red," Gus says. Thumbs through the book. Returns to the dedication. "Well, ain't that a kick in the head. You and Mary really are a thing."

Red nods. Feels good to tell Gus about it. More than his therapy downstairs last night.

"We haven't talked much since Wil left," Red says. "But we're still a...thing. I guess."

Gus folds his hands. Leans back in his chair. Seems satisfied to come upon this news. Proud of himself.

"So what's the deal?" Gus says.

Red says, "Mary and Jon were at the end of their marriage anyway. Wil comes over to help clear a frozen grain bin Jon rents to Joe. Then the accident happens. Jon dies."

Gus refills Red's cup of coffee. "Yep, I know about that part already."

Red says, "Watching Jon die did something to Wil. He stays with Mary for a while. Starts pulling out his eyelashes. Sleepwalking at night. Not in a normal way, either."

"What do you mean?" Gus says.

"Mary said he'd pound on windows at night. Shout nonsense. Ran in the prairie in his bare feet. No kidding, middle of the night," Red says.

Gus looks surprised. "All this in his sleep?" he says.

"Right. The doctors diagnosed him with post-traumatic stress disorder, PTSD. Probably from watching that accident. The eyelash pulling, that's a symptom. Trichotillomania," Red says.

"Was there any treatment for this? Therapy?" Gus says.

"Not around here. Wil's too stubborn anyway. He had a hard time believing what he did at night. Couldn't remember doing them. Hell, couldn't remember half the things he did. Mary would show him the broken windows. The cuts on his body. Wil only admitted to weird dreams," Red says.

Gus plucks an eyelash out. Jerks upright in his seat.

"Why would you want to pull out your eyelashes?" Gus says.

"I guess it feels good to Wil. A release. I read a couple articles about it," Red says.

"What about the book?"

"Mary called me whenever Wil was acting up. One thing lead to another. Grieving widow. A helpful lawman. You get the picture," Red says. "Got her the book as a means to our new life. Wil offing Joe and Elma put a wrench into that."

Gus rifles the pages of the book. "Damn. I had no idea."

Red stares at the ceiling again. Eyes trace the outline of water stains where the wind pushed the rain inside a couple years back. Keeps his face out of view.

"Wil came and went. Worked some odd jobs. Practically lived at the bar in Betrug. I kept an eye on him, follow him around. He'd clear squatters off fields. Out-staters. Meth heads. Got rougher and rougher with people. He met up with Joe one day. Wound up killing both him and Elma," Red says. Exhales loud and long. "Can't help but feel responsible for this mess."

"Damn, Red. I had no idea," Gus says. "You have no reason to feel guilty, though."

"I shouldn't, but I do. I actually trailed Wil out to Joe's place. That's why it was such a coincidence when I spotted Wil tearing out of there. I just didn't know how to tell you until now," Red says. "The blood may as well be on my hands. It happened on my watch."

"Now I get why you were so eager to hire help to find Wil," Gus says. Thinks of the red envelope. The land grab the feds offered him. "It's better that other people are handling it now."

Gus offers another donut to Red. They eat for a bit. Silence.

"You ever wonder about Joe? Seems kind of odd, doesn't it?" Gus says.

"How's that?" Red says.

"Joe rents a grain bin from Jon. Jon dies clearing the bin. Wil kills Joe," Gus says.

"I think about it all the time," Red says. Takes a bite of donut to disguise the look on his face.

"Maybe there's more to why Wil killed Joe than we know," Gus says.

Red doesn't respond. Chews his food. Thinks how this confession should feel cathartic. It doesn't.

There's still plenty left to feel guilty about.

Chapter 70

W orm. Or, as the oil rig's tool pusher, Taw, says, "another shit worm."

Worm is the term for a new guy on the rig. Can't pass myself off as anything else. Never worked a rig.

Especially when I have to ask what a "tool pusher" does. Taw laughs. Slaps a beefy hand on my back. It hurts. It's supposed to hurt. I don't show it.

"Means I push you around, tool," Taw says.

He could do it, too. As solid and tall as the rig itself. Gnarled and meaty as a big toe. An infected toe. Reeks.

I tell Taw I'm here to replace Lou's tour. I'm the sub for *a lot* of Lou did, I emphasize. Hope that's enough of a hint for the dope, but not the prostitution.

"Tour" is another rig term. I say it like "tower." Les told me about that. Sounds more legit. Not sure if it even made a difference just now.

Taw is full-time, unlike the workers cycling in and out. Stays at the rig. Works 12 hours at a time. There's a square building on skids next to the rig. Taw lives there, but we all use the changing room inside. There's an office, electricity and water there, too.

I use the changing room to slip on coveralls. Try not to let the dope in my jeans pocket slip out. But not the revolver.

Sam's back at the Lou's RV. Parked next to the other trucks by the rig. Told her to stay still. That maybe this will all blow over. She downed a couple pills. Slipped back to bed. Tucked the gun under a pillow.

Good thing, too. Taw's got a certain vibe about him. Something in the way he walks. Keeps checking the horizon. Talks too fast. Like he's trying to trip me up on something.

Taw asks me where I'm from. If I brought a lunch.

Whether I've filed my paperwork.

I lie about the paperwork. But I take the chance to ask about fracking. Been meaning to get a proper rundown anyway.

"You know how high the Sears Tower is?" Taw says.

It's not called that anymore, but I don't correct him.

"I guess so. Really high, right?" I say.

"Right. If you took five of those, that's how deep down the oil shale is. 'Bout one and a half miles," Taw says.

The bore hole is lined in a steel casing. Turns horizontal once it hits the shale. To appease "the hippies," as Taw says, they add extra cement to keep out the ground water.

Then they shock the shale. Forms cracks in it called "fissures."

A proppant, water and chemical mix is pumped into the fissures. This makes the cracks open up more.

Proppant is a special kind of silica sand. Or a resin-coated type of sand. Sometimes it's man-made ceramics.

"What kind of chemicals they use?" I say.

"Barely any. Only one percent of the mix. Ninety-nine percent is sand and water," Taw says.

"No. I mean what are the chemicals?" I say.

Taw continues. Pretends I didn't ask the question.

The mixture is pumped out. Some stays behind. They keep the fissures open.

Oil and natural gas flow out the fissures. It's pumped into big reservoir tanks. Trucks are constantly filling up at them.

That's the thing about the rig. I thought it'd be just the platform and pipes. But it's a bunch of things.

There are the natural gas reservoirs. The sand reservoirs. The water tanks. Storage for the recovered proppant, water and chemical mix. The housing unit. And all the trucks that go with it. The traffic is constant.

From there, it's as simple as making a billion dollars.

Taw says there's enough natural gas on the Bakken Formation for 100 years. Maybe more. It'll cut oil imports. Make the country energy independent. Right here in North Dakota.

"Those camel jockeys overseas, they don't like what I do. That's why I do it," Taw says.

"So what do I do?" I say.

Taw points at the pipes on the rig. Explains how Lou used to help the roughnecks "trip" pipes. This involves putting in or taking out sections of piping at the well. All 1.5 miles of it.

"I'll be tripping pipe?" I say. Think back to that injured worker. His shredded arm.

I'm relieved when Taw says no.

"Worms don't trip pipe. You're on clean up," Taw says.

Clean up doesn't sound so bad. A quick job.

"OK. What am I cleaning?" I say.

Taw scrapes the grime from his boots.

"Mud," he says.

I take another gander at the rig. It looks gray at first. But I see it now. The gray is from a sheet of mud. It's from the mix. The pipes bring it up. Slop it around.

Guess it won't be quick after all.

"Any other questions?" Taw says. "I got to get this crew going."

"Yeah. You the only full-time guy on the rig?"

"This is my rig. That answer your question?" Taw says.

"Yeah, I'm good," I say.

The place is full of potential buyers. If the workers are getting cycled in and out, they'll want to go as hard as possible in the shortest amount of time. Bingo.

Taw's probably more inclined to sex. I'll watch him for that. Keep him away from the RV.

"Good. You're ready to start," Taw says. "Oh, I almost

forgot. One more thing you should know, shit worm."

"What's that?" I say.

Taw slaps me on the back. Even harder than before.

"Everything here can kill you," he says.

Chapter 71

I try to keep an eye on the RV. Taw makes sure I'm too busy for that. Has one of the guys give me a pressure washer. A bucket. A broom.

"Get cleaning, worm," the roughneck says.

It's dirty work. Mud is everywhere. The pressure washer does a fine job. Too fine. It blows the mud back onto me. I'm soaked through my coveralls after just five minutes. Should've worn another set of clothes.

I think to ask some questions. To get a feel for "the market" for Les. But I never get a word out. Don't want the mud to get in my mouth.

The washing is interrupted a few hours later. A roughneck walks up. Motions to a pallet. It's stacked with 80-pound bags.

"Take the bags there," the roughneck says and points. "Empty them into that machine there."

I'm not sure what's inside these bags. But I know one thing. After moving 20 of them, I'm bone-bending exhausted. Good thing there are only 30 more on the pallet.

Over and over, I empty the bags into the machine. My stomach growls. I glance at a clock. Just about lunch time. I could slip away, check up on Sam.

But no one is interested in lunch. The work only picks up. I spot a roughneck eating chips on the way to a portable toilet. Looks like that's it.

I finish with the bags. Head over to the toilet. Figure I'll go inside. Then quick run over to the RV.

I pass by the roughneck coming out of the toilet. He walks with a limp. Nods to me.

"You Lou's replacement?" he says.

"Yeah. Filling in for him," I say.

"Good. He was a shitty worker. A real ginzel."

Ginzel. Not sure what it means, but it's probably not good.

"How's that?" I say.

"Couldn't focus on nothing. But Taw kept him on anyway. The guys liked him around anyway," the roughneck says.

"Oh, OK," I say.

The roughneck cracks his neck. "Did Lou tell you about anything else? Other things he did out here?"

I get where he's going. We go behind the toilet. I make a quick sale. Even if everyone knows about this stuff, it's better to not make it obvious.

I slip back into view. That's when something catches my eye.

The door to the RV. It's open.

Chapter 72

*S*am wakes to a creaking sound. Thinks it's coming from the muscles in her neck. It's not.

She tries to rub the opiate fog from her eyes. The tactic of staying numb for whatever unpleasantness awaits is working too well.

"Who there?" Sam says.

Words don't work. Her brain is still sleeping.

There's a cautious footstep outside the bedroom. Heel. Toe. Then it stops.

Sam glances at the bedroom door. It's more of a paneled divider. The latch is unlocked. Forgot to lock it before passing out.

Heel. Toe.

Heel. Toe.

The footsteps sound heavy. Like they belong to someone big.

Sam fights through sleepiness. Runs a hand under the sheets. She remembers the revolver, the Smith & Wesson 60. Just not sure where she put it.

Heel. Toe.

Panic burns off Sam's mental fog.

"Wil? Is that you, Wil?" she says.

No reply.

Heel. Toe.

Whoever it is, he's right outside the divider. Sam's hand finds the revolver. But it's too late. And she's too groggy. Her hand accidentally scoots the revolver onto the floor. It lands with a thump.

Sam hears the divider. It's sliding open.

Her fingers search the floor for the gun. She finds it. Lifts it up as a figure enters the room.

Sam's gut says to shoot. The feeling's vetoed by her eyes. She can't make out who's standing there. Oxycodone still has her vision in its jaws.

Heel. Toe.

The figure is at the foot of the bed.

Chapter 73

"Who's there?" Sam says.

"Holy shit, Sam, put the gun down. It's me," I say.

Sam squints. Rubs her eyes. Puts the revolver down.

"Good to hear," Sam says. Her speech slurs.

"Was someone in here?" I say. "The outside door was open. Are you OK?"

The mud is heavy on my coveralls. I'm making a mess. But I don't care.

Sam looks around.

"Don't remember anyone," she says.

"Are you OK, though?" I say.

"I think so," she says.

I step outside the bedroom. Sure looks like someone was here. The kitchen area is a mess. Compartments are open. Nothing is where I left it.

I make a mental checklist. Start going through it. Hard to tell if anything's missing. This is Lou's RV, after all.

Wait.

The condoms.

There's an empty package in the garbage. I can't see a used sheath. But the packaging is there.

Sam doesn't see it. I debate whether it's worth telling her.

What am I thinking? Of course it's worth it. She should know.

"There is one thing missing," I say.

"What's that?" Sam says from the bedroom.

"A condom," I say.

Her face goes even blanker.

"Shit," she says.

"Are you sure you're OK? I was keeping an eye out. I didn't see anyone come in. I'm sorry," I say.

Sam closes the divider. I hear her shuffle clothing off. Then silence.

"I'm OK," she says.

"Are you sure?" I say.

"Yeah. Must not've liked what they seen," Sam says.

I don't reply. Not sure what to say.

Sam puts her clothes back on. Opens the divider.

I want to hug her. Can't. I'm filthy.

I start to say something but stop.

There's a knock at the door.

Chapter 74

"The fuck you doing?"

It's Taw. He's not happy. Barges into the RV.

"Just checking something," I say. "What are you doing? This isn't your RV."

Sam closes the divider. I move to block the view.

"Checking what exactly?" Taw says. "I saw you walk in here like it's your break or something. No one leaves the rig without me saying so, shit worm."

I hesitate. Can't tell if he knows about Sam.

"I'll get back to it," I say.

Taw raises a hand.

"This isn't your RV. It's Lou's. Not the best worker, but he was worth keeping around," Taw says. "You know what I mean?"

That stops me. The way he says it. He knows.

Gotta play this cool.

"Yeah? We got things in common, I guess," I say.

"I guess you do," Taw says. Takes a step toward me. His frame fills up the narrow RV. "Lou owes me some money."

"That a fact?" I say. Stand in place.

"Yeah. Seeing as how I'm a partner and all," Taw says.

"In what?" I say.

"You know what I'm talking about, shit worm. He'd bring in the dope and the whore. Pay me for the privilege of pushing it here. Like I told you. This is my rig," Taw says.

I feel the dope in my pocket again. And the money. It all presses hard against my leg.

I'm not sure how far to take this situation. Les will want to know about Taw taking a cut. That's worth

225

something. But handing Les's money over without permission is a line I don't feel like crossing.

"I'm not Lou," I say.

"You don't want to pay up, fine. I'm reasonable," Taw says. "How about me and the crew take a run at the pussy you've got behind that door instead? Lou always set that up for us."

My bones ache from half a day of work. Not sure how anyone could fuck after a shift. Of course, I'm not cranked on meth, either.

"Not interested," I say.

"I don't remember making an offer," Taw says. "I want something, I take it."

He's too big for me to stop. If he wants into the bedroom, he'll just go. I need to buy him off for now. Slip away after work. Tell Les what's up. Ride that line between keeping both Les and Taw happy – and Sam and me healthy.

"How about this instead?" I say. Reach into my coveralls. Pull out a single baggie.

Taw grabs it from my hand. Stuffs it into a pocket.

"The rest of it. Give it to me," he says.

The choice is down to Taw or Les. Who do I want to risk pissing off?

It's not a hard decision. Les isn't bearing down on me like a grizzly bear with an ear infection.

I empty my pockets into Taw's massive paw. The dope. The money. Everything.

"Now you're playing fair," Taw says. "My crew will still be by for samples on that whore later. Then we're even."

He slaps me on the back. I know what they'll be sampling.

"Even," I say.

Chapter 75

*T*aw leaves. Sam opens the divider.

"We got what we need. We'll let Les know what's up," I say. "I'll go back to the rig. Change out of these clothes. Then we'll take off."

Sam looks around. Doesn't find whatever it is she's after.

"Why would we do that?" she says.

"Didn't you hear him? They're coming for you. A bunch of them. Why would you want to stay?" I say.

"Because we're dead if we go back to Les empty handed," Sam says. Thumps a finger on my chest. "We need to get that dope and that money back, and then some."

I don't want her out here. She knows it.

"How do you suppose we do it then?" I say.

"Only two ways," Sam says. "Either take the stuff back or earn the money some other way."

I check the clock. Four hours until the crew switches out. The "samples" Taw mentioned, it didn't sound like he intended on paying cash for them. Especially when he and the crew come back cranked on dope.

There's no way Sam and I could take them all on with just the revolver, either.

Making a run for it sounds good. But who knows how long we'd make it before Les found us again.

What to do?

"Neither way sounds good," I say. "I'll find an idea. Or maybe one will find me."

"Figure it out," Sam says. Heads back to the bedroom.

"Keep that gun close," I say. A reminder more for my sake than hers.

"No shit," Sam says. Closes the divider with a snap.

Time to get to work.

Chapter 76

R ed knocks on the door. Chips of paint flutter to the ground.

"Mary?" he says. Throat hoarse. Palms greasy. "Come on, Mary. Stop it with the silent treatment."

Red knocks again. Rests his knuckles on the paneling. Watches a spider trek across his fist.

Mary replies with a knock on the window next to the door. Red shuffles to meet her. Places an open hand on the glass.

"Mary, please, can we talk? Let me come in," Red says.

Mary Reynolds brushes aside her long, braided hair. Doesn't look like she's slept a minute in weeks. Probably because she hasn't.

"You said this was going to be easy," Mary says. "Why did you lie?"

"I didn't lie. Things got complicated, that's all. Wil shooting Joe and Elma, that wasn't part of my plan. *Our* plan," Red says. His hand trembles on the glass. "I'm trying to fix that."

"Then why aren't you out there trying to find Wil?" Mary says. Raises a hand on the other side of the window to meet Red's. Then decides against it.

"I hired a person to help me. She didn't work out," Red says.

"Then why aren't *you* out there trying to find Wil?" Mary says, repeating herself. "Or is that complicated, too?"

Red takes his hand off the window. Rubs his eyes.

"Yeah, it's complicated," Red says. "But that doesn't mean we can't be together. To live life together. You've just got to sign that paperwork. Sell the farm. Then we can run away. Go anywhere. Do anything."

Mary slams a fist against the glass. The entire pane shakes.

"Now is not the time to think about the money," she says. "Bring my boy back. You owe me that. And I want you to do it. Not some federal agency so I never see him again outside a courtroom. Then we can talk about the money."

Mary pulls away from the window. Lets loose a muffled scream. Something crashes. Probably more books.

Red walks back to his truck. Takes slow. Deliberate. Steps. Thinks how Jane said her plans changed.

And how his have, too.

Chapter 77

*B*ack to pressure washing.

Taw makes sure I do a good job. Cracks jokes when the washer is running. I can't hear them.

Then it's on to the pallets again. And fetching random tools. A wrench the size of my leg. A hammer Thor would envy. Carts of things I can only identify by weight.

It's like they're trying to wear me down. It's working.

The repetitive work gives me time to think, though. I need a plan. And it needs to work before that dope disappears up the crew's noses. I spot them hunched over. Rise with a pep in their step. All courtesy of Taw.

Meth is shit, but I'm starting to understand why it's so popular here. Could use a little jolt myself.

I mean, fuck, look at that prairie. They say if you stare at a void it eventually stares back. Well, ladies and gentlemen, this is it. And that wind, that's the prairie inhaling, not exhaling. Sucks the energy from you. I've got nothing left.

"The hell you staring at?" Taw says. He's right next to me now.

I must've started that long gaze that comes with exhaustion. Didn't realize it.

"Nothing," I say.

"Back to work, shit worm," Taw says.

I finish cleaning. Coil up the pressure washer before the sun goes down. Figure I'll get off the rig before Taw and the others.

I quick change into a fresh set of clothes. Bolt over to the RV. I still don't have a plan. Try thinking of one on the way over. Too tired to do even that.

After putting a foot inside the RV, I realize I don't need one. Sam screaming from the bedroom is plan enough.

Chapter 78

T aw is hunched over Sam. Pants around his ankles. They're clean. He must've changed at the rig. Not sure why that matters, but I notice it.

Sam's body scrambles underneath his weight. She's trying to pull her shirt down over her naked waist. A line of blood runs down her bare leg.

Taw fights her with one hand. In the other is a Bowie knife. About a six-inch blade. Not sure why I notice that. He doesn't notice me, though.

Sam makes eye contact for a brief moment. Then they shift to the floor.

I look down and left. I'm back at the grain bin. I see Taw's thick body fall from the top of the grain bin. Crushes my father.

I reach to the ground by the grain bin. Pick up a revolver. That look in my father's eyes. It's the same one sick cattle give before they're shot. Like they're saying, "Seriously? This is how I die?" I've put down so many sick animals. I know it well.

It was hard at first, those mercy shots, being I was young. But I convinced myself. Told myself the animals were in misery. Put them down quickly. To spare their suffering.

But I didn't at the grain bin. I stood there, mouth open, breathing deep. Natural. Watching my father's organs burst one by one. He choked as they came up and out his mouth.

Seriously?

Seriously.

No more suffering. Make it stop. Mercy kill. Mercy. Kill. Mercy.

Kill.

Kill.

I squeeze the revolver in my hand. I'm back in the RV. Watching Taw try to tear Sam apart. Standing there, mouth open, breathing deep. Not going to let it happen again. Going to do something this time. Can't watch another person die in front of me, crushed under the weight of bad luck.

"Taw," I say. Stoic. Robotic. Unnatural.

He stops. Turns his head to me.

I stab the revolver's barrel into Taw's left eye. It pops out, and I'm back at the grain bin. Watching my father's do the same. Taw's hand around my wrist returns me to the RV. He's leagues stronger than me.

I pull the trigger.

Chapter 79

The shot is cleaner than expected. I watch it all in slow motion. Like one of those documentaries about high-speed photography.

In one frame, the revolver barrel is in Taw's eye socket. Little by little, the back of his skull flakes away. Like a chick pecking out of an egg.

Tunnel vision fixates my eyes on Taw's face. It's a common effect, I've read, in high stress situations. It gives me the focus to bring my other hand up. Push Taw away from the bed a millisecond after the shot.

I see the top of the grain bin, too. The proverbial light at the end of the tunnel seeps through. Where the frozen grain fell.

I blink and adjust my eyes. The light isn't coming from the top of the grain bin. It's shining through a jagged hole in the RV wall where the mushroomed bullet passed through. A bright beam of light points to Taw's gore on my shirt. The bed. The wall.

It's dark out, though. There's only one explanation for the light. Headlights. Aimed at the RV.

I hear a chorus of doors slamming. Feet rushing. The crew will be here any second.

Sam's a mess, literally and figuratively. She dodged most of the gore, but she's still bleeding. My eyes follow the red trail up her bare leg. It slips under her long shirt and toward her waist.

"What's up with you?" I say.

It's way too casual a thing to say in this moment. I know that. But my brain isn't catching up to the situation. For some reason, I try to lift the shirt up.

"No," Sam says. Squats my hand away.

That's when I notice the wound on her chest. A red dampness turns the cloth of her shirt into a sponge.

"What happened?" I say.

Sam doesn't respond. Just crawls into the fetal position. Tucks everything under that shirt.

I hear shouting outside. Very close.

I rush toward the side entry door. Need to lock up before the crew can get inside.

Too late.

Chapter 80

Three roughnecks shovel into the RV like a snowplow clearing a path. All huge.

I try closing the door on them. Doesn't work. They could come through the wall if they wanted.

I stop resisting and let them enter. Start barking before they can react. Doesn't even matter if the words make sense. It's more important to throw them off balance.

"Shut the fuck up," I say. Aim the revolver between the first roughneck's eyes. "Who's got it?"

That catches him off guard. He stammers. Tries to make sense of me.

Being a strong arm for farmers, I learned a lot about this moment. That in between time that lasts only a fraction of a second. Things can either go to shit or roses. It all depends on who does what in that tiny moment of hesitation. And how each person perceives it.

I read the meth in his eyes. It's in the way he can't seem to focus. He isn't here to logically unpack the situation. He's here to fuck something up. That's enough justification for me.

I kill him.

I pull the trigger and I fucking kill him.

This time the full metal jacket bullet exits at the front of the RV after passing through the roughneck's head. Puts a hole in windshield.

The other two roughnecks go blank. Like their faces forgot how to look.

"You were coming for samples, right? Right?" I say to them. Can't tell if the bullet nicked their arms or it's just the blood from the first one.

Neither makes a move. Their minds are on pause.

"Samples, you motherfuckers? Samples?" I say. Shouting so loud I can't hear myself anymore.

I think one of them shakes his head. Can't tell.

"I want your money. Your dope. Everything. Now," I say.

They tear out their pockets. Baggies of meth, pills and all manner of ingestible sin hit the floor. Money, wallets, truck keys, too. Right down to the lint.

They keep clawing at their pockets even though they're empty. I tell them to stop.

"Now get the fuck out," I say.

They turn to leave. I stop them.

"Hold it," I say. "Say you're sorry to my friend."

The words don't make sense to me. So I say them louder. Grow more incoherent with each repetition.

I see that look in their eyes. Like they're saying, "Seriously?"

Brings me back to the grain bin.

"Say you're sorry," I say again. Start mumbling.

And the eyes.

"Get over there and say you're sorry."

And the sight.

"Say you're fucking sorry."

And the smell.

"Do it. You won't get another chance."

And the wind.

"Fuck...just...I'm sorry, OK? Watching you die like that. Standing there. Fuck...I'm sorry...just...fuck."

And the guilt. Oh, the guilt.

"I'll kill you to get rid of it."

The two men shuffle over to the bedroom. Sam looks up.

"Sorry," the men say as quiet as moonlight painting the prairie.

It's not good enough.

"Say, 'I'm sorry I didn't try harder to save you,'" I say.

They repeat it, more or less.

"Get out," I say.

They repeat that, too.

"No, I mean get out. Leave. Now," I say. They do it.

Then I sit down next to Sam. Study her face. She starts sobbing.

I weave our arms together. And I cry with her.

Chapter 81

W e don't stay like that for long. There's more noise outside.

I unwrap from Sam. Pick up the revolver.

"Wait here," I say.

I head out. Step over the bodies to get to the door.

A half-circle of workers forms 10 yards out from the RV. They look as stunned as the two I kicked out.

I make the revolver obvious. Hold it out and down from my side.

"What?" I say.

One of them speaks up when the other don't.

"Where's Taw?" he says.

No sense in hiding what they already know.

"I killed him. Any other questions?" I say.

"What about Stu?"

Must be the other dead guy.

"I killed Stu, too," I say.

Seems blunt, but this is how to talk to oil workers. Direct. No pulled punches. It's the same as the cadence on the rig. No bullshit. Just say what you mean. Keeps people alive. Or dead, in this case.

"Why?" the worker says.

"They were hurting my friend inside," I say.

"Hurting a whore?" the worker says like that's not possible.

"Maybe Taw told you there was a whore in there," I say. Rotate the revolver so it reflects off the headlights. "But there ain't no more. Understand?"

No one moves. That's answer enough.

"What now?" the worker says.

"Get some sleep. Come back tomorrow. Work like

normal," I say.

"No. What about the energy shots?" the worker says. There's a starved look in his eyes. Like dry cattle staring at an empty trough.

"What energy shots?" I say.

"That oil isn't gonna pull itself out of the ground," the worker says.

I get what he's talking about. This is why I hate meth. Makes you more concerned with it than things like, oh, say, the two corpses in the RV.

I head back into the RV. Return and make the sales. Take the workers for all they have left. Their faces light up. Perfect time to make demands.

"You want more energy shots? We need an agreement. Anyone asks, you say Taw and Stu died taking a nap in the RV. Taw had a cigarette, lit the place on fire. It was an accident. Understand?" I say.

They nod.

I head back into the RV. Fetch truck keys from Taw's pocket. Wrap Sam in a blanket and help her out.

"Get her into Taw's truck. Turn the heat on and keep her warm," I say to the workers. "Does anyone have a spare can of gas?"

One of the workers raises his hand.

"Go get it," I say.

"Why?" the worker says.

"You're going to help me burn this RV to the ground," I say.

Chapter 82

"Well done," Les says from the other side of the fire.

We're back at the Man Camp now.

Les sneezes. Wonder if he's getting a cold. Certainly spends enough time outside. Always wearing that thin, blue "Navy Vet" cap. No hair underneath it, either.

"Well done?" Sam says.

We're in fresh clothes now. Our skin still smells like the RV fire. Like a mix between rotting barbecue and burning plastic.

"Seriously. Well done," Les says. Laughs. "That's how I hear you cooked the RV."

That word. *Seriously.* Are people really saying it that much? Or am I just hearing them say it?

Les sneezes again. Someone passes him a bottle.

I retell what happened. Just in case Les didn't hear the first time. About how I put two workers down for attacking Sam. Then torched the evidence in front of witnesses.

No sense in hiding the truth. Not that Les would necessarily give a shit. Or maybe he would. Hard to tell.

"No need to repeat yourself," Les says. "You came back with more money than you went with. That means it was a good day. And burning Lou's RV was a nice bonus. He ended up dead in the end anyway. Couldn't handle the cane."

He pulls from the bottle. Passes it to Sam. She downs most of it.

"Easy now," Les says. Motions for it back.

Sam ignores the request. Polishes the liquor off anyway. The hot stress radiating from her face could melt coal. She tosses the bottle into the night outside the fire.

"Hmmm," Les says. Stares at Sam. Extends his hand into the darkness. It's immediately filled with a fresh bottle.

"What do we do now?" I say.

"You're going back to the rig. Do your worm work like nothing happened. Move that dope," Les says.

"You're not worried they're going to report us?" I say.

"Not in the least. Workers are just meat for the grinder. The company will send replacements. There's no way that rig is going to stop," Les says.

I crack my neck with a quick jerk. Can't tell if Les is setting us up. Take the fall if the police show up.

I look at Sam. How she's so vacant. Can't imagine her going back.

"We've done our due there. Everything's set up to sell. How about sending someone else like you said you would?" I say to Les. "We can take care of business for you in the Man Camp or something."

Les looks at Sam but talks to me.

"I changed my mind. I like your style too much. I need someone out there willing to get their hands dirty," Les says. Shifts to talking to Sam. "But you, Sam, should stay behind. Let Doc check you out. Don't worry, though. You can get back to work once the stitches are in."

He says it like he's talking about a truck with a flat tire. That's when it really sinks in. We're going to die here if we don't leave. Things went from too boring to too eventful in a hurry. I wanted some action, but not like this. Prefer the way things used to be back in Betrug, shit shoveling for locals. Probably not the only one in North Dakota to feel that way after getting a taste of the boom, lured in by the chance to get a piece of the action.

Sam going to Doc would only add another bar in this jail cell of a Man Camp. She must already know this, because she's shaking her head.

"I can get better in our RV," Sam says. "Need some rest."

"Just let Doc check you out quick. Make sure everything is OK," Les says.

"No, thanks," Sam says.

Les sits upright in his wheelchair.

"Go there in the morning. Or tonight even," he says.

Sam stays silent. Stares at the fire.

"What do you have against doctors?" Les says. "You worried about him poking places he shouldn't? He's very good. A decent guy."

"I just want some sleep," Sam says.

Les pokes at the dirt with his cane. Draws an X. Thinks. Or wants to look like he's thinking.

"Fine. But you're not going anywhere tomorrow, Sam. Stay in your RV and rest," Les says. Points his cane at me. "I'll send some guys to make sure no one bothers her. If you don't go out to that rig alone tomorrow, I'll castrate you myself. You hear me?"

I nod. He's making it harder and harder to leave.

"I get it," I say.

"Then get this," Les says. Tosses a brown paper bag to me.

I catch it. Look inside. More dope. A *lot* more dope.

"Congratulations, you're officially a partner. Not something I let a lot of people in on. You're running the business on that rig. Keep the rig's energy up. The oil companies will look the other way so long as things keep humming along. They like hard workers," Les says. Looks at Sam. "So do I."

We have got to get the hell out of here.

Chapter 83

R ed drains the flask. Tastes like old sink and spray paint.

He leans over. Looks at the dead steer in the pasture. Too fresh to bloat much yet. The morning wind keeps the stench down.

"You need a vet, not a sheriff," Red says to the woman next to him.

It's Lori. Late 60s. Hard as they come on the prairie. Face like baked clay and hands to match. Cuts from the wind cured by the sun.

She rents pasture from Joe and Elma. Or used to anyway. Now the bank owns the land.

Lori's cattle keep busting out of the fence. Hump it across the road and into a wheat field. Happens all the time. Old Man Zed pisses shit when it does. He owns the wheat.

That's where the term "mend fences" originated. Farmers would reconcile after a fence was repaired. That's what Red's heard anyway.

Looks like that won't be happening. Not this time. Probably Zed popped a cow in Lori's pasture for good measure. Not a rational thing to do. Not uncommon, either.

Red digs with his fingers by the steer's ear. Feels for a small, round circle. An entry point. Nothing. Pokes around the other vital areas. Nothing again.

"Unless you keep the Eucharist in there, you put that liquor away when you're on my property," Lori says.

Red shrugs. Finishes it off. Stuffs it in his back pocket.

"And unless you have a reason I'm here, I'll be leaving your property," he says.

Lori points to the far side of the pasture. Her finger traces the outline of a new power substation.

"Ever since that substation went in on county land, my cows give me less milk. The cattle get sick," Lori says. Kicks at the dirt. "There's stray voltage."

"Stray voltage?" Red says.

"An electric current running underground. It happened in Minnesota once. Wabasha County, near where my sons live in Rochester," Lori says. Lets out a loud breath through gritted teeth. "Do something about it."

Red rubs his jaw. Lets his thoughts drift off to Mary.

"Not much I can do," he says.

"But it's county land. I don't understand how you're so helpless," Lori says. "This stray voltage isn't just making my herd sick anymore. It's killing them. Isn't that worth something?"

Red ignores the comment. Surveys the prairie. As flat and rough as a bastard file. The fall weather scrubs the terrain a grayish yellow.

His eyes fall to the family cemetery. It rests on the other side of the fence. Been there since the 1800s. It rises five feet above everything else. A plateau of tombstones.

It's a testament to generations of deep tilling and overgrazing. Better practices in more recent times managed to keep the dead from spilling out onto the fields.

"I don't know," Red says.

"You don't know?" Lori says. "Maybe this stray voltage is getting to you."

"Maybe it is," Red says. Snaps back into focus. "Call your insurance company, Lori. Call the USDA RMA. File the claim. Explain the situation. If things are how you say, they'll take the lead on it."

Red starts back for his truck. Lori follows.

"My family's been running cattle and milking cows for

more than 100 years. What if this drives me out of the business?" Lori says as Red gets into his truck.

"Then you better pray they find oil on your property," Red says. Shuts the door.

He drives until Lori is out of sight. Pulls over, opens a beer, closes his eyes and drinks.

Chapter 84

R ed opens his eyes when the can goes dry as his throat. Looks in the rearview mirror. Spots a windmill in the distance.

It's new. Just like everything else in North Dakota. Energy. Land. Money. The ways those three things work together. What they make folks do to themselves. To each other. All new.

He thinks back to his last conversation with Gus. What was it Gus'd said? "Don't feel guilty."

That's not going to work anymore.

Red puts the truck back into drive. Feels the alcohol pool in his foot. It sinks into the accelerator.

The truck makes a U-turn. Red takes a two-track shortcut straight toward Gus's house.

Chapter 85

I park Taw's truck in plain view near to the smoldering RV. Make sure everyone knows who I am. The other vehicles park as far from the wreck as possible.

The workers get the point. No one says anything. I find the pressure washer. Get back to washing the endless tide of mud off the rig.

Taw's replacement is already working. I ignore him. He returns the favor. Looks the other way when I slip a baggie to a couple workers.

The rig is silent otherwise.

I wonder how Sam is holding up. She's by herself back at the Man Camp. Sleeping off yesterday.

Wish I was, too. Despite the exhaustion, I couldn't keep my eyes shut last night. Waited up with the revolver while Sam slept. Kept thinking someone would come through the door.

No one ever did. Never could cure myself of the anticipation, though. So I stayed up. Feel worse today than yesterday by a mile.

A worker hollers to me for help. By name. Doesn't call me "worm."

He needs me to unload a few pallets. Each one sports stacks of bags piled 10 high. Feel like they weigh as much as me.

"Cut open the bags. Dump them in there," the worker says over the blistering machinery.

"In there" is what looks like a cement mixer. I ask what's in the bags.

"It gets combined with the frac sand and the water," the worker says. "We pump it underground. Then we pump it back up."

"Yeah, I know that. But what is this stuff in the bag?" I say.

"It's a chemical. It holds open the fractures so we can get the oil out," the worker says.

"What kind of chemical?" I say.

I'm not sure why I'm curious. Maybe want to get my mind off yesterday.

"Who gives a shit? These pallets aren't going to unload themselves," he says.

Can't argue with that.

I cut a bag open. Hoist it up to my chest. A fine powder peppers the air as I dump it into the mixer.

I breathe deep and go for the next bag. Whatever is in there can't be worse than what's in my pocket.

The worker agrees. Buys dope off me when we're through. Looks like he needs it. I watch him come back to life.

"Thanks, man. I needed an energy shot," he says.

That term, they keep using it. Makes meth sound nicer. Reasonable. Maybe even to me.

I head back to the pressure washer. Palm the wad of bagged up dope in my pocket. I couldn't be more tired. And it's not like anyone has a digital scale out here. No one would notice a quick bump missing from a bag.

I walk past the pressure washer. Keep going to the truck. Make sure no one is watching.

I spill a bit of powder onto the hood of the truck. The crystals wink at me in the light of the morning sun.

I'm too tired to think twice. Shape the meth into a tiny line. Lean down.

But the prairie wind doesn't ever get tired. A well-placed gust puffs the dope away. Like an invisible hand wiped the hood clean.

I look at the rig. Think about those bags. The dope in

my pocket. The cash and revolver in my other pocket. Sam back at the RV. Les and the Man Camp. The people I killed yesterday. The oil boom. The unrelenting prairie wind.

I rub my eyes. Head back to the rig. Only 10 more hours before I can see Sam again.

Chapter 86

"Something bothering you, Red?" Gus says from the doorway to his house. Sniffs at the sheriff. "You look a little flush."

Red stamps his feet in place. Rocks back and forth on all 16 inches of Gus's doormat.

"Was out at Lori's place. She...uh...lost a cow," Red says.

Gus opens the door wider. Red moves to walk inside, but Gus shuffles out first. Closes the door behind him.

"Can't I come in?" Red says.

"And talk about a steer? If it was half as messed up as you look, we've got plenty to talk about. But let's do it on the porch. The family went into town. I was about to head out to spray for wormwood on the four-wheeler," Gus says.

Red walks away a few feet. Walks back. "I can't do this anymore."

"What? The sheriff thing?" Gus says.

"No. This Wil thing. Being here and not there. Letting other people handle things. Not knowing what's going on. I can't do it," Red says.

Gus thinks about his conversation with Tom and Beth. About the red envelope. And the land deal.

Keep Red away until the investigation closes, they'd said. Gus would have first dibs on some hot property for cheap. The land value is set to skyrocket, but no one has a clue about it. Except for the feds, apparently. And now Gus.

Gus had pressed the agents for more information. They kept quiet on the specifics. But they did say it would be a parcel on the Reynolds property. As in Mary Reynolds, Wil's mother. That was the deal. Take it or leave it.

Gus couldn't see a reason not to take the agents on their word. The badges checked out. They talked like federals. Land values did skyrocket overnight. All the time, in fact, as the oil companies focused on expanding their reach.

The red envelope from the agents is the fail-safe in all this. Gus thinks to where he stashed it away. In the gun safe downstairs? Yes, next to a box of shells and the agents' business cards.

"Calm down," Gus says. "Why don't you take a breather? Come out with me on the four-wheelers. It'll feel good to get out."

Red rubs a hand on the back of his neck. "There's no time for wormwood. We have to find Wil," he says.

"Stop talking like that. The feds have it under control," Gus says.

"How do you know? I sure as hell haven't heard from them lately. Have you?" Red says.

Gus flinches. Takes a sec to read Red. Does he know about the meeting with Tom and Beth?

No. Red's eyes are manic. Not their usual metallurgy of steel and vinegar. The one that could drill holes for fence posts in the prairie.

"Can't say they've been in touch with me, either," Gus says. Clears his throat. "Hey, let's go into Betrug for lunch. My treat. You can tell me why it's so important to find Wil now."

Red pulls out his flask. Takes a pull. Remembers it's empty.

"Sure. And then I'm leaving," Red says. "You coming with me? Figure I'll start in Minot. Work my way to Williston. You always wanted to play cops and robbers. Now's your chance."

"I'm staying around here. You should, too," Gus says.

Recites the combination to the gun safe in his head.

"You need to settle down first. Then we'll talk about Wil. Let me grab my wallet from downstairs," Gus says in the most unassuming voice he can muster. Turns to go back in the house.

"You keep your wallet downstairs?" Red says.

"Yeah. Was doing laundry just now," Gus says. It's a weak excuse. Passes Red's boozy muster anyway.

Gus hurries inside. Throws on a light jacket. Opens the gun safe. Stuffs the red envelope into his deep left jacket pocket. A .45 Ruger Blackhawk revolver loaded with jacketed hollow points goes into the right one.

"Ready to go?" Gus says as he returns to Red.

Chapter 87

*T*he Betrug Café is too empty. Not enough people around to prevent a confrontation. Defeats the purpose of bringing a hot Red into the cool neutraility of town in the first place, Gus thinks.

Red seems to calm down as they place their orders. No pacing. No drawing attention to himself. He knows well enough not to do that.

"You OK?" Gus says. Still trying to read Red.

Gus thumbs the red envelope in his pocket. Orders a light lunch. Sandwich. Salad. Slice of pie. Coffee. Another slice of pie. It's light for him anyway.

"No, I'm not OK," Red says. Pauses to order. One burger. Two beers.

The waitress raises an eyebrow.

"You sure about those beers, sheriff?" she says.

"I don't remember asking for your fucking opinion," Red says. Growls into the table as he says it.

The waitress huffs. Leaves without responding.

"Was that really necessary? You sure you're OK?" Gus says. Keeps his voice down.

"I just told you I'm not," Red says. Bites at a fingernail. "Things are changing around here."

Gus shifts in his seat. Feels the Blackhawk rub against his side from inside the jacket.

"Yeah, times are changing. Everything. Everyone. You used to be the one telling *me* to watch my mouth. Now you're cursing out waitresses. Real noble, Red," Gus says. Thinks about his land deal with the federal agents. "Is this a money thing? Is that what's going on?"

Red stays silent. The food shows up a few minutes later, minus the beers. Red starts to protest, but Gus cuts him off.

"Just bring him the beer. I'll keep him in line," Gus says to waitress.

They start eating as she brings over the beers.

"Money changes people, right? Makes them do bad things. Do you think those people are worth forgiving?" Red says.

"What do you mean?" Gus says.

"Like if I told you something. You wouldn't hold it against me, right?" Red says.

Gus sighs. Rolls his eyes.

"I don't know, Red. I guess it depends on what you're going to tell me," he says. "My kids try to pull this stuff on me. A pre-approved confession. Gets exhausting."

Red looks Gus straight in the eyes. It's the first time today he's shown that much focus.

"I need to know you're on my side, Gus. That we'll stick together no matter what," Red says.

Gus imagines what's in the red envelope. Comes up blank. Maybe Red already knows what's in it. Maybe not. The curiosity burns a hole in his pocket.

"Why are you hesitating?" Red says.

"I wasn't," Gus says. It's a lie.

Red's eyes break away from Gus. Return to their manic state.

"Never mind then," Red says.

"No, Red, listen. I wasn't hesitating. You have my support, OK? You're the sheriff. I'm the deputy. I got your back," Gus says.

Red stands up from the booth. Drops a few bills on the table.

"Not anymore you aren't," Red says.

"You're firing me?" Gus says.

"I thought I could trust you," Red says.

"Sit down. Let's talk about this. What's going on?" Gus says.

"Goodbye, Gus," Red says. Heads for the door.

Gus jumps up from the booth. Follows him out the café. He could pull out the red envelope or the revolver.

He'll let Red decide which one he grabs first.

Chapter 88

Gus cuts Red off at the truck.

"Hey, hold on," Gus says. Puts an arm between Red and the door. "You shouldn't be driving anyway."

"I told you to leave me alone," Red says.

"Fine. I will. But give me one minute. Can you calm down for that? Just one minute," Gus says.

Red pushes Gus's arm aside. Opens the door.

Gus runs around to the passenger door. Gets inside.

"Get the hell out of my truck," Red says.

Gus decides it's time. Slips a hand into his pocket. Pulls out the red envelope. Wags it in the air.

"This. Do you know what this is?" Gus says. Not as if he even knows.

"It looks like a laminated piece of red paper. I got no time for magic tricks, Gus."

"Maybe it will change your mind," Gus says.

He tears at the perforations stitched into the envelope. Pauses. Hands it to Red.

"You should open it," Gus says.

"What's this about?" Red says.

"Find out. Open it," Gus says.

Gus slips a hand inside his jacket as Red takes the envelope. Wraps his fingers around the revolver's grip. Just for security. If what the federal agents said was true, this land deal could make him rich. And his grandkids' grandkids.

But only if Red stays put. The agents didn't mention how. Just that he couldn't go looking for Wil.

The last time Gus used the revolver on something, it was to drop a hog. It stayed put, too. One shot behind the ear. Just rolled over and died. Wasn't much farther away than Red is now.

Red fumbles with the envelope. Takes a minute to figure out how to get it open. Flips it upside down. Shakes out what's inside.

It's a photograph.

Red starts to say something. Stops. Has a good look at the photo.

Gus leans over to see. Red hides it from view.

"Where'd you get this?" Red says.

"Let me see what it is," Gus says.

"Not until you tell me where you got it," Red says.

That's when Red notices Gus's conspicuous hand inside the jacket.

"Take your hand out of your jacket," Red says.

Gus scans Red's body. Can't tell if he's carrying a firearm, too.

"Relax, I just have an itch," Gus says.

"Then take your hand out of your jacket," Red says.

"Show me that photo first," Gus says.

"Tell me where you got it from," Red says.

They stare at each other like two fence posts on the prairie. Neither budges. Not until the wind rocks the truck.

That's when one of them makes a move.

Chapter 89

G us takes his hand out from the jacket. No sense in playing cowboy. The café isn't more than 30 feet away.

"Fine. See?" Gus says. Shows Red his empty palms.

Red turns the photo so Gus can see.

"Now tell me. Where did you get this?" Red says. Sounds as sober as a judge.

Gus leans over to see. It's a color photo of Red. He's in the cab of his truck next to a...

Transvestite?

The man next to Red – and it is a man – is pulling up a pair of pants. But everything about him looks like a woman. Except for one thing. A penis between his legs.

Red knows when the photo was taken. In Minnesota, when he met "Jane" to talk about Wil. It's a fail-safe. A guarantee. Something to keep Red in line.

"Why do you have this photo, Gus?" Red says. "Did you take it?"

Gus looks as surprised as Red.

"No, I didn't take it. Someone gave it to me," Gus says.

"Who? The same person who wrote this?" Red says. Turns the photo over.

Printed in small type on the back of the photo are these words: "This goes to the newspaper if you don't stop. – Jane."

"Holy shit, Red. You and a prostitute?" Gus says.

"No. Me and Jane. Or someone who works for Jane. From our meeting in Minnesota. But we sure as hell weren't doing what this picture makes it look like. Now tell me where you got this," Red says.

Gus tells Red about the meeting with the federal

agents, Tom and Beth. Leaves out the part about the land deal.

"And you never told me?" Red says.

"Look, I didn't know. They just showed up and gave me an envelope. Told me what to do with it. Shit, I'm running scared here, OK? There's nothing in the reserve deputy pamphlet on how to deal with this," Gus says in a rush.

"Yeah, well, get in line. The whole state of North Dakota is in the same position," Red says. "Just another reason I couldn't trust you to tell time."

"Red, look ..." Gus says.

"You're going to give me the phone number for those federal agents," Red says. Starts the truck. "Then I'm finding Wil. There's a reason Jane wants me to stay put. But I just don't give a damn anymore."

Gus starts to say something. Red cuts him off. Pulls open Gus's jacket. Grabs the revolver.

"You're such a prairie dog, Gus. You know that?" Red says. Switches the gun to his left hand. Aims it at Gus. Uses his right hand to drive the truck out of Betrug.

"It ain't like that, Red. Not at all," Gus says.

"We're going back to your place. You're getting me those phone numbers. Your wife and kids home?" Red says.

Gus stammers. His mind can't break the gaze of the revolver.

"Uh, no. They went to Bismarck, like I told you before," Gus says.

"Good," Red says.

Chapter 90

R ed guides Gus down the basement stairs with the Blackhawk.

"The business cards are in there," Gus says. Points to the gun safe.

"Bullshit. You want me to let you open a gun safe?" Red says. Keeps the revolver aimed at Gus's vitals.

"You can open it if you want. The combination is 19-1-13-9-19-1-7-21-25. Just, please, let me see my family again," Gus says.

"Fine. Stand over there," Red says. Herds Gus into a corner. Returns to the safe. "Now tell me the numbers again. And don't fucking cry on me."

But Gus can't help it. It's not his family he thinks about as he tears up, though. It's the thought of missing the land opportunity. The money. It hurts more than the chance of missing his wife and kids.

He always told himself money didn't matter in life. Doing right by family matters. It's a nice saying, but not when this kind of money is on the line.

"If you only knew why I had to do this. You'd understand," Red says. Opens the safe. Finds the business cards. Pockets them. Turns to face Gus.

"Me, too," Gus says. His right fist cracks Red's nose like a padlock popping open.

Red takes the punch without stumbling. That gives Gus enough time to seed another knuckle into Red's jaw.

But not a third. Red has a moment before dizziness melts his vision. Shoots Gus in the leg with the revolver.

The .45 caliber hollow point scores a fistful of meat from Gus's outer thigh. The fragments terminate as pockmarks in the basement walls. No magical ricochet like in the movies.

Red slides up against the wall. Gus does the same on the opposite side of the basement. Neither talks for a few minutes. Just breathe through the creeping pain in their wounds.

"Sorry," Gus says finally. Threads off his belt. Wraps it like a tourniquet around his upper thigh.

"Why'd you hit me?" Red says. Blood from his nose drools off his chin. "Why do you give two shits whether I leave to find Wil?"

Gus sighs. No sense in hiding it now.

"The federal agents, Tom and Beth, they made me a deal. Said if I kept you here I'd get first dibs on some hot property," Gus says.

"What kind of dibs?" Red says.

"Said there was going to be a plot of land coming on sale soon. I could buy it for almost nothing. They said the price would go way up after that. Guaranteed. I could sell it, keep my family comfortable for generations," Gus says.

Red digs into his pocket. It's like a trough for the blood from his nose. Finds the business card, pulls it out.

"What property were they talking about?" Red says.

Gus hobbles to his feet. Tests whether he can walk with the tourniquet. Nope.

"I need a doctor," Gus says with wide eyes.

"The property, Gus. What property were they talking about?" Red says.

Gus hesitates. Coughs. It sounds forced.

"You don't tell me, I'm leaving you in this basement," Red says.

"Fine, fine. It's the Reynolds place. Now get me the hell to a doctor," Gus says.

Red squints away the look of shock in his eyes. Looks for a landline phone so Gus can't see. Finds one and tosses the receiver to Gus.

The cord is long enough to stretch across the

basement. Not an uncommon sight on the prairie. The cell towers constructed for the oil fields are changing that.

"What's this?" Gus says.

Red says, "You're calling those agents. Then we'll see about getting you to a doctor."

Chapter 91

*B*eth's cell phone rings. She nods to Tom to turn the car radio down.

They've been driving for hours with no real destination. Just waiting for Jane to call. And listening to the radio. Tom pulled rank to listen to a swap meet. Said it was like hearing the real Mayberry.

A voice starts speaking as soon as Beth picks up. Monotone. No hint of gender or race. It's Jane. But she's more robotic than before. Almost like a recording.

"I detected the envelope opened," Jane says.

Beth puts the call on speaker. Motions for Tom to pull the car over.

"Understood. What does that mean for us?" Beth says.

"In 10 seconds I'll transfer this call to Gus's home phone. It's trying to call you now," Jane says. "It might mean Red is staying put. It might mean Red saw the contents, doesn't care and is headed out to find Wil anyway. In either case, get Gus to meet you."

"What should we do if we meet Red?" Beth says.

"Kill him," Jane says.

Tom tries to get a word in but can't. Jane ends the call.

The phone rings again. It's a Betrug landline. Beth answers.

"Yeah, Gus here," Gus says. His wet breathing is steady as a waterbed. "Listen, I had to open the envelope."

Tom gives Beth a look. They're both thinking the same thing.

"That's OK. That's why we gave it to you," Beth says. Keeps her tone friendly. No sign of suspicion in her voice. "And how did it go?"

"Well...it...it sure scared Red into doing the right

thing. He says he's not going anywhere. So...so don't give that photo to the newspaper," Gus says.

"So long as he stays put, that won't happen. You can tell Red that," Beth says. "Do you want to meet up again?"

"Yeah, yeah, exactly. Let's meet," Gus says.

"Where and when should we meet? It's up to you," Beth says.

There's a pause. Like Gus puts his hand over the phone and talks with someone else. It's not a tight grip, though. Beth can hear two distinct voices talking in murmurs.

"Let's meet tonight at 8. How about the park in Betrug? Where they had the pumpkin festival," Gus says.

"Sounds good. We'll see you there," Beth says. Ends the call.

Beth's tone changes back to its normal stoicism.

"Red knows what's up," she says.

"Meet at a park to keep it public. Do it at night to make it private. The best of both worlds. I expect Red will come armed," Tom says. Pulls the car back onto the road. "Do we call Jane?"

"No. I'm sure she's been listening," Beth says.

"We've been sitting with our thumbs up our asses waiting on Jane to deliver her end of the deal. We need to know more about Wil's location and everything else she promised. Better happen after tonight. Tired of being her lap dog," Tom says.

"Don't forget about that paperwork we're supposed to get him to sign, too," Beth says.

"About that. Did you open the envelope it came in? Do we know what's in it?" Tom says.

"Not yet. We're supposed to wait for instructions. Looks like Jane knows when the envelopes are opened," Beth says.

"Fuck Jane. Once we get Wil we're done," Tom says.

He turns the radio on. The ag report delivers the latest pork belly prices.

Beth flicks it back off.

"After all this, you're ready to blow her off?" Beth says. "You didn't feel that way before. We need to trust the Bureau. They gave this the green light."

Tom pulls the car onto the road. Passes a tractor driving slower than wheat growing.

"Trust the Bureau, sure. But how do you know we can trust her? I've been doing this for years. I've never come across anything like Jane. Know why? Hackers weren't around 25 years ago. That's probably what this is about. We'll wind up with egg all over our faces," Tom says.

"Fine. We'll call the Bureau again," Beth says. Dials a number on her cell phone. The phone loses reception as soon as she presses Call. She doesn't look surprised. Jane's in control.

"It's probably your shit government phone. Use mine. It's a slightly different shit government phone," Tom says. Passes his cell phone to Beth. She tries the same numbers.

"Same thing," Beth says.

Tom pulls the car over. Tries the numbers for himself on both phones. Same result.

"How do we know this isn't just crappy reception? We're basically on the moon as far as cell towers are concerned," Tom says.

Beth takes her phone back. Dials their motel in Betrug. It connects.

"We can only call the places Jane wants us to call," Beth says after hanging up. "She's in charge."

"Funny. I thought the Bureau was in charge," Tom says. "Can we only go where Jane wants, too? What would happen if we skipped that meeting?"

"I don't know. I don't want to find out," Beth says. "I think Jane's on a different level."

Tom pulls the car back onto the road. Passes a sign for Betrug. It's five miles ahead.

"We always have the choice. It's not like there's some invisible hand pulling the strings that's going to reach out and slap me," Tom says.

Beth thinks she might show him a visible one. His humor grows more taxing each day.

"You're not seriously thinking of skipping the meeting, are you?" she says.

"What's the worst that could happen? I'm calling Jane's bluff. Fuck her. You go. I'll stay at the motel. Get packed. We're leaving. Getting back on the trail instead of getting punked by some hacker. I'm not holding my breath for Jane to deliver," Tom says.

Five miles later, Tom parks the car at the motel. Tosses the keys to Beth.

"I'm taking a nap. Get me a sandwich from the gas station, will you?" he says in a tone to remind Beth he's the veteran of the pair.

"Don't hold your breath," Beth says under hers.

Chapter 92

"You're a horseshit liar, Gus. Would've been less transparent if you'd just handed me the phone," Red says.

He tears the phone cord from the basement wall. It pops out like an unraveled button.

"Can we go to the doctor now?" Gus says. Tightens the belt around his thigh with a loud grunt.

"Yeah, I suppose I should get my nose fixed up. Wouldn't want to bleed all over tonight's meeting," Red says.

"What about me?" Gus says.

"You get to stay here," Red says. Puts a foot on the first tread of the stairs going up.

"What? Why?" Gus says. Tries to hobble off the wall. No use.

"You want to know what this is all really about?" Red says.

"I told you my thing. You tell me yours," Gus says.

Red takes his foot off the step.

"Me and you, we got something in common. That Reynolds land and money. You don't want to know more," he says.

"Sure I do," Gus says.

Red shakes his head. "When you told me you got cut into that Reynolds land, it means someone, like Jane, is planning on me being dead soon. Because that land and that money, it should be mine."

Gus coughs. "My family won't be back until tomorrow. I hurt too much to walk. You can't just leave me here to suffer."

Red starts up the stairs. Pauses.

"I don't have the heart to kill you, Gus. But I don't give a damn enough to save you, either," Red says. Unloads the Blackhawk revolver. Tosses it down the stairs next to Gus. He'll use his own .45 Colt Anaconda revolver. Prefers it. "Here's your gun back. Just so you can't call me a thief among everything else you're bound to say about me."

Red reaches the top of the stairs. Listens to Gus's panicked breathing.

"Good luck," Red says.

Chapter 93

*T*om keeps his word about skipping the meeting. Tells Beth as much after she returns to the motel.

"You couldn't find the time to pick up a sandwich?" he says to Beth from the bed. Stretched out. Socks off.

The digital clock on the nightstand reads 7:49 p.m. Eleven minutes to the meeting.

"I was clearing the park. Marking the blind spots. So, no, I didn't have time to feed you," Beth says.

Beth loads another magazine full with cartridges. Slips it into the mag pouch next to the Glock 23 holstered on her belt.

The belt holds her loose dress shirt in place. The shirt hides the ballistics vest underneath. But she doesn't hide her disbelief at Tom.

"You can't even give me support for this? Cover the blind spots?" Beth says. "That's enough to get you terminated."

"So is willingly giving some hacker the time of day," Tom says. Finds the TV remote control. Flips on the ag report. "This really is funny stuff. Just look at how these people are dressed."

Beth does a final check of her gear. Pats herself from head to toe.

"If I'm not back by 9, could you find it within yourself to check on me?" Beth says.

Tom laughs. "When you're back at 8:05, could you find it within yourself to pick up supper?" he says.

"Don't hold your breath," Beth says.

Chapter 94

R ed waits until 8:05 p.m. to make himself known. He's watched Beth wait by a bench for 10 minutes.

"I thought there were two of you," Red says.

The oversized bandage over his nose looks downright theatric. He found time to see a doctor, albeit a horse doctor. Told a lie about getting on the wrong side of a horse's ass. Close enough.

No sign of the blood now. Except for his boots.

Beth notices them as Red approaches. It's a go-to trick for reading a person. People usually have fresh clothes to wear. But they don't switch footwear often. Shoes are the real storytellers about a person. Income. Vocation. Location. Recent activity. Plenty of soul in those soles.

"And I thought you were supposed to be Gus," Beth says. Makes it obvious she's looking at Red's boots.

"I was inspecting a dead cow earlier today. You can look up now," Red says.

He stops 10 feet from Beth. Close enough so they don't have to shout. Far enough away for wiggle room.

"A dead cow. I see," Beth says.

"People around here, they still call the sheriff about these things. They like it when problems are solved. Especially by someone they can trust. Who knows the people. The area," Red says.

"I get it, sheriff. You don't like me. That's fine," Beth says. "You wanted to talk. So let's talk."

Red continues his line of thought.

"That's not something I'll be able to say much longer. That I know the land. The people. You're standing here. I don't know you. Homicides? Never knew much about them until now. And the land? That oil patch isn't getting smaller. They should just rename this state Saudi Dakota and be done with it," Red says.

Beth cuts off Red's waxing philosophy. Boils things down to the dirt.

"Where's Gus, sheriff?" she says.

"Gus is fine. I didn't kill him if that's what you mean," Red says.

"Is he hurt?" Beth says.

"I said he's fine. Now I've got a question. Where's Wil?" Red says.

"I don't know. If I did, I wouldn't be standing here right now," Beth says.

"Let's try this then. Where'd you get that photograph you gave to Gus?" Red says.

Beth watches Red's hands. They hang loose from his sides.

"That doesn't matter. What matters is that you give up trying to find him. Let us do our job," she says.

Beth crosses her hands at the waist. All the better to reach the holstered pistol on her belt beneath her jacket.

"Oh, I think it matters quite a bit. Because there's only way one you would have it," Red says. Clears his throat. "Jane."

Beth winces at the name. Sends the reaction to her big toe where it can't be seen. Presses down in her shoe.

"Jane? I don't know what you're talking about," Beth says. It's a weak lie. Of course she knows about how Red hired Jane.

"If I wanted bullshit, I'd go back to that dead cow from this morning," Red says. "You're working with Jane. She gave you the photo. Stop lying."

Red reaches in to his pocket. Beth mimics the action. Goes for the Glock 23.

"Hold on, hold on. I'm not going to shoot you. I'll let

you know if I do," Red says. Pulls out the photo.

Beth relaxes. Keeps her hand on the holster anyway.

"See. That's me meeting with Jane. Or someone working for Jane," Red says.

He hands the photo to Beth. Returns to his 10-foot buffer.

Beth studies the image. It's Red in the cab of a truck. A feminine man gets dressed beside him. Or maybe it's a woman with a prosthetic penis. Hard to tell.

"This is what was in the red envelope we gave to Gus?" Beth says.

"Right. And the person in the photo is the one I talked to when I set everything up with Jane," Red says.

"Are you sure?" Beth says. Notices the smell of ammonia cleaner from the photo. There's still a bit of dried blood on a corner.

"I know what it looks like. Me and a hooker or something. But it's not. This is what Jane does. She always has something on you. A way to keep you in line," Red says.

Beth hands the photo back. It's clear Red won't leave without it.

"Fair enough. Yes, we're working with Jane. She wants you to stay put. I suggest you do," Beth says.

Red scans the park. Notes the blind spots.

"You should know Jane has a safeguard for you, too. You wouldn't be working with her if she didn't," he says.

Beth follows Red's eyes. Watches as they pause on each blind spot. Trees. Benches. Vehicles. Buildings. She's already made a mental map of them.

"How can you be so sure?" Beth says.

"Because this isn't the first time I've worked with her," Red says.

His eyes return to Beth. He notices the way it takes her pupils a moment to meet his.

"Do tell," Beth says.

Red says, "Right when the oil boom started up, I get this grant from the Department of Homeland Security. It'll pay me overtime to keep watch on prospectors at the oil patch on weekends. Make sure equipment and infrastructure doesn't get hit by terrorists.

"So one night I'm out monitoring this new oil rig after hours. I see this guy poking around. Bald guy. Got a cap that reads Navy Vet on it. Never forget it.

"I stop him. See what's up. He says he's with one of the fracking companies. But his ID doesn't check out. I try to haul him in. Off he goes.

"I call up DHS. Tell them what happened. They say this guy is an environmental terrorist. A real shithead, too. Bombs. Sabotage. Kidnapping. Oil fracking is his latest target.

"It's out of my league, so DHS taps this Jane person to go find him. She brings in the cloak and dagger bullshit. Kind of like how there is now. But the whole thing winds up botched. The wrong people got hurt. This Navy vet guy disappears somehow. We never find him.

"I make sure the whole thing is covered up. Tidy up the loose ends. Pay respect to the locals Jane indirectly killed. In return for my silence, Jane offers me a shitload of money. All I have to do is convince the owners of a particular property to sell to an oil company. That also hasn't happened."

Beth nods. "The Reynolds property," she says.

"Exactly," Red says. Conveniently forgets to mention how he'd planned to "convince" the owners to sell. And all the ways it went wrong.

Beth purses her lips. "So why did you call Jane to find Wil?" she says.

"Because I wanted to stay ahead of fed assholes like you," Red says. "And because Jane had skin in the game anyway."

"Or maybe because you want Wil out of the way. Might help you make a land deal, pocket some cash," Beth says.

Red shakes his head.

"It's not like that. Mary Reynolds is still alive. She's the one that can sell that property, not Wil. I just want Wil back before he's hauled off to prison. For my sake. For Mary's sake. For Betrug's sake. It's certainly not for Jane's sake. Or yours," Red says.

Beth makes a connection. Jane must be planning on Mary stepping to the background, or undergroud, soon. Why else give Beth papers for Wil to sign off on? They must be for the land sale.

But what's so important about selling the Reynolds property that Jane would go through all this trouble? Beth's not sure, but it makes her glad she packed extra magazines.

"About that. What is Jane? I'm curious to know what you think," Beth says. "Both DHS and the FBI hired her. She must be someone special."

"I don't know who or what Jane is," Red says. "But I think we've made it to the part where we stop the small talk."

Beth raises an eyebrow. "Good. So you've decided to stay in Betrug. You're not going after Wil," she says.

Red's eyes take another sweep of the blind spots. Expects the other agent to show up. Beth's thinking the same thing.

"Actually, you're going to tell me where Wil is. Then I'm going to find him," Red says.

"Jane apparently knows, but she hasn't told me," Beth says.

Red grits his teeth. Feels his vision blur. Doesn't need his eyes to know she's telling the truth. Or at least enough of the truth. He's stuck. But that's why he brought the revolver.

"You know where the saying, 'It's a draw,' comes from? It means the first person to draw their weapon wins," Red says. It's not true, but it buys time. "And I don't think you have anyone backing you up."

Beth controls each breath in and out. Smooth and steady. Hopes Tom is listening somewhere in dark.

Chapter 95

R ed's the faster draw. Aims his Colt Anaconda at Beth's chest.

"Don't lie to me. Where is he?" Red says.

Beth gauges the distance between them. It's less than 21 feet. Her training reminds her that she might still get the drop on Red. It's called the Tueller Drill.

But the Tueller Drill doesn't consider someone who already has the revolver up. It has to be holstered. That's not the case here.

No, she can't get the drop on Red.

"Red, listen to me. I don't know. Jane knows. She said if I keep you here, she'll let me know. That's it. End of story," Beth says.

She offers to unholster her pistol and place it on the ground. Red agrees. Beth shows him her palms after setting the firearm down.

"I don't have a reason to lie," Beth says.

Red waits. Listens for movement in the park.

Nothing.

"That's what Jane said, huh? I have to stay here. Then you find out," Red says. "Fine. I'll stay. But only on one condition."

"Name it," Beth says.

"You're staying with me. Or rather, I'm staying with you," Red says.

"What?"

"You're going to get in my truck. I'll drive you to wherever you're staying. When Jane calls you with the information, you'll let me know what's up. That clear?" Red says.

Beth shakes her head. Thinks about the cell phone in

her pocket. How it didn't connect before. How Jane likes putting people on a particular goat path. Give them the illusion of choice.

"I don't think Jane works like that. She expects things to go a certain way," Beth says. Thinks back to Tom in the motel. "I wouldn't want to test her on that."

"I really don't give a damn at this point," Red says. Nods to the pistol on the ground. "For every step I take forward, you take one step back. That clear? None of this kicking the gun toward me Hollywood crap."

Beth follows Red's orders. He walks forward as she retreats.

"Now get in the truck. You're driving," Red says after picking up Beth's Glock.

It's a short drive from the park to the Betrug Motel. Red keeps his revolver trained on Beth the whole time.

Beth scans the parking lot for Tom. No sign of him. Bastard. Splitting up is always a bad idea.

Red watches her eyes.

"Pretty shitty partner you've got," Red says. Walks toward a motel room door facing the parking lot. "I can relate. Gus was just as worthless when I needed him most, too."

He motions for Beth to open the motel door.

Beth works the lock. Holds her breath. Prays Tom doesn't let her down once again.

Red pushes her to the side. Slips inside the room in two steps. Pivots into a corner so his back isn't exposed to Beth.

Beth exhales. There's Tom, inside the motel room. Finally.

Except her breath doesn't come out naturally. It makes the words, "Holy shit."

Red stumbles backward out of the room. Bumps up against Beth. She ignores it. Hard to focus on anything except the sight in front of them.

Tom is naked and hog-tied on the bed. The belt from his pants is coiled around his neck so tight it nearly meets in the center of his throat.

A fresh sandwich sits on a beige plate atop the nightstand. Propped against it is a note. It reads, "Don't hold your breath" in bold typeface.

Red starts to say something. The ringing from the room phone cuts him off.

Chapter 96

Beth holds up a hand to let Red know she'll answer the phone. Picks it up and listens.

"I never liked your partner," Jane says.

"I can see that," Beth says. Watches Red pace the room.

"Your partner died from autoerotic asphyxiation. While eating a sandwich. Got it?" Jane says.

"Understood," Beth says. Stares at Tom's body with the kind of morbid curiosity that sent her to the Bureau in the first place.

"Tell Red he can expect the same if he doesn't cooperate. That's on top of the photo the newspaper will now be running. You will receive instructions on where to find Wil in the morning," Jane says. Ends the call.

Beth sets the phone down. Debates what to do with Red. It only takes a glimpse of Tom's over-inflated, purple-black face to make a decision.

"Well?" Red says. The Python dangles in his right hand.

"I wait for further instructions," Beth says. "And you wait here."

"Bullshit," Red says. Looks up at the ceiling. "You hear that, Jane?"

Beth picks up the note. Looks it over. There's nothing exceptional about it. Save for one thing.

"Red, you should know something. That note says, 'Don't hold your breath.' I said it tonight when I was frustrated with Tom when he decided to stay here instead of go to the meeting," Beth says.

"So?" Red says.

Beth wags the note in front of Red.

"So Jane heard that. It had a meaning no one else could've known about. Or even heard," Beth says. Points to the sandwich. "He wanted supper instead of helping me. It means you'll end up dead if you don't stay in Betrug. You have to do things a certain way."

Red rolls his eyes.

"This is why I hate dealing with federals. If you even are one," Red says. "For all I know, you offed your partner for pissing you off, then met me in the park. You made up a conversation on the phone just now. You're Jane."

"I swear to you. I did no such thing," Beth says. Thinks how Red's theory is certainly plausible, if not a little paranoid.

"Good for you then," Red says. Turns to leave. "You could already guess this, but I'll just state the obvious anyway. When you finally do leave to get Wil, you'll see a truck in your rearview mirror. That's me."

"I'm telling you, Red. Don't. Jane will kill you," Beth says.

"Jane? You mean you, right? I'm not so worried," Red says. "I've got your gun."

He pauses. Waits for a reaction from Beth. Sees none. She's telling the truth as far as he can tell. Complicates things. Good thing he has twice the firepower now.

"I suppose you'll tell me not to hold my breath," Red says as he leaves.

"No. I wish you good luck, sheriff. Seriously," Beth says.

Chapter 97

*S*am waits until the sun goes down to leave the RV. Or at least try to leave the RV. Can't stand being cooped up. The Man Camp loses a minute of sunlight a day now.

Wil isn't back yet. Good. Time to keep things moving forward.

She pulls on a heavy jacket. Heads outside. Notices the two men by the black trucks. The ones monitoring the RV since dawn.

Her insides feel bruised. Nothing on her face shows it. Walks with purpose up to the men. They weren't expecting that.

"Les sent you here to watch me, right?" Sam says. "Well, here I am."

One of the men shrugs. Picks something out of his teeth. Examines his thumbnail. Wipes something on his pants.

"Yep. There you are, girlies," he says. Pluralizes "girly" for some reason. It's like his mangled face can't end a sentence without an "s."

Sam moves a step backward. Takes another look at the scars cutting a reddish brown across the man's face. He looks like an infection scraped off a horse hoof, but still familiar. Clearly going blind in one cloudy eye.

"I'm bad luck. The last guy who followed me around shot himself in the face," Sam says.

"So I've heards," the man says.

The scrawny guy with the shotgun. It's him. He survived somehow. Didn't take long for Les to push him back out to work. Sam almost feels bad for him. More so for the sake of herself.

Sam scans for a shotgun. Nope. He must've wised up. Graduated to handguns. Or maybe the shotguns are in the truck.

The three stand there for a while. Sam. The scrawny guy. One of Les's random strong arms. Fiery and silent, like the last sliver of sunshine on the horizon.

"I feel like going for a walk," Sam says. Feels the raccoon jewelry brush against her sternum as she turns away.

"Not allowed, girlies," the scrawny guy says. Hacks something onto the ground in front of Sam's foot.

Sam tenses up. Wants to finish fucking up the scrawny guy's face. Files the feeling away for another time. It'll come soon enough.

"Have it your way *thens*," Sam says. Smiles to herself as she walks back to the RV.

Chapter 98

I get back to the RV at the Man Camp late. Too late for supper. Sam already ate. So it's granola bars and Tang again. Too bad. After today, I could go for a burger.

I hit the shower. Change into fresh clothes. Get the mud from the rig out of my skin.

"You always going to be this late?" Sam says after I'm done.

"Maybe. Hard to say," I say. Open a granola bar. "Moved a lot of Les's dope. Powders and pills. First one gets them to work. Second one keeps them working."

"Meth and pain pills. Like peas and carrots," Sam says. Takes a seat across from me. "What else?"

I finish the granola bar. Open another two.

"I'm still pressure washing. Help where they need it," I say.

Sam strokes the raccoon penis jewelry around her neck. Watches me eat.

"I didn't mean work. I mean you. Anything else you want to talk about?" she says.

It's hard to remember yesterday. Feels like trying to recall a boring movie.

"You want to talk about yesterday? Can't say I remember much," I say.

"I didn't ask if you remembered yesterday," Sam says. "Do you feel OK? That's what I mean."

I look for another box of granola bars. Find one and pop it open.

"I'm fine, I guess," I say.

"So you're fine with yesterday?" Sam says.

"Yeah. I'm fine," I say.

Sam doesn't look satisfied with the answer. It's like she's waiting for something. I'm too tired to guess.

"Maybe you'll ask how I'm doing," Sam says.

I swallow a bar in mid chew.

"OK. How are you doing?" I say.

Sam rolls her eyes. "You're missing the point. Never mind," she says.

It's not like that at all. I realize I should've asked. But with this weary fog I'm in, my brain isn't catching up to my mouth.

"Hey," I say. My hand touches hers. We cradle the jewelry together. "How are you?"

Sam lets a breath out. "Fine," she says.

I don't believe her. She wants me to press her for more. But I'm no good at this budding relationship bullshit.

"Good," I say back. There. Settled.

"Holy shit, you're dense," Sam says. Gets up from the small table.

I rub my eyes.

"No," I say. "Just tired."

"Easy for you to say. You didn't have some guy on top of you. Some guy cutting you. Some guy underneath your clothes. No. You played hero. Then you went back to work like it never happened," Sam says.

"You want to talk about shutting down? You never told me what he even did," I say.

Now we're both standing up.

"Does it even matter what he did at this point?" Sam says. "You walk in here like you don't even care. Like it's just another day."

How are we arguing right now? What happened? Wish she'd just tell me what she wants.

"I do care," I say.

"You're not showing it," Sam says.

Showing it in the right way is more like it. Because I do care. But it's only been 24 hours since it all happened. Is there a manual for these things I didn't read?

"If you need to talk about something, let's talk about something," I say. "You want to get outta here, let's get outta here. But tell me what you want."

Sam shakes her head.

"You don't understand," she says. "I've had all day to think about what happened to me. All day. There's nothing else to do. This is difficult for me."

No more decoding. I go straight out and say what I'm thinking.

"You think you're the only one Taw was hurting? When I saw you all bloody underneath him, it's like I was being hurt, too," I say. "I killed Taw, Sam. I fucking killed him. And I killed a guy coming to help him. Do you mean to tell me I don't care about you? Seriously, Sam?"

I surprise myself with that bit. Feels strange to say I killed someone. But the phrase has a familiar ring to it. Like I've thought it before.

I shelve the thought. Because the admission of how much I care about Sam trumps everything. Sends a warm shiver into my dead muscles.

Maybe that's the reaction she wanted all along.

I keep going. Why the hell not? It's all true.

"I've never felt like I could trust someone like you," I say. "It's almost like it was…"

Sam finishes my sentence.

"Meant to be," she says and laughs. "That is so cliché. But it's true. It does feel that way."

I crack a smile, too. It's good to see her laugh. Especially when there's no reason for her to do it. Not after yesterday.

"You took the words right out of my mouth," I say.

"Another cliché," Sam says.

I hug her. Not sure if kissing her is the right thing considering yesterday. But making sense is the least of anyone's concerns on the Bakken. I do it anyway.

"That's what I needed from you," Sam says.

Her voice tiptoes over the words. Like it's walking on the first ice of the season on a frozen lake.

I smile and hug her again. Not too tight. Her body is still tender.

Sam gives my hand a squeeze. "There's some microwave pizza in the cooler. You want some?" she says.

"You sit down. I got it," I say.

It isn't fancy, but it's a meal. More importantly, we eat it together. Not two people sitting and eating. Together.

Chapter 99

A fter pizza, Sam tells me how the Man Camp is clearing out. She watched the soft-sided campers come down. A whole row of trucks left in the afternoon. Each looked like a scene from *The Grapes of Wrath*.

"Winter is coming. It's always nasty. Most of the workers probably want real housing," I say.

"I thought there weren't enough hotels and dorms?" Sam says.

"There aren't. That's why some people will tough it out here," I say. "We're in a nice RV. We'll be OK for the time being."

"You want to stay the winter?" Sam says.

"It's like you said before. We make as much money as fast as we can. Then we leave. Hopefully that happens before the big snow hits," I say.

"You're not worried Les is going to keep us here anyway?" Sam says.

I clear the paper plates from the table. Dump them in the trash.

"Maybe. Why do you ask?" I say.

"Two guys watched the RV all day," Sam says. "One of them is that scrawny guy who blasted himself in the face with his shotgun."

I stop clearing the table. "Seriously?" I say.

"He's his usual asshole self. Face is all messed up, though. Like horror movie bad," Sam says. "You didn't get hassled coming into the Man Camp tonight, did you?"

"Nope. Did those guys give you trouble?" I say.

"Wouldn't let me take a walk," Sam says. Perks up her eyebrows. "Sort of an off topic question, but what about your nightmares? Those getting better or worse?"

I forgot about those. Mostly because I haven't had one in a while.

The thought of the shadow people makes me pull an eyelash out. Sam notices. I turn away so she can't see me eat it. Make it look like I raise my hand to my mouth to think.

"Fuck the nightmares, how long do we have before Les makes you go back?" I say.

Sam is a commodity out here. With the shortage of women on the prairie, he can't afford to wait for long.

"Couple weeks, if Les allows it. Most likely much less than that. Sewed my own stitches today so I didn't have to visit the camp doctor," Sam says. Quiets her voice. I can barely hear her. "They'll want an inspection of me. To test me for readiness."

My face mimics Sam's "no fucking way" look.

"Two weeks. That's not much time," I say. Then realize what I missed earlier. "Wait, did you say you left the RV? Asked to go for a walk?"

Sam's eyes look away from mine.

Damn it.

"What the hell, Sam? They're going to think you're ready to go back," I say.

"I went to tell those guys to fuck off," Sam says.

It's hard to blame her for being herself. But still. Damn it. It sabotages the timeline. It's almost like she wanted to expedite the situation. Why? I have no fucking clue. Makes no sense.

"They're going to come for you a lot sooner. We don't have two weeks. We have two days. Or two hours," I say. Run a hand through my hair. "Why'd you do that?"

"Didn't think it was a big deal. Walking around is one thing," Sam says. "Doing...*that*...is another."

"These people don't think like that," I say.

Sam grabs my arm. Squeezes it.

"Wil, listen. They can't do that. They can't do the inspection," she says.

There's something off in the way she says it. A real fear. But there's something beneath it, too. A monotony. Almost like she doesn't mind having this conversation. Scripted concern.

I don't mention it, though. That's not the issue. The issue is how we get the hell out of here in a matter of hours, not days.

"Promise me you won't let that inspection happen," Sam says.

Les's guy gave me more rounds for the revolver. I'm already in this deep. Wad of money in my left pocket. Gun in my right. Only person I've ever really cared about in front of me.

Yeah, this is a promise I can make.

I take Sam's face into my hands. Look right into her eyes.

"I promise," I say. "Best thing to do is for me to work the rig tomorrow. Not raise any suspicions with Les. Then make a clean break for it once I get back."

I kiss her. It's soft. And long. Like the threads on a prairie smoke flower before the wind carries it away.

Chapter 100

R ed cracks his neck. Long night in the truck parked at the motel. He stayed up watching. Waiting. Didn't want Beth to slip away unnoticed.

He walks to Beth's door. Tries the handle. It's locked. No surprise there. He knocks three times. No noise from inside.

Red heads back to his truck. The park is only a few blocks away. Beth could've walked it in the night when Red inevitably slept a couple minutes. Or she might've snuck out some other way. Time to check it out.

Red fires up the truck and heads out. His hunch pays off.

Chapter 101

B eth is 10 feet from her car at the park when Red pulls up. Blocks the front end of the car with his truck. Not that it does much good. Beth could still back out. But it gets her attention.

Red rolls down the window. Holds the grip of Beth's Glock 23 out. It's a stupid thing to do. The barrel points back at Red. He doesn't seem to care.

"Looking for this?" Red says.

Red holds the Glock out in his left hand. His right holds the Colt Anaconda revolver below the door. The hand is invisible to Beth. Not a stupid thing to do.

"You're giving me back my gun?" Beth says.

"Come on. Take it," Red says. Wags the pistol.

Beth takes a step toward the truck. Pauses. "Why?" she says.

"Because I don't want you pulling a fast one on me to get the gun back anyway. Focus on finding Wil. Not me," Red says.

Beth takes another step toward the truck. Gauges how easy it would be for Red to pull her inside. Chances aren't in Red's favor. But he could pin her against the side regardless.

"Get out of the truck. Leave it on the ground. When I take a step forward, you take a step back. Remember that?" Beth says.

"We don't have time for this. Just take it," Red says. "Trust me. If I wanted to hurt you, I'd've done it by now. You have to be well enough to get me to Wil. And you can't be well if you're not armed. Not around here."

Beth doesn't move.

"Show me your other hand," she says.

Red rolls his eyes. Releases the revolver. Raises his right hand like he's taking an oath.

"You want me to swear on the Bible next?" he says. Returns his hand to the revolver out of view.

Beth grabs her pistol back in mid-sentence. Red doesn't flinch.

"Good. Now we can get on with things," Red says. "Jane must've called you with directions to Wil, right?"

"She did," Beth says. Racks the slide on the Glock.

"Now hear me out on this. I got an idea," Red says. Tightens his grip on the revolver. "What if we worked together on this? I know the area. The people. You're down a partner anyway. Maybe we can both walk away from this happy. What do you think?"

He barely finishes his sentence before Beth puts a bullet in Red.

Chapter 102

The next day at the rig is rough. The machinery is in no mood to work. Neither are the people.

One guy complains of knee problems. I sell him a few pills. Help him get through the day. He leaves cash for me under some gloves.

Thankfully, the water runs out before we can do more drilling. Happens all the time. That means waiting for a water truck. It's always late. Too much demand.

There's not much for the workers, either. I hear there's a shortage of well water. Kind of odd considering there's plenty for private wells.

In a painful, ironic twist, there's too much natural gas. It's burned off right at the rig. Thing is, there's a propane shortage for the grain dryers a mile away. So the farmers use natural gas pumped in from outside the state. Just as bizarre as everything else out here.

They say you can see the glow from the natural gas burn offs from space. I don't doubt it. The nighttime is never black anymore. Now there's a permanent sunset across the horizons. Or sunrise. Depends on your perspective.

The workers bitch about going into town for bottled water. Somehow they always come back with liquor instead.

But not today. Today everyone's thirsty. Crack open jugs of water. Drink up.

I know dehydration when I see it. A few of the workers look rough. The chalky lips. Tired eyes. Slow reflexes. Those aren't things suited for an oil rig.

So it's no surprise when one of them loses a pair of toes.

It starts with a sharp shout on the other side of the rig. We all rush to the worker. Looks like his foot is a cake, and the machinery just cut a slice.

Steel-toed boots, they do that. The plate dents if it's hit hard enough. Can turn the inside of a boot into a knife. Take your toes clean off. Which is what's happening here.

The worker literally walks it off. If he's in pain, he's doing a great job of hiding it. But then I recognize him as the one with the knee problems. Now I know what happened.

"Didn't feel a thing," he says. Turns to me. "Thanks for that."

Never mind the fact I sold him the reason he probably got hurt in the first place.

A couple guys help him off the rig. One of them shoots me a look. Turns the dope in my pocket to lead. I feel it sag against my hip.

Someone yells to take a break off the rig. There'll be a safety inspection. That means naptime. Not much else to do anyway.

I sell a few more pills. Help the workers relax. We spread out in the shadow of the rig to avoid the sun. The fall afternoons still get warm.

I'm asleep a bit when I wake to the soft strums of a guitar. It's coming from the other side of the shade.

And that's when I realize how deep in shit I actually am.

Chapter 103

I recognize the fingers playing the guitar. It's Moe. One of Les's guys. Missing two fingers at the knuckles on his fretting hand. He plays for us around the fire back at the Man Camp.

Moe's at the wrong rig, though. Works at one 15 miles from here. Maybe the sun is in my eyes. Something's off.

I take a seat next to him.

"Moe?" I say.

"Hey, man," Moe says.

"Don't you work on a different rig? What are you doing here?" I say.

"Les sent me. Said I should make sure you make it back to the Man Camp," Moe says as plain as describing grass.

He plucks a couple strings. They're black from his filthy hands.

"Why?" I say.

Moe twists a machine head back and forth. Tries to tune the D string. Always tuning.

"Said you needed to be monitored. For your own good," he says.

How kind of Les to send a dunce. Probably the last favor he'll ever do for me.

I mask the growing panic in my gut with an eyelash. Making a clean break is going to be a lot more difficult. Meatheads like Moe might be dense, but they're dedicated all the same.

"Good to see you, Moe. You taking requests?" I say. Change the subject.

"You think I'm good enough to take requests? Oh, thanks, man. I appreciate that," Moe says. "But, no, I'm not taking requests."

Nothing more to say from me then. I rise. Moe grabs at my wrist. Looks me in the eyes like a dog under a dinner table.

"Got any?" he says.

I nod. Drop him a small baggie.

"I owe you one, brother," Moe says.

"You owe Les," I say.

"It'll all work out," Moe says.

What a sick game Les rigged. As sick as the junkie spin cycle itself. Up and down. Up and down. Up and down. It'll catch Moe soon enough.

Moe's guitar licks start smooth. Strong. Pleasant. Then they flutter into a frantic cacophony. The music dissipates into noise.

I tune it out. Head back to the rig. The safety inspection is over. Time to get back to work.

I feel the revolver shift in my pocket as I fire up the pressure washer. There's only going to be one way out of here.

PART THREE: EXTRACT

Chapter 104

The two men with the black truck are back, including the scrawny guy. They park 50 yards from the RV.

Sam watches them through a crack in the blinds. Hopes they can't see her eyes pacing back and forth.

The pair yell to someone in the distance. Sam picks out a few words here and there. Can't make sense of anything.

One of them pulls a knife out. Shows it to the other one. It's a small hunting folder. A Buck 110.

The sight of the knife turns Sam's wounds hot. She holds a hand over them. Feels the heat creeping through her skin. Infection. She didn't tell Wil, though. That would mean camp doctors.

Sam pops a few ibuprofen tablets. Keeps the inflammation down. It's the only legitimate medicine in the RV. It'll have to do until they can leave. Then she'll see a real doctor. All in due time.

The two men saunter out of view. Sam scribbles on a piece of paper. Helps her think. Starts on the semblance of a plan. But there's no time to do that.

Open air and the scrawy guy replace where the side door of the RV used to hang. The scabs on his face contort into a grin.

"It's time, girlies," he says.

Chapter 105

*L*es flags me down on the way into the Man Camp. Waves the blue Navy Vet hat in the light of the horseshoe pit.

I stop the truck. Roll down the window. Play it cool.

"Did Moe show up?" Les says from his wheelchair. Works himself up alongside my door.

"Right behind me," I say.

"Good," Les says.

Moe drives by right on cue. He waves out the window. Les returns the gesture.

I debate whether to ask why Moe was sent out in the first place. Decide against it. Don't want to raise suspicions.

Turns out Les already has his. Two burly guys show up on the passenger side. One has a shotgun. The other is opening the door.

I raise an eyebrow to Les.

"These guys need a ride?" I say.

Les points his cane at my face.

"Why don't you come on out of there?" he says.

"What's going on?" I say.

"You'll see in a minute. No need to get upset or anything. Just come on out," Les says.

I exit the truck. Les keeps the cane trained on my face.

The guy in the cab follows right behind me. Digs into my pockets. Pulls out the revolver, the dope and the cash.

"Les?" I say. "What's this about?"

Les lowers the cane.

"This is for your own good. Wouldn't want you acting like an idiot," he says.

"Acting like an idiot about what?" I say.

Les sighs. Or laughs. Hard to tell.

"Growing up, we kept chickens in the backyard. Rhode Island Reds. Great egg-laying hens," Les says. "But eventually those hens went dry. No use in keeping them around."

The guy with the shotgun searches the bed of the truck. Nothing back there but tools.

"One day a big grocery store opened nearby. Suddenly we had cheap eggs and cheaper meat. Having our own hens wasn't as important," Les says.

Not sure where the latest edition of Les's Fables is headed.

"There a point to this story?" I say.

"Yes. It's to distract you while my guy searches your truck," Les says. Nods to the guy with the shotgun. "Anything?"

"Nothing," comes the reply.

"Good," Les says. Wipes at his face with his hand. "I forget the rest of this story, but it's relevant."

"Meaning?" I say.

"Meaning that I'm going to fuck test your lady friend," Les says. "And you shouldn't be upset about it. Nothing personal. Strictly business."

The wind picks up when he says it. I think I'm hearing him wrong. Ask him to repeat it.

He does. That's what I thought he'd said.

"Seems to me she healed up real quick. Just yesterday, she asked to take a walk. I need to make sure she's serviceable," Les says. "Sure, these workers would plug a gopher hole. A few probably have. But still, I'm trying to be a good capitalist here. And this disarming you, this is just a precaution. For my protection and yours. You understand."

I play along in hopes of buying us more time.

"You don't want to be in this same predictament again

316

ISONSON

in a few days. Why not allow some extra time? Might help in the long run," I say.

It's the best I can think to say. It's not enough. Les is still humping that civilization building delusion.

"You've got to understand what pussy's worth out here. The companies won't admit it, but whoring has a long history with any boom. It's integral to the success of the boom itself. The whores wind up pregnant, so they start hospitals and schools. That sends a signal to the legit businesses. Helps settle the boom. These oil companies, they get it. They depend on people like me to deliver. In return, I get to run a Man Camp and whatever else I please. The objective is bigger than you or me," Les says.

I can't even see Les anymore. He's just a black dot in my vision.

I think of Sam. Pluck an eyelash.

The black dot squiggles. Grows arms. Legs. Like the shadow people who come out at night.

I pluck another eyelash.

"What are you doing? Pulling your eyelashes out?" Les says.

I slip the lashes onto my tongue. Swallow.

The hot panic in my gut cools. I can see Les again.

Les says, "Here's the deal. I'm going to go stick a hot brand on that cow. You can have your gun back in the morning. If she's ready, she'll join you out at the rig. Can fuck in your truck."

"What if she's not ready?" I say.

"Then she won't be worth a damn after I'm through with her anyway. Probably drop her off in Minot somewhere. Winter's coming soon. Can't afford dead weight in the Man Camp," Les says.

"I see," I say. Think of how good it will feel to kill him. That is if Sam doesn't get him first.

Les motions to the burly men.

"They'll be seeing you to your RV," he says. "Keep watch over you all night. Again, it's just a precaution. Keep a cool head and you'll be fine."

It's going to be long night. Or a short one.

Chapter 106

O ne. Two. Three. Four.
One guard for each side of my RV. Les isn't playing around.

They stand about 50 yards away on each side.

One. Two. Three. Four.

Four black dots in my vision. Like four shadow people.

I know they're guards. My mind sees them differently. Projects my subconcious into the night. The shadow people are back. Even after the sky turns black I can see them. Darker than dark. Blacker than black. Holes in the night.

Sleep is out of the question. I go through the RV instead. Try to find anything that could be used as a weapon.

Les's guys already sifted through everything. No knives. No clubs. Not even a can opener. Must've done the search after they knocked the door down.

They half-assed the door. It's hanging in place with duct tape. Good. It'll make it easier for me to leave. Because Sam is somewhere in the camp. And there's no way in hell I'm spending the night in here.

I'm right back where I was before I came to the Man Camp. Able to look out at the world. See the illusion of choices in front of me. But stuck like flies in a jar.

Seriously.

Like flies in a jar.

Seriously.

I look out at the shadow people. They stack on top of each other. Like acrobats. Make a tower. No. A silo. Or a grain bin. I know this is my imagination. I let it play out anyway.

My fingers go for an eyelash. There's nothing left. I hook the edge of the lid with the corner of my black fingernail. Dig until the tender skin is dirty red.

It mimics the feeling of plucking a lash. The pain is sharper, though. Cuts all the way down to my feet. Unzips a hole in me big enough to slide a coffin through. Or two. Stacked like sentences on a page. Like a grain bin.

Joe.

Elma.

I killed them.

I remember everything.

Chapter 107

*S*am knows she's naked on a blanket. She just can't see it.

The room could not be darker. Blacker than the night. The kind that brings blindness. Are her eyes shut? Or open?

This is Les's luxury RV. She knows that much. And she's in the bedroom.

She pulls at the restraints around her ankles. They're anchored to the bedframe. Positioned to keep her ankles apart.

Sam tries to wiggle her toes. They've long since stopped responding. Feels like they're missing. But they're there. She'd helped cinch the restraints onto her ankles.

She's the one who cut the lights and undressed herself. Who told Les's guys she "wanted to prove herself." Then jerked both of them off in the dark. They left without restraining her hands. Perfect.

There's a noise outside the room. The jagged creak of a door. Then wheels. A grunt. Footsteps.

Footsteps?

They shuffle and scrape the floor.

Sam palms the one thing she has on. Tumbles the lucky raccoon penis jewelry around her neck. Its slim profile curves upward like a saber.

The door opens. A fire of light ignites the room.

Chapter 108

M y mind slips back to that day. *The* day. One year ago. A cold, windy fall day. Kind of like this one.

My arms mimic the motions played out in the memory. It must look like I'm dancing to the guards outside. But I need this. I need to feel it.

In the memory, I stand next to my father outside the grain bin. It's a couple hundred yards from the house. He slips me a disgruntled look.

"Been a while since you've been home," he says. "You find work yet?"

Work. Always the work questions.

"Yeah. Odd jobs here and there," I say.

He doesn't know the half of it. I'd broken into a storage shed the night before. Stole a bunch of hydraulic fluid for a tractor. Sold it at a discount to another farmer. Then got shitfaced.

"I'd keep you busy around here," my father says. "Put you to work. You know that."

An offer of more work. It's as far as he ever went with being generous.

But he and my mother fight too much. Money. Contracts. Sign this. Don't sign that. It's constant.

I'm too old to stick around through that bullshit. But I'm still too young to turn down an offer of breakfast.

Of course, there's a trade off. I have to help with the grain bin before we eat.

"What's up with the grain bin?" I say.

"Red, the sheriff, he was out here the other day. Wants to rent it over the winter. Might sublet it to Joe for a few things," my father says. "But there's a chunk of ice and grain frozen at the top. Need to get inside. Just get a quick look at the problem."

I survey the grain bin. Old and small. Probably the worst one in our inventory. The grain goes in at the top. Comes out a shoot in the bottom. There's a door on the side for surveying problems inside. Happens a lot this time of year.

"Why's he want to rent this one? Why not one of the newer grain bins?" I say.

This one leaks like a sieve. That's probably what caused the frozen chunk up top.

"Beats me," my father says. "But it's money. Honest money. Not like that funny contract your mother wanted me to sign."

So that's what they've been arguing about lately.

My stomach makes a sound like a coffee grinder. I glance over to the house in the distance.

I turn my head back to my father. He's opening the side door to the grain bin.

I can already tell that something is wrong. There's a scraping sound at the top of the grain bin. I open my mouth to warn my father.

Too late.

Chapter 109

T he next memory feels less like a movie. More like a painting. I'm at an art exhibit. Stare at three coffee mugs on the wall. Each one has "Seriously!?" printed on it in bold, black letters. They're Joe's mugs. Won them from a TV game show.

Two mugs rest in the hands of Joe and Elma inside a pair of coffins twisting their way into my gut. The third mug dangles off the pinkie of my father.

I killed Joe and Elma. And I may as well have killed my father.

Guilt swallows my gut. Makes me feel hollow. Sucks at the backside of my skin. Pulls it close. Like my outsides are folding into my insides.

It's my fault.

I should've warned my father.

I shouldn't have killed Joe.

I shouldn't have killed Elma.

Now I know why I had a hard time remembering these things. My mind protected itself. Good reason, too. I want to vomit.

I'm back at the RV now. Look out the window. The shadow people have turned back into guards. One of them makes his way toward the RV door.

One other thing I know. I killed those oil workers, too. My fate is sealed. At best, I'll end up in prison. At worst, I'll wind up dead tonight.

I think about my choices. They're only illusions. I know what's going to happen.

I walk to the RV door. I'll leave. Give the guards a fight. Hopefully find Sam before she's torn to pieces.

Or maybe she'll find me first, turn the whole damsel-in-distress bullshit on its end.

I ball my right hand into a fist. Then do a silent count.

One.

Two.

Three.

I open the door. Step out into the night. Feel the invisible hand of the wind push me forward. What I see vacuums the air from my lungs. In front of me isn't a guard.

It's Sheriff Red.

Chapter 110

"Wil?" Red says.

He seems as surprised as me. But relieved, too. And hollow. Exhausted. Exasperated.

"Red?" I say.

I wonder if this is my imagination. A memory painting the sheriff into the night. But there aren't shadow people around. Just a damp, bloody Red.

His limp left arm dangles in a rusty red sling fashioned from a seat belt and a T-shirt. The left side of his body, from shoulder to foot, is the same color as the sling. I see the red is darkest at his left shoulder.

A thick bandage hides his nose. He breathes through his mouth instead. A gurgle growls from somewhere behind his throat.

"Let me in before they see me," Red says.

I hesitate. Do a quick check for weapons. He probably has one. But I can't see it. I let him in.

Red empties himself onto the table in the kitchenette. Breathes deep. Closes his eyes.

The room takes on a smell like sour beach. Salty. Warm. Polluted.

I give Red time to breathe. He opens his eyes. Slides into a chair. Leaves a greasy streak on the table.

"Been running," Red says.

"I can see that," I say.

I also see the handle of a revolver poised like a snake in his pocket.

I don't show my guest any courtesy. My hand tugs the revolver out. Red's face flushes crimson for a second. He's too tired to protest. Just shakes his head.

"You planning on shooting me?" Red says.

"Depends. You here to arrest me?" I say. Keep the revolver pointed at the floor. It's a Colt Anaconda in .45. Never shot one before. I'm a fast learner.

"I had to outrun an FBI agent to get here. Been shot. Driven off the road. Ran over. Slapped around. Nearly killed every mile. But I made it," Red says. "This FBI agent, she's the one who wants to arrest you. I just want to talk."

"About what?" I say.

"You killed two too many people back in Betrug, Wil. The FBI got involved. Out of my hands," Red says. Coughs. "But I had to find you. Make peace with you."

I raise the revolver. Aim it at his head. Not that I plan on killing him. I just don't know what else to do. Need a platform to bargain with in this confusion.

"Seriously, Wil, listen to me. I'm not here to bring you in. I just need to explain things," Red says. "At least let me do that. Then you can kill me. And I can go to the grave at least half in peace."

I keep the revolver up. Think about the epiphany a few moments before. Try to keep the emotion off my face.

"I'm listening," I say.

Chapter 111

R ed lays it out. Barely breathes between sentences. The revolver in my hand raises and lowers with my temper. Gets quite the workout.

Red says, "I'd been taking federal grant money for overtime for a while. The county's been getting them since 9-11. Supposed to pay for extra patrols around sensitive areas. ICBM sites on the prairie. Power plants. Railroads. Standard stuff.

"The money was few and far between, though. Until the oil prospectors showed up. Lots of them. Suddenly people started caring about North Dakota again.

"The hippie freaks were next. Trying to get a head start on the fracking. They weren't flower children. More like the hardcore kind. Eco-terrorists. They weren't fucking around.

"Dumb bastards. I shipped most of them back to the West Coast. But then I run into this one guy. He was something else."

Red coughs. I toss him a bottle of water. Use my free hand to do it. Glance out the window. The guards seem unaware of Red's visit. They might in a minute depending.

Red takes a drink. Continues.

"This guy, he was the real deal. Some sort of veteran, so he knew what he was doing. Turns out he's more than I can handle. So I call up DHS, Department of Homeland Security. They refer me to a private contractor. Someone they say can 'take care of problems like him.'

"I get phone calls from someone called Jane. Jane gives me instructions. What to do. Where to go. Who to break. There was a ton of collateral damage. People went missing. Turned up dead in ditches. Couldn't go anywhere without being tracked. Just really bizarre stuff.

"Folks around town, they started noticing. A few innocent folks got hurt. I didn't like that. Beat on the hippies, the eco-terrorists, all you want. But leave my Betrug neighbors out of it.

"So I walked away from it. Told Jane I was done. And after all that trouble, Jane never caught the guy. He got the hell beat out of him. But he lived another day."

It sounds a lot like Les. I keep quiet. Let Red talk.

Red says, "Here's where the shit hits the proverbial fan. DHS and Jane, they weren't going to let me off easy. Said they'd pin all that mayhem on me. Make *me* out to be the eco-terrorist as a fall guy to cover their own asses.

"We struck up a deal instead. An oil company needed land from a particular Betrug farm family. Not to drill on, though. To make a road. The company wanted the entire parcel, too. Seems the owners weren't interested in selling. But the road was a keystone for a larger project. The company needed that land. Without it, this project was dead.

"So if I helped convince the land owners to sell, Jane and DHS wouldn't stick me in prison for the mess that eco-terrorist guy made. Care to take a guess which family owned that farm?"

I wish Red hadn't asked. I don't kill him before he can tell me the answer. But it's really fucking hard.

"*My* family's farm," I say.

I crack my neck. Check the window. The guards moved out of sight.

Red's story makes some sense now. My folks always fought about a contract. Must've been the one with the oil company for that road.

Red says, "Your father wanted no part of that contract. Your mother did, though. Neither would budge. That wasn't the answer Jane wanted to hear.

"Now listen, Wil. This is important. I didn't mean for things to go the way they did. But everything fell into place. Your mother and I, we'd been...you know. Things weren't good with your folks in the first place."

I should just shoot the motherfucker. But I wait. I'll do it at the end. I want to hear him say it.

Red says, "I'm not proud of the way I became involved with your mother, Mary. But we fell in love. Between the DHS and Jane thing, the affair and the big money that contract could bring in, everything lined up. The only thing in the way of the good life for us was your father. Your mother and I, we came up with a plan. I rented a grain bin. Covered my tracks a little bit by saying it was for Joe. Then I ..."

My ears don't even register what Red says. Tune it out. My brain already knows by now. Red rigged the grain bin. Set it up so that frozen grain chunk would crush my father as soon as he stepped inside.

I don't hear anything. I just see those eyes. My father's eyes. Right before he died. The surprise. Like they're saying, "Seriously? This is how I die?"

Then I see the same look in Joe. In Elma. And everyone else I've killed since the grain bin.

The only person I've pointed a gun at and haven't seen the look in is sitting in front of me. That's about to change.

My ears go back to working again.

"...I put in my report it was a freak accident. After that, the plan was to marry your mother. Then sign the contract. Take the money. Run away together. I used the cover of comforting a widow so people didn't suspect anything when I went over there," Red says.

I cut him off.

"Did my mother sign the contract yet?" I say.

That's the only reaction he'll get from me.

Red says, "No, she didn't sign. Your mother had a

harder time with all this than we thought going into it. You should've visited with her more. It would've helped."

After what Red just told me, I'd be surprised if I ever speak to my mother again.

I chew on my chapped lips for a few long seconds. Taste the sliver of blood backwashing onto my tongue.

"What about Joe hiring me to kill Elma?" I say. "That part of the plan, too?"

Red shakes his head.

"I kept a tail on you for good measure. Was in the Betrug bar that day you talked to Joe," he says. "But I swear I had nothing to do with that. It just sort of happened. Joe wasn't exactly on the straight and narrow himself. Not the worst thing that you popped him, honestly. And Elma, well, she would've exited this planet in a bad way no matter what."

I think back to that day. One shotgun. Two point-blank shots. My derailed train of thought.

"All of this started with the grain bin accident you set up," I say. "My mind's been a mess ever since. Maybe I wouldn't've killed Joe and Elma. Wouldn't've ran off to the Bakken. Wouldn't be standing here right now."

Red opens his mouth to say something. Stops when I cock the revolver. And there it is, that look, one more time.

Chapter 112

*T*he Colt Anaconda is a double-action revolver. Cocking the hammer isn't necessary. I could've just pulled the trigger and ended this shithead. But I want to watch Red squirm.

Red's nerves dance in the chair. He's shaking.

"What else you got to say?" I say.

Red chokes. Takes a drink of water.

"I'm sorry. I am so, so sorry. I'm 100 percent responsible for murdering your father," Red says. "It's why I wanted to find you. I had to tell you. I'd take it back if I could. But I didn't have a choice. Even if your mother got a divorce, there was no guarantee that land would've been sold."

No, asshole. You're responsible for everything. Sounds like some people in town might feel the same way.

"So that's it then? You just wanted to talk?" I say.

"Your mother wants you back at the farm one last time. I know it's hard, but consider going back with me. Not for my sake. For hers," Red says.

I shake my head. Laugh because I don't know what else to do.

"I don't owe her anything. And I'm sure as hell not going anywhere with you," I say. Hear a loud truck drive by in the distance. Switch topics. "Who's this other person coming to get me?"

"She's an FBI agent. She's working with Jane. One of them will get you in the end," Red says. Cracks a pathetic attempt at a convincing smile. "But maybe you and I can honor your mother's wishes with a visit anyway."

"Wait. So how did this Jane get involved with me? I thought Jane was just for the eco-terrorist guy," I say.

"I called her. I wanted her to find you before the FBI did. I needed to tell you what had happened," Red says. "But then Jane and the FBI started working together anyway. I about died trying to outrun them here."

I keep the revolver on him and an ear to how quiet the night outside the RV becomes.

"So Jane, the same person you say rained hell on Betrug, now wants me? And you called her to do it?" I say. "Holy shit, Red. Why have I not killed you yet?"

"You'll get your chance to kill me. But first, let's see your mother," Red says. Sweaty and desperate. "Come on. What do you say?"

I don't give him a kiss off. No final words. No acknowledgement.

I just pull the trigger.

Chapter 113

I 'm not aiming at Red when I fire the revolver. His time will come later.

I spin on my heel toward the door. It's one of Les's guards, the scrawny guy. There's a pump shotgun in his hands again. Good for him. Face is seriously fucked up, though.

Seriously.

The scrawny guy says something just before I fire. Maybe a threat. Or an offer of a beer.

I'm beyond listening at this point. Don't care. Unleash the .45's bark and bite. Finish the surgery on his face in one shot. He won't be getting up this time.

Enough of the Midwestern guilt. I won't feel bad about anything. This isn't a situation I asked for in the first place. Never had a choice. These aren't nice times. This isn't a nice place. I'm not a nice person.

My mind hasn't felt this clear in a long time. Seriously.

Red bolts up out of the chair. "What did you just do?" he says.

"Sit the fuck back down," I say. Decide he'll be staying here. Don't want him slowing me down.

Nearly plant a bullet in him as I say it. But I don't. Not yet. I need to find Sam first. Also need a way to get around those guards. I can hear them shouting somewhere in the distance.

I pop the cylinder out of the .45. Count the cartridges. Five unfired. One with a dented primer, fired.

I change my mind about Red.

"Stand up," I say. Poke him in the ribs with the revolver.

Red stands. Raises his right hand as a show of

surrender.

"You got here how?" I say.

"I've got a truck," Red says.

"Give me your keys," I say.

Red doesn't hesitate. Tosses the keys to me.

"Take me to the truck. Walk in front of me. No questions. Do what I say," I say.

I stuff the revolver into my pocket. Pick up the scrawny guy's pump shotgun. Take stock of the ammunition. Two slugs in the magazine. One in the chamber.

With the revolver, that brings the ammo count to eight. Not much compared to the dozen or so guards Les keeps around.

Not sure why I'm focusing on math at a time like this, but it keeps the tunnel vision away. My blood bubbles with adrenaline.

I grab Red's arm in the sling. Swing him in front of me. Push him out the door. Follow a few steps behind.

The other guards are on scene. One is straight ahead. The other two come from the left. All sport shotguns. Fifty yards and closing. All illuminated by truck headlights.

I'm not too worried. They must be horseshit guards to have let Red slip into my RV anyway. That's the kind of reliability meth gets you.

The thought only crosses my mind for a split second. I empty the shotgun into the two guards on the left. Aim. Fire. Pump. Repeat. My targets are too stupid to not stand there in shock as I drill exit wounds through their backs wide enough for a fist.

I cycle through twice on empty before realizing it. Time to get moving again.

I scramble into the night. Stick Red between me and the guards approaching on the right. They open up. Nothing connects.

Our 50-yard head start turns into 75. Then 100. Soon enough we're at Red's truck. It's hidden behind a small hill of trash.

"I drive," I say. Stop Red from opening the passenger door. Point to the bed of the truck. "You get in the back."

"What?" Red says.

"You deaf? Get in the back," I say. "And make sure you catch any shots at the cab."

Red winces. Climbs into the bed. Have a nice ride, asshole.

I toss the shotgun onto the seat in the cab. Fire up the truck.

I kill the lights, though. A truck is a lot bigger than a person. No sense in giving them an even better target. There's a bit of light from inside the Man Camp anyway.

Now to figure out where the hell they've got Sam.

Chapter 114

I hit something big with the truck. Person big. Or maybe just a pile of trash. Hard to see without the lights.

I glance back at Red. He's still there. Clings to the sides of the truck bed with his good arm for dear life.

Another volley of gunfire detonates behind us as I pull into a main Man Camp artery. It keeps my foot on the gas. Les's guys don't seem to care about collateral damage. Figures.

I turn the wheel by memory. Cut across a narrow aisle of tattered campers and shitty RVs. Red shouts something. I can't hear.

I realize too late he's trying to warn me. The truck hammers through a quilt of power cords and garden hoses. The Man Camp is stitched together with them.

The force of the truck tugs at the web. Campers and RVs tip into the aisle behind the truck. Everything slows to a crawl. A shotgun slug vaporizes a side view mirror.

I beat the gas pedal with my foot. There's a pop either from the truck or the mess in the aisle. Either way, I'm moving again. The tires churn in the clay as the truck careens forward.

I quick look back at Red. He's plastered against the bottom of bed. Tries to stay small to avoid the gunfire. Looks like he lost his arm sling. Oh well.

I finally turn on the headlights. Much better. The wreckage behind me will keep the guards away for a bit. But the headlights only illuminate the fact I have no clue where I am.

I've driven through the Man Camp plenty of times. But I just toppled several of the landmarks I normally use. It's only night, prairie and heaps of roughneck trash now.

I drive to the edge of the Man Camp, head up a small hill and make a quick U-turn. Gives me a better view. It about knocks Red out. He's hanging on like a rat in speedboat.

I spot a line of dancing flashlights in the distance. It's headed for me. Les's guys.

My eyes follow the lights back into the Man Camp. Les keeps his RV surrounded by his strong arms. That must be where they're keeping Sam. Follow the flashlights and I'll find Les. Or so I hope.

I gun the truck straight into the line of flashlights. Outlines of surprised faces scurry out of the way. There's a report from a shotgun somewhere. I just go faster.

I swerve to clip the first one. He's standing next to a pile of trash at the entrance to an aisle. In an instant he's on top of the heap.

There's another one up ahead. He's frozen in place. Probably never faced down a truck before. *Thump.* And he now he won't have to worry about doing it again.

I watch the rest of the flashlights go out. They'll probably wait me out. Start shooting once I stop. It's going to be tricky to get out of this place.

I spot Les's RV straight ahead. Or rather, I see the reflection of a wheelchair next to an RV. Must be him.

I hit the brakes, but not too hard. Let the truck coast into the wheelchair first. The mangled metal rockets off into the night.

I'm already out the door, revolver in hand, when the truck finally stops. Red moans something from the bed. I'm surprised he can even breathe.

"Stay here. Just have to make a quick stop," I say to him.

Red starts crying about something. I'm moving too fast to hear or care.

My legs sprint to the RV door. Adrenaline convinces me it'd be quicker to kick it in. My foot hits too hard. Make a hole in it instead.

I try the handle instead. It's unlocked. So much for dramatics.

I'm prepared for something awful inside. But I'm still surprised by what I see.

Chapter 115

The inside of the RV is too quiet. Too still. And tense. Like a mirror paused in free fall. Then I spot her.

Sam stands in the kitchen area. Hands limp at her side. Damp sundress sucks at her pores. Bright red coats her right hand up to her elbow.

She offers me a crooked, knotted up smile.

"About fucking time my ride showed up," Sam says.

The sight is so bizarre I'm almost surprised when she talks.

"You OK?" I say.

"Yeah. Fine," Sam says.

I scan the RV. No signs of Les. The door to the bedroom is shut, though.

"Anyone else here with you?" I say.

"Just Les. He's in the bedroom. Won't be coming out for a while," Sam says. Gives a faux look of confusion. "Say, I think I lost my lucky raccoon penis. You see it around here?"

I match her look. Only mine is genuine.

"I guess not," I say.

"Oh, silly me," Sam says. "It must've slipped up Les's dickhole when I went down on him. Talk about a coincidence, huh?"

Holy shit. That's brutal. The thought of the long, thin raccoon penis jewelry curving up like that makes me wince. I feel it in my own crotch.

"Oh, OK," I say.

Sam raises her red hand.

"I just gave it a twist," she says. "And pulled."

Holy shit.

"I think I get it," I say. "Is he dead?"

"If he's not, he wishes he was," Sam says. Seems satisfied.

I look out the window. Spot flashlights headed our way.

"We need to get going. Les's guys are going to be here any second," I say.

Sam laughs.

"So serious," she says.

We bail out of the RV. Red's moved himself into the cab of the truck. I make him ride bitch between me and Sam.

Red offers a weak wave hi as I start up the truck. Looks a cough away from death.

"Who's this?" Sam says.

I pass the Anaconda to her.

"I'll explain later. If he moves, kill him," I say.

I watch Red's eyes fix on Sam. He stares hard at her. Like he's not sure if he recognizes her. Sam does her best to avoid eye contact.

The report from a shotgun behind us has me hitting the gas. Dumb bastard puts a hole through the window of another RV next to us. Terrible shots, those guys.

Time to get the hell out of the Man Camp.

Chapter 116

*B*eth counts the shotgun blasts. Force of habit. Her training drilled it into her head. Count shells in. Count shells out.

She also learned how to manage pain. Red left her with a seriously bruised leg. Got into a scuffle at a gas station. Red ambushed her. Grabbed the directions to Wil. Not even a bullet-busted shoulder kept him off her trail.

Beth stays crouched on top of a hill overlooking the Man Camp. An earpiece connected to her cell phone keeps her informed.

Jane.

"Truck. Three inside. One shotgun. No shells. One revolver. Five shells," Jane says in Beth's ear. "They're leaving the camp now."

Jane's voice sounds deep and labored. Like a boombox low on batteries.

Beth stays quiet. The hill isn't so far away that no one could hear.

"They'll head to Wil's family farm. Go there," Jane says. "Make him sign the contract. Then do what you will with Wil. I'll deliver you the eco-terrorist at the same time."

Jane says it like Beth has options. "... do what you will." But Beth knows she doesn't have options. There's only one. She'll arrest Wil and make a career of it. Everything is icing on the proverbial cake. Provided Jane comes through on handling Tom's demise.

"I've already taken care of loose ends at the FBI," Jane says. "Don't worry about cover stories. Or your dead partner. You'll be fine as long as Wil signs."

Eerie timing. As if Jane could read Beth's mind.

345

Maybe she can. Jane seems to operate on supernatural levels of technology. It's like that old Arthur C. Clarke quote. Advanced technology is indistinguishable from magic.

Beth wants to ask what will happen if Wil doesn't sign. But she already knows the answer. Makes her wonder how she'll handle things being outgunned.

Jane has an answer for that, too. More uncanny timing.

"Don't worry about back up, either," Jane says. "You'll be covered. Just keep him alive. Get him to sign."

Beth thinks of the spare mag pouches on her belt. Mentally counts the shells inside. Should be enough. Hopefully.

She watches a line of headlights follow Wil's truck out of the Man Camp. They dim from view as the wind conjures the first snowflakes of the fall.

"Get back on the road. I'll give you directions," Jane says. "You failed with the sheriff. You let him get ahead of you. This is your last chance. Now hang up the phone."

Beth follows orders. Hangs up. Limps back to her car. Hopes her leg feels better in a hurry.

It's not like she has a choice.

Chapter 117

Back at his house, Gus picks up the phone. Uses his good hand to do it. Even though Red shot him in the leg, the horse doctor said to favor the whole side. It'll help the stitches heal.

"You're not out of this yet," the voice on the phone says.

Gus doesn't recognize it. Can make an educated guess anyway.

"Jane?" Gus says. Tries to hide the surprise in his voice. Wife and kids are home.

"The land the FBI agents promised you, you still want it," Jane says like a statement, not a question.

Gus clears his throat. Even that causes him to wince. The stitches on his leg are already too loose. The horse doctor used a big needle.

"I'm in no shape to do anything," Gus says.

"Yes, you are," Jane says.

"No, seriously, I'm not," Gus says.

"I don't remember asking you a question," Jane says.

"Yeah, well, I don't remember ... uh," Gus says. Tries to think of a snappy comeback. Fails.

There's a pause from Jane. Then a beep. Static takes over the line.

Gus wonders if he should hang up. Jane comes back before he can.

"You will go to the Reynolds farm. Wil's parent's place. You won't get land. But you will get money for your trouble. You can collect it there," Jane says.

"What do you mean?" Gus says. Waves away his curious wife.

"The money will be waiting inside for you. Easy as

that. You deserve compensation for your troubles. You performed well," Jane says. "But bring a gun. Just in case."

Gus looks out the window. The yard light highlights the start of a snowstorm. The glow forms a sort of yellow snow globe floating in mid-air.

He thinks about the last time he went out on a limb for money. Things didn't go so well. But this doesn't sound too bad. No strings attached.

"I just go over to the house, right? The money will be waiting for me in what, a briefcase or something?" Gus says.

"Yes. On the kitchen table," Jane says.

Gus shrugs to himself.

"Sounds easy enough. You want me to leave right now?" he says. "The weather is picking up."

"It's now or never. Hurry," Jane says.

"The way you say it, I don't have much of a choice," Gus says.

"No. You don't have a choice. Now. Or *never*," Jane says.

"I could always choose never."

Jane raises her voice. It doesn't sound angrier. Just louder. Like someone turned the volume up on a speaker.

"The last person who mocked me didn't live to tell about it," she says.

"Fine, fine. I'm leaving," Gus says.

He hobbles downstairs. Comes back up with Safety, his single-shot shotgun. Kisses the kids goodbye. Makes up an excuse for his wife about why he has to leave. It's as flimsy as how he told her he'd accidentally shot himself in the leg.

It's the last time they'll see him alive.

Chapter 118

*M*ary Reynolds gets up from dinner. Same as last night. And the night before. Soup. Hasn't stocked up since Jon died. Answers the ringing phone on the wall.

"Mary," a voice says.

"Who is this?" Mary says.

"A friend," Jane says. "I can't talk long. There's someone coming to your house. He has a gun. He's looking for money. Don't trust anything he says. I thought you should know."

Mary starts to say something. The line goes dead before she can.

Something catches her eye outside. Headlights. They creep toward the house. Could be Red coming back with Wil. Not likely, though. He would've called.

It's probably one of those oil company people. Still trying to get her to sign that contract. They stopped being polite months ago. Probably sending some strong arm to rough her up.

Mary doesn't think twice to go for the shotgun leaning against the disheveled bookcase.

Chapter 119

I slow the truck. We're on the main drag back to Betrug. Snow's making it hard to tell if we're even moving.

The line of trucks in pursuit fell out of sight a while ago. Doesn't mean they aren't close. Visibility is down to about six inches. Most of the drive's been by memory. Seems to be working better than before.

I hit the high beams. Try to cut open the flaky night. Just makes things worse.

"Should we pull over?" Red says.

It's the first thing anyone's said since we left.

"Who are you again?" Sam says.

She keeps the revolver pressed into Red's battered side.

"I'm a sheriff. Name's Red," he says.

"Where's your badge?" Sam says.

"Left it at home."

"What kind of sheriff are you?"

I don't get why Sam's being so tense with Red. Then again, why shouldn't she? Wouldn't anyone who's just cored out the inside of a dick with another dick be a little on edge?

"He's who he says he is. I know him," I say.

That gets an eyebrow from Sam.

"What are you two? Friends?" she says. "Didn't you tell me to shoot him if he tries anything?"

"I don't know. Are we friends, Wil?" Red says. Attempts a smile. Face is a little too bruised for that.

What a bastard, trying to game Sam. I let my silence do the talking.

"We're not pulling over, are we?" Sam says.

"Like hell we are," I say. "We're going back to my folks' place."

"What's there?" Sam says.

"Not much. But it's not here," I say. "Then we can sort out a little issue. My mother, Red and I are going to have a little talk."

Red frowns. Now it's his turn to go quiet.

"What issue?" Sam says. Pokes Red with an elbow.

I'm starting to notice how often she asks questions. Nothing wrong with that. Just an observation.

"You care if I tell her?" Red says to me.

I laugh. Should've shot him when I had the chance. Now he's just playing the martyr.

"How considerate, you asshole," I say. "Please, go right ahead."

Red sighs. Still avoids making eye contact with Sam.

"There's an oil company that wants the property. Needs to build a road. Very important," Red says. "They're willing to pay a shitload of money for the rights. But first Wil's mother needs to sign the contract."

Sam looks to me. "Why didn't you tell me about this?" she says.

"Honestly, I needed Red to remind me. He showed up out of the blue. Told me all about it," I say. "Warned me even. The FBI is coming for me."

"For what?" Sam says.

"I took a shotgun to ..." I start to say. Then change my mind. "... far. Too far. Let's leave it at that."

Sam's not satisfied.

"Actually, let's not. What's going on?" Sam says. "You remember that I'm the one with the gun, right?"

Red chimes in before I can respond.

"It's my fault. I got Wil into some trouble," he says.

Fuck it. No sense in hiding the truth. Not after everything at the Man Camp. It's not like we're a truckload of angels here.

"Yeah, it is your fault," I say. "But here's what happened."

Red and I take turns laying everything out. We don't hold anything back.

Sam hears how my parents fought over that contract. How Red and my mother had an affair, then conspired to kill my father in a grain bin "accident" in order to get the contract signed. How they said Joe had rented the grain bin to make Red look better when he moved in on my mother. How in a coincidence I wound up killing Joe and Elma. How I fled, coming back to reality at that bathroom where I met Sam.

Red fesses up to all this, as he should. Explains how he worked with Jane earlier to put the pin on an eco-terrorist, likely Les. And how he called Jane to find me once he realized the FBI would take over my case. But Jane switched sides on him, working instead with two FBI agents.

"It's not enough to make up what I've done. But I wanted Wil to know that grain bin wasn't his fault. My conscious got the best of me. Wil won't believe me, but it did," Red says. "That's why I wanted to find him before the FBI. To tell him. So he wouldn't live his life thinking he caused his father's death."

The snow outside picks up. I turn the windshield defrosters up.

"And you didn't remember any of this?" Sam says to me.

"What was that word you used, Red? PDFT?" I say.

"PTSD. Post-traumatic stress disorder. Probably a result of watching your father die. Messed with your memory," Red says.

"Is that why you were pulling out your eyelashes?" Sam says.

My eyelid twitches. That anxiety in my gut is gone. Talking with Red did something to me. A bit of closure. No urge to pull an eyelash out now.

"Yeah, I guess it was. I didn't even realize it," I say.

I don't mention the shadow people. No sense in that. Just loose threads from my misfiring brain. I think.

"So what's the deal with this contract now?" Sam says.

"Mary, Wil's mother, never signed it after all. Had a harder time with everything than we thought," Red says.

"Couldn't Wil just sign it?" Sam says.

I shrug. Guess I hadn't thought of that before. Not a high priority for me in the grand scheme of things. Won't be talking to my mother after everything blows over anyway.

"Not as long as Mary is alive," Red says. Chews the words for a second. Shakes the feeling away.

I clear my throat. Turn the wipers on. The snow is getting wet. Clumpy. Like driving through cottage cheese.

I change the topic.

"Hopefully Les's guys lose us in this snow. We'll bug out at my folks' house. Then get the hell off the prairie," I say. Nod to Red. "Oh, and probably shoot this bastard."

"Sounds like a plan," Sam says. Elbows Red. "Sound like a plan to you, sheriff?"

Red chuckles. Tries to disarm the question. Not so set on dying anymore. Not like he was back at the Man Camp, all soaked in guilt. Damn. He got over that in a hurry.

"Think how that'll hurt your mother, Wil," Red says. "You two can take off. I won't turn you in to the FBI. Promise."

"Go to hell, Red," I say.

Thirty minutes later, I swing the truck into the driveway. The headlights reveal something I wasn't expecting.

Someone beat us here.

Chapter 120

*T*he snow traces a set of tire tracks leading into the driveway up ahead. Look fresh.

I slow the truck to a crawl. I don't stop, though. That's just asking to get stuck. Snow's getting deep.

"Probably that FBI agent," Red says. Cradles his bad arm. "Maybe you should turn around."

"No one asked you, asshole," Sam says for me.

I glance at the time on the dashboard. Midnight. We've been on the road for three hours. Should've been less. The wind beats on the snow. Seems like each flake could come though the windshield.

And it might. That wind is screaming. This truck is shitty.

"To hell with it. I gotta piss," I say.

I give the accelerator a gentle nudge. The "low gas" light flickers on the dashboard. Good thing the driveway is mostly downhill.

Chapter 121

W alls of white buttress the house up ahead. Looks more like an oversized snow fort. That's how snow works on the prairie. Two inches can look like two feet. Snow piles up on whatever stops it.

Like the house itself, the snow drifts point east. Everything does. The trees around the house. The outbuildings across the yard. The few spears of grass treading above the snow.

I keep the truck in the tracks pressed into the driveway. Come to a stop in the driveway behind another truck. Snow melts on its hot hood.

My eyes trace the route of a second set of tire tracks. They just keep going past the driveway. Not unusual. People cut through the driveway to get to the section lines. It's legal to drive section lines in North Dakota. Some folks take that to mean they can trespass. And others just don't give a shit.

"Gus," Red says.

"What?" I say.

I kill the headlights. Leave the truck running.

"That's Gus's truck," Red says.

"Who's Gus?" Sam says.

"My deputy. Former deputy," Red says. Rubs his hands together. Even I can feel him clam up. It's not from the cold outside. "Guys, this is not good."

"Great. We can say hi," Sam says. Motions the revolver toward the house.

Red frowns as I turn off the truck. I keep my eyes on his.

"How many rounds you got in that revolver?" I say. Need a reminder. The counting is comforting. Might just be a replacement for pulling out my eyelashes, though.

Sam pops open the Anaconda's cylinder. "Five of six," she says.

I think to the shotgun behind the seat. It's empty.

"Red, you keep any ammo in here I don't know about?" I say.

"In the glove box," Red says.

Sam clicks the glove box open. Finds one stray .45 shell mixed in with moldy cigars and paperwork.

"Some sheriff you are," she says. "You run around with one spare in the glove box?"

"It's all I got," Red says.

Sam picks the lone empty casing from the cylinder with her fingernail. Loads in the replacement.

"Ready?" she says.

"Let's go," I say.

I exit through the passenger side behind Red and Sam. The wind's too strong on my door.

It only takes a second for the snow to coat our faces. Have to hide them under our arms. Wish I could look around a bit before going inside. No use.

We shuffle up to the wide deck that skirts the front door. I let Red take the first fall on the narrow stairs. Snow coats the first crooked step. I should know. My bad measuring made it that way.

I open the door. Step aside. Sam shoves Red through first. Good thinking. Because the scene inside makes me wish I had that shotgun.

Chapter 122

Sam flicks on a dim light as we enter the kitchen. I breathe deep. Look like a doper doing it with a nose coated in white powder. Smells like home.

The lingering aroma of meat and potatoes. The damp cure coming up from the basement. Earth peppered into the walls from a lifetime of prairie wind. Home.

Red calls into the house. Sam keeps the revolver up. Stays behind him. Keeps her back to the wall.

"Gus? You there?" Red says. Wipes the snow from his forehead. "Mary? Hello?"

There's a noise from upstairs. Or maybe it's from in front of us. Sounds more like a raccoon than a person. Too many feet moving too quickly.

"Gus?" Red says.

Silence.

Red turns back to us. "He must be here. No way he's outside," he says.

"I'm right here," a voice says from the dark.

It's coming from the living room adjacent to the kitchen.

Chapter 123

"I'm surprised you remember me, Red," Gus says. Gus stays in the dark of the living room. Still as a rock pile. Can only see the outline of him and a shotgun.

Red takes a step forward.

"Stop," Gus says. "Take another step, I'll shoot."

"You're not a real popular guy, Red," Sam says.

"Who the hell are you?" Gus says to Sam.

She squints at the living room.

"I had the same question. Can't make you out in the dark," Sam says.

"I can see you just fine. And I prefer to stay over here," Gus says from the shadows. "I'm a reserve deputy sheriff. About to be sheriff by default any minute. Are you Jane by chance?"

Sam shakes her head. "My name is Sam," she says.

"Sam's a boy's name," Gus says.

"Yeah, well, Gus's an ugly name," Sam says.

I want to snort a laugh. Too busy inching away from Gus's voice.

Gus's outline shifts. Like he's trying to keep his weight on one side.

"You here to give me my money or what, Red?" Gus says.

Red shows Gus his palms before speaking. "We don't have any money," he says.

"Then why'd I get a call telling me to come here to get the money?" Gus says.

Another voice from the darkness of the living room, this one female, chimes in.

"No one's getting any money," the voice says.

Chapter 124

Now it's Gus's turn to be in the crosshairs. His voice shows it. It breaks as he talks.

"Who's there?" Gus says into the darkness. "I've got a gun."

"So do I," the voice says. "I'm behind you."

I keep inching myself toward the front door. This is no place to be caught unarmed.

Red's face looks like he just shit his pants. Twice.

Sam stays put. Squeezes the Anaconda tight. Looks amused by what's happening. Tiny smile peeks out of the corner of her mouth.

"My name is FBI Special Agent Beth Haen. I'm one of the agents you talked to from before," Beth says. Her voice is full, solid. Someone here to take control. Still out of view, though.

"Oh, so you're here to give me my money," Gus says. Sounds like every bumpkin prairie dog ever.

I watch Sam's eyes dart between Gus and Red.

"No. I'm here to give you two choices, Gus," Beth says from the dark. "You can leave now. Or I can shoot you dead right here. It's up to you."

"That's the second time tonight I've had someone threaten me with a gun," Gus says. "Didn't work out so well for the first one."

"You didn't hurt Mary did you?" Red says. Looks around the room.

"She didn't give me a choice. Cracked a shot off as soon as I pulled up. So I shot back. Hit her pretty good. She ran off. Might be outside. Might be inside. No idea where she ended up," Gus says. "Now what about my money?"

Red's rage shoots tremors across his body. Can't say I feel the same way. Not after what he told me.

I hear Gus shuffle toward a wall. A hand scratches at it for a light switch.

"Stop what you're doing," Beth says.

A red laser sight cuts across the living room. It connects Beth's position to Gus's sterum. Casts two crimson shadows over the dark room.

"What about my money?" Gus says again.

"Hey, Red. You want me to shoot this Gus guy or what?" Sam says with a smile. She's enjoying every second of this train wreck. Turns to me. "Or maybe I shoot Red? What do you think?"

"Everyone just stop. Now," Beth says. "No talking. No moving. No one gets hurt."

Gus's fingernails claw at the wall. It's no use. The light switch for the living room is in the kitchen. Chalk it up to the mysterious art of prairie wiring. It's closer to Red than to Gus.

Red's breathing gets labored. Panicked. His hands twitch. Face contorts.

"Gus. Stop. Moving," Beth says again.

"Just a minute," Gus says.

Red can't help himself. He darts his hand to the light switch. Flicks it on.

The switch may as well have been attached to Beth's pistol. Both it and the light fill the living room at the same time.

Chapter 125

I see it all in hyper detail for reasons I can't explain. The light shows me everything frame by frame. I can even spot Beth's first bullet rifling in midair. My vision tunnels in on it. It's followed by two more.

Two leaden mushrooms blossom against Gus's chest. The third catches his head on the way down.

Back in real time, I look to Sam. She keeps the revolver on Red. No change in expression. Still masking that smile.

Seeing her confidence keeps me loose. I can't help but match her smile. She glances back at me. I let out the nervous laugh I held in before. The way this night's been, it seems appropriate.

Red remains frozen at the light switch. Beth's attention shifts to him.

"Not a step forward. Not a single step," Beth says.

A weak "hi" is all Red can say. I remember how he mentioned outrunning an FBI agent. Beth must be it. She looks a flinch away from putting him down.

"Seriously, Red. Is there anyone who doesn't want to kill you?" Sam says.

I help Beth along. Better for her to do it than Sam. Or me.

"Kill him," I say to Beth. "He's not worth the linoleum he's standing on."

Beth doesn't break her gaze.

"I'm not here to kill Red. I just want him out of my way," Beth says. "My business is with you, Wil."

Red contorts his head toward me. "Run while you can. Get as far away as possible," he says. Has trouble forming the words through clenched teeth.

There's a genuine ring to his warning. Not sure how far I'd get anyway. Truck's out of gas. Storm's upgrading into a blizzard. Better to take my chances with Beth in here.

Just need to clear something up first.

"Would someone please shoot this mumbling fuck already?" I say.

Red stops breathing. His frantic eyes shift between Sam and Beth.

"Works for me," Sam says. Ends Red's life with a messy shot to the head.

Chapter 126

G ory debris from the shot litters the kitchen. Use my sleeve to wipe the bits from my face. Just smears more of Red's red. My shirt is freckled with the container of his final thoughts.

"Thank you," I say to Sam.

"You're welcome," she says back. Wipes a smudge of grease from her cheek.

I turn to Beth. Time to take control of the situation.

"The guy had it coming. You understand," I say.

"I know," Beth says. She's calm. Steady breaths.

"And another thing. We just saw you kill that deputy," I say. "That makes the score tied in this shit storm. Don't think we won't rat on you if you try to haul us in."

"I know," Beth says again.

Both she and Sam realize they're aiming their handguns at a corpse. Shift to training their barrels at each other.

"You sure know a lot. Good for you. Now let's talk about you putting down that gun," Sam says. Smiles wide.

"In a minute," Beth says.

"No. Right now," Sam says.

Beth's gaze travels past Sam. Looks out the kitchen window. "There's someone coming up the driveway," she says.

I turn to look. Well, I'll be damned.

Turns out we didn't lose Les's guys after all.

Chapter 127

H eadlights from five tan trucks stop outside the house. A sixth vehicle pulls up behind them. A black SUV.

A dozen guys pile out of the caravan. Each one has a shotgun, a handgun or both. One of them is hoisted down into a busted looking wheelchair.

Les.

"Shit. Les is here," I say. Turn to Sam. "I thought you took care of him."

"I thought I did, too," she says. Not smiling anymore. Looks shocked.

Beth picks up on Sam's shift in demeanor.

"What do these people want?" Beth says.

"They're from the Man Camp and they're here to kill us. And probably you," Sam says.

"Hand me Gus's shotgun," I say to Beth.

Beth doesn't move.

"We can get back to killing each other later. Trust me," I say. Start for Gus's body.

Beth waves me off. Uses a free hand to pass me Gus's single-shot Winchester 37 shotgun. Tosses a few shells.

I load up while Sam locks the front door. Beth latches the back door on the far side of the living room. Must've slipped in that way earlier.

I start counting again. Sam's revolver has five rounds left. I carry four shotgun shells in my pocket and one in the gun. Beth's probably packing an Old West range war's worth of magazines. But we're still outgunned.

I turn off the lights to give us some cover. The house is sheeted in the gray, snowy night.

The interior immediately returns to illumination. Headlights outside fire high beams through the windows.

At most, we have six seconds to decide what to do next.

"We hole up in the basement and hope for the best," I say. "Or we make a run for it."

From a crouched position on the floor, Beth starts to say something.

Scratch that. We have two seconds.

Les's small army is shouldering its way through the front and back doors.

Chapter 128

*L*es's beefy toadies barrel in like stampeding cattle. Anything in the way is plowed to the side. Furniture. Lamps. Tables. Books. Corpses.

Sam, Beth and I back up in reaction. Intersect in the living room. Get sandwiched between human haybales on either side.

The room goes silent. Stays that way until the creak of a wobbly wheelchair rusts the fragile air. The crowd in the kitchen parts. Reveals a deadly pale Les. Wears a wool blanket over his lap.

"Some weather we're having," Les says. Voice is cracked, slow and low. Painkillers. Lots of them.

"How's the crotch?" I say.

"Fuck you," Les says. Scowls.

"I'd say the same to you, but a raccoon already did," Sam says to Les with the kind of evil grin that could light a fire all on its own.

"You're dead tonight, bitch," Les says. Points his steel cane.

"What a coincidence. I was just thinking the same thing. Right before I corkscrewed that penis up inside you. It's still there, isn't it?" Sam says.

Les's eyes sag as he barks back. It's too unintelligible to make out. A couple of his goons raise an eyebrow.

Sam seems to get it, though. Trains the revolver on Les's chest.

"Your guys can kill me. But you're going to hell with them," Sam says. "Unless you feel like running away while you still can. Excuse me. *Wheeling* away."

I listen to Beth breathe beside me. Still cool as the breeze. Steady. Wish I could say the same. I don't share

371

Sam's attitude about death. Wish this shotgun wasn't a single-shot.

"This is going to feel good," Les says. Turns to his latest sergeant-at-arms. "Shoot all three of them. But don't quite kill them. I want to personally beat the last breath out of each one."

Les aims his cane at Sam's face. Then mine.

I feel my face making that "seriously?" expression. It's only fitting. The prairie howl outside sounds like a long oil train out of the Bakken. It'll sweep me up after they kill me. Provide a proper burial under the snow.

My mind shifts back to that day at the grain bin. Instead of guilt, instead of panic, instead of fear, I feel peace. There's comfort in the strong cradle of compression forming around my chest. Almost cathartic to feel the weight of the grain crush me.

I exit my thoughts. Return to reality. Only a second's gone by. Everyone in the room is still poised, guns ready.

That's when the phone on the kitchen wall rings. I don't think Les would've picked up had Beth not flinched at the sound.

"Who the hell is this?" Les says as forcefully as someone on painkillers can into the phone.

Les listens. His pale face turns from irritated to stoic. Holds the phone up for the room to hear.

"Thank you for showing up, everyone," a metallic voice says from the phone.

Chapter 129

No one in the house makes a sound. Even the wind quiets down for the call.

"For those who don't know, my name is Jane," the voice says. The tone shifts from robotic to a regal female. "My thanks for disposing of Red, Gus and Mary earlier. Their usefulness had expired."

So Gus did kill my mother. Hard to say how I feel about that.

Sam's eyes scan the room. "Are you calling from inside the house, Jane?" she says.

"No," Jane says.

"So where are you calling from?" Sam says.

"Be quiet, Sam," Jane says.

"You know my name?" Sam says.

"I know all of your names. And I have you like flies in a jar," Jane says.

Les remains silent. Unlike everyone else, he stares at the floor.

"So who are you, Jane?" Sam says.

"Let's say I'm like the wind. An invisible hand that guides what needs to happen," Jane says.

Sam doesn't let up. Only one thinking clearly.

"Still doesn't answer my question, chief," Sam says. "Who are you working for?"

"You don't need to know the specifics," Jane says. "I'm done talking to Sam. Now I'll address Les."

Les could hang up the phone. The defeated look on his face lets everyone know he won't. Somehow finds the strength to address me.

"Remember how I said around the fire that in the beginning there were the raiders? The ones that eventually formed governments and pulled the strings with invisible hands? Well, Jane is it," Les says. "We can talk about the invisible hand guiding the economy. Write off things like the oil boom as a happenstance of that ghost in the machine. Except the invisible hand isn't just a concept. It's made up of real people directing events for their own purposes. And unless there are people like me, trying to wrestle control away and restart civilization on our own terms, the invisible hand gets to do whatever they want. That was my vision. And I'm sorry you can't be a part of it."

Les sounds as delusional as every other out-stater that comes here expecting to change the world. Always pushing a vision instead of making the money they came out to make in the first place. Even if he's right, so what? Doesn't change anything. I'm still festering in this clusterfuck of guns and cold sweat.

"Nice to finally catch up with you, Les," Jane says through the phone. "Let me clarify for everyone. Les came to the Bakken as an eco-terrorist. Tried to blow up oil rigs. Kidnap prospectors. Wore that Navy veteran hat to avoid suspicions. Not that he ever served. Of course, this was when he could still walk more than five steps at a time."

Les stays silent. His little dissertation on conspiracy theories drained him.

"My, shall we say, *employers* were alerted to Les's presence. They weren't too happy. I used the late Sheriff Red to coordinate a response," Jane says. "Les got away somehow. But not before Red put him in that wheelchair.

"Red owed me one after that. So I had him focus on the contract that wasn't getting signed at the Reynolds household. The one you're standing in right now. I needed the father, the stubborn one, out of the way if he didn't choose to sign.

"Everyone thinks they have a choice. Sign or don't sign. Do this or don't do that. Go here or go there. Rich or poor. But it's just an illusion when the end has been predetermined by people like me, the ones who present the choices in the first place. You exist in *my* world."

The guns in the room shift in their respective hands. Itchy trigger fingers don't mesh well with philosophical diatribes.

Sam fires out a question.

"So was Wil and I running into Les's Man Camp just a coincidence? Or did you arrange for that, too?" Sam says.

"Individuals who don't pattern well, like Wil, are harder to contain. That the two of you wound up in that Man Camp was just a pleasant coincidence. One that we'll be happy to bring to a conclusion in a moment," Jane says.

"We?" Sam says.

The word barely escapes her lips. The room swims in a flood of gunfire. But it's not coming from inside the house.

Chapter 130

The windows of the house shatter simultaneously. A blast of wind shovels snow inside. A cannon of cold joins the blisters of gunfire coming from outside. Headlights from the trucks illuminate the unreal carnage like an old film projector.

The gunfire drills holes in the heads of Les's men. They let loose a couple stray shots on the way to the floor. The kitchen and living rooms look like the containers under the grates in a slaughterhouse.

The shots skirt around Sam, Beth and I. We stay frozen in place. There isn't enough time to react anyway. The three of us look like parasites huddled inside an intestinal infection.

A second later the shooting stops. Les still holds the phone in his hand. The bullets missed him, too. They didn't spare the walls and floor, though. Drywall dust and sawdust hang in the air.

It's just the four of us now. And Jane on the phone.

"Are you there?" Jane says.

Les looks at Sam. Then at me. Seems to have a hard time believing any of us are still alive.

"Here," Les says into the phone.

"I know what this looks like. But in time you'll understand why I am in the right. I am the good guys. You are the bad guys," Jane says. "Now give the phone to Beth, the FBI agent."

Les wheels himself forward. Passes the phone to Beth. She keeps one hand on her pistol as she takes it.

I scan the shattered windows. No sign of anyone outside. Hard to see anything with the headlights and weather.

Beth palms the greasy phone over her ear for a minute or so. Hands it back to Les.

He holds the receiver up for us to listen. Jane resumes.

"It's time to wrap this up," Jane says. "Beth has a contract with her. The Betrug Café in town opens in about an hour. Beth, Wil and Sam will get in a truck. Head into town. Someone will be waiting for you at the café. That person will go over the contract. Wil will sign it. Donuts and coffee are on me. Doesn't that sound nice?"

I clear my throat. Start to say something. Then I stop. My thinking is getting foggy again. It's like that snowstorm outside blew its way into my brain. Hell, the wind is strong enough, that might've happened.

Sam elbows me. "I don't think we have a choice here," she says.

"Yeah, I guess not," I say.

It helps to have her nudge me along. Straightens out my head.

"OK, Jane. Me, Sam and this FBI person. We'll go into town. Sure," I say.

The math doesn't add up in Les's favor. His face twists into a snarl.

"What about me?" Les says into the phone.

"My people will be coming for you. We're going to have a little talk," Jane says.

Les drops the phone. Reaches under the blanket on his lap. Hoists a big bore revolver hidden between his legs.

"You people can go to hell," Les says. Aims the gun at Beth's chest.

Four shots stab holes in my eardrums. One from Les. One from Sam. One from Beth. And one from outside in the snowstorm.

Four shots. Two connections.

Les slumps in his wheelchair. Slinks to the floor. Beth takes a deep breath from the floor. It's her last.

Sam keeps her revolver on Les. Empties another two rounds into him. Pointless, but satisfying nonetheless. Nothing's rational in this room.

It takes a couple minutes of letting the adrenaline burn off for us to realize Jane's been talking.

"Pick up the phone," Jane says.

I pick up the phone. Hold it up so both Sam and I can hear.

"I'm here," I say.

"Change of plans. The contract is tucked inside Beth's jacket. Get it," Jane says.

Sam rifles through Beth's pants pockets. I wave her toward the jacket. Her cool veneer finally cracks. Nerves are getting to her.

"She's got it," I say after Sam shows me.

I expected the contract to be thicker. It's only a few sheets zipped inside a plastic bag. Not very impressive considering all the trouble it's caused.

"Good. Now find a set of keys for a truck outside," Jane says.

"Wait a minute. How do I know I'm not walking into a trap? Isn't the FBI trying to arrest me?" I say.

"Don't worry about that anymore. Sign that contract. Collect your money. Live out your life somewhere warmer. Free and clear. Just don't come back here," Jane says.

"And if I don't sign?" I say.

"Your life will quickly become much more difficult," Jane says.

Sam searches the warm pockets closest to her for keys. Comes up with a set for the black SUV.

"Keys. Got them," I say into the phone.

"Good. Head into town. Bring the contract," Jane says. "Go to the Betrug Café. Your contact will meet you there. You'll know when you see the person. No reason to go in armed."

Sam and I are in no shape to walk around town. Both soaked in gore.

"We're messy," I say.

"You're right. We want you clean at the signing ceremony," Jane says. "Check into the motel in town. I'll make the arrangements. Room 27 will be unlocked when you arrive. A fresh change of clothes will be waiting. Clean up. Then head over to the Betrug Café. It opens in a few hours."

The cold gets to Sam. She shivers. It's that or shock.

"Can't we just stay here?" Sam says.

I don't know who would want to do that. This place is a mortuary.

"No. Just go," Jane says.

We pick our way over the bodies. Head out the door.

I squint into the wind outside. Try to find whoever did all that shooting. No signs of life anywhere. Or of my mother's body. Fine by me. Too much snow anyway.

I fire up the SUV. No issues. Sam buckles in next to me. Closes her eyes. Stays quiet as the SUV heads out.

I pause the vehicle at the top of the driveway hill. Take a look in the mirror. Review the splintered image of the house peaking through the blowing snow. Feel the last vestiges of nostalgia. Only lasts a second.

Feels good to drive away. I'm not going to miss this place.

PART FOUR: PROFIT

Chapter 131

Jane lives up to her word about the motel in Betrug. Room 27 and fresh clothes are waiting for us.

Sam and I stay quiet. Take turns in the shower. The warm water rekindles the light in our eyes.

It takes every ounce of soap in the room, but we manage to get clean. The fresh clothes are perfect. Flannel shirts and jeans.

We get a bit of much-needed shut-eye, then head out. The café opens soon.

Sam breaks the weary silence as I start up the SUV.

"So are you going to sign?" Sam says.

It's not like I have a real choice. Like a fly in a jar.

"Definitely. Let's get some money. Get the hell out of here," I say. "Besides, Jane will clear my name. Get the FBI off my trail. Only choice I have is to sign."

Then I pause. Think back to my father. How he resisted signing. I wonder why? Did he see something I don't?

If the money didn't sway him, maybe something else did. Self-determination? Going against the grain? Just being stubborn?

No. Not those things. Something inside me knows the answer already. Just don't want to admit it.

He wanted to keep the property to give to me. To pass down. Just like the generations before. Tradition. It mattered to him more than money.

Not only that, but it offered me a shot at redemption. A future. Hope that I'd sort things out. And now I have that chance. That choice.

Makes me rethink what I just told Sam.

"Good. Sign it," Sam says. "Sell the property. Take the money. We can start a new life together."

I spot the Betrug Café up ahead. An orange OPEN placard faces the street. I spot a luxury car in the parking lot. Too fancy for Betrug. Must be the person we're supposed to meet.

"Or I could keep driving," I say. "Maybe Jane lied. Maybe this is all a trap. This might be the last time we're free."

Sam looks shocked. "What are you talking about?" she says. "Just sign the damn thing. Be done with it."

I think about what Jane said. About the illusion of choice. How we're like flies trapped in a jar.

"What if I just delayed the choice? Stayed in limbo? Nothing would get decided either way," I say.

"Now you're just being ridiculous," Sam says.

She has a point. I do, too. But I turn into the Betrug Café anyway.

Sam gives me a final lecture before we exit the SUV. The decision is still mine in the end. Nothing anyone says can move that pen for me.

We enter the café. A single man sits inside. New blue jeans. Snappy sport coat. Dyed brown hair. Shiny cowboy boots. Million-dollar grin. Trying and failing to fit in on the prairie.

The man stands to greet us like he rehearsed it the night before.

"You must be Wil," he says. Voice is steady and smooth. "Would you and your friend care for a cup of coffee?"

Chapter 132

I shake the man's cool, manicured hand.
"Have we met before?" I say.
"Oh, I doubt it," the man says.
He turns to Sam. Gives her a warm hug.
"And you are?" he says.
"Sam. Hi," Sam says.
"Very nice to meet you. Please call me Cal," Cal says.
"You buy those boots on the drive over here?" Sam says as we sit down.
Cal chuckles. Raises his hands in the air.
"Guilty. I'm a total fish out of the water," Cal says. "I didn't realize no one wears cowboy boots around here. My feet are killing me."
A waitress comes over. Sets down three mugs and a coffee carafe.
Cal looks up at the waitress. "I'm sorry, I thought I ordered orange juice? It's on the menu," he says.
"All out of orange juice," the waitress says. "We have coffee, though."
Cal shrugs. Pours the hot liquid for us. We don't touch it.
"Hungry at all?" Cal says.
"Not really," I say. Especially after last night.
"Too late," he says. "I already ordered."
The waitress brings out heaping plates of bacon, sausage, pancakes and scrambled eggs. Cal scoops food onto smaller plates for us. Motions for us to eat.
"Please. You must be hungry at this time of the morning," Cal says.
I don't even pick up a fork. Sam stares at Cal.
Cal takes a couple pity bites of food. Shows his palms.

"Guys, relax. Enjoy this moment. Have a pancake. You can't sign paperwork on an empty stomach," Cal says.

Sam and I both open our mouths to say something. She gets it out first.

"Are you clueless?" she says.

I know Sam wants me to sign the contract. She's not acting like it with Cal. But I can see how she can't help herself. Last night was brutal. This guy's a total nob.

Cal takes Sam's question in stride.

"Clueless about what?" he says.

"Jane? Les? The Man Camp? Red? Gus? Everything," Sam says. "You're sitting there like it's no big deal. Are you in on this?"

Cal clears his throat. Takes a sip of coffee.

"I don't know those people. Our company runs a few Man Camps. Trailers, dorms and campgrounds. Very clean. Very nice," Cal says. "And I am in on this. The contract, that is. I'm the one who mailed it out."

I don't get the sense he's lying. It's clear he's a glad hand. An oil company hack. He has no idea what it took to get to this moment.

I unfold the contract onto the table.

"Let's talk. Maybe I'll find my appetite," I say.

Chapter 133

*C*al smoothes out my contract. Pulls out his own copy from a briefcase on the floor.

"As you might guess, the energy company I represent does a lot of these contracts. We've been able to simplify the legalese so it's easier to understand," Cal says.

"You dumbed it down for us prairie dogs," I say.

I can't help myself either. After last night, it's fun to take a dig at the poor sap.

"Believe it or not, almost everyone is turned off by huge contracts, not just NorDak folks. It's just a courtesy. Meant no offense," Cal says.

NorDak. I think he meant NoDak.

"Then why'd you make the print so small?" I say.

Cal smiles. It's the same rehearsed one from before.

"To fit it onto a smaller number of pages. We're a green company. Committed to reducing waste," Cal says. "Fracking is clean. Efficient. Practical. The fuel extracted keeps energy prices affordable. The country relies less on foreign energy sourced through unregulated, environmentally unfriendly practices. Fracking is good for the economy and the planet."

Good for him. He can memorize his company's pamphelts.

I squint. Read over a few sections on the contract.

"Maybe you can simplify something for me. What's this road you want to build about?" Sam says.

"Oh, it's much more than just a road," Cal says. "Your property sits in a critical junction of several road, rail and pipeline projects. You could say it's the keystone. Developing it will expedite shipping into the future. More oil products on the market mean lower prices for consumers. Everyone wins."

"How far into the future does this contract cover?" I say.

"Indefinitely, as the contract stipulates," Cal says.

Sam takes a loud sip of coffee. Nudges me.

"Tell me more about these lower prices for consumers," she says.

Cal hits his well-groomed stride.

"This project will help people across all income levels afford natural gas and oil products. That means fewer people going cold in the winter. The elderly won't have to choose between paying heat and electricity. Farmers using grain dryers, like the ones around here, won't go broke during propane shortages. That means lower food prices for everyone," Cal says. "You might say selling this property is an act of charity for millions of fellow Americans. But instead of parting with your money to do it, you walk away with a check."

Now I know why they sent Cal to this meeting. He might be a slick hack, but he's an effective one. My father wanted to give me a legacy to inherit and pass on. This is even better. And I'm wealthier for it.

Just so long as the price is right.

"About the money. How much am I looking at getting?" I say.

My mouth won't close after he tells me. Neither will Sam's. The number is more than I could spend in two lifetimes.

"Is that all at once or spread out?" I say.

"That's just the upfront sum. You'll also pull royalties on energy extraction if we find oil," Cal says. Piles a pancake onto my plate. "Eat up, Wil. Your mouth looks hungry."

My stomach wakes up. I fork the food into my mouth. Best tasting pancake I've ever had.

Cal lays a gold pen in front of me.

"All you have to do is sign," he says. "Picture it, Wil. You'd be young. Rich. Carefree. The two of you can travel the world. Do anything you want."

I pluck the pen. Twirl it in my fingers.

Sam watches me. I glance at her.

"Do it," she says. Links an arm in with mine. Runs a palm over my back. Feels like an invisible hand is giving me a back rub.

I think about my father. The generations of family that worked that farm.

I think about Sam. My feelings toward her.

I think about Jane. About her threats.

I think about the people I've killed. And then don't. Don't want to right now.

I think about the contract. Everyone associated with it is dead. Everyone except me.

"Everything OK, Wil?" Cal says. His eyes shift between me and the gold pen.

I fold a strip of bacon into my mouth. Give it a greasy crunch.

Sam and Cal watch me tap the pen on the table. I match the beat to the clock ticking on the wall.

"Nasty winter this year. That's what they're predicting," I say.

"Oh, yeah?" Cal says.

My body feels like it could float away.

"Seriously," I say and sign the contract.

Chapter 134

I give Sam a long kiss before hitting the shower at the motel. We can hardly contain ourselves. I don't know whether to laugh or cry, jump or sit. Another shower sounds fitting for some reason.

Sam sets my copy of the contract on the nightstand. Flips the gold pen down next to it. Cal let us keep it. Told us it's made of real gold. Imagine that. Quite an upgrade from the gold paint of Sam's raccoon penis jewelry.

I slip off my clothes before the door shuts. Not too worried if Sam can see me. We'll be getting to know each other a lot better in a minute.

Chapter 135

Sam pauses at the nightstand. The latest edition of the *Betrug Bugle* perches on the edge. Front page photo shows Sheriff Red. He's in his truck next to a transvestite.

Jane's ace in the hole. Now on display for all of Betrug to see.

Sam picks up the newspaper. Studies the photo. Spends a long time staring at the transvestite. Sets the paper back down.

Red was hard to pattern, as Jane would say. But there would be no loose ends. No potential risks running free in the world. How soon before Jane would come for Wil?

Not long.

The phone on the nightstand rings. Sam jumps at the sound. Looks around before picking up the receiver. Listens but does not speak.

She hangs up. Reaches her free hand into her pocket. Walks toward the shower. Wraps a hand around the Anaconda.

Only two shots left.

Chapter 136

SIX MONTHS LATER

*T*he waitress opens the *Betrug Bugle*. Leans against the counter at the Betrug Café.

"What are you reading?" says a man in overalls with a burly beard. Takes a seat on the other side of the counter.

"About that old Reynolds place. The one they sold," the waitress says. "Guess they're building a road through it. And some other stuff."

"Really? That's too bad. The market wants what it wants, I guess," the man says. Points to the menu. Licks his lips. "Say, you got any pie left?"

"You want pumpkin or apple?" the waitress says.

"Pumpkin," the man says.

"Sorry, we only have apple. How many pieces you want?" the waitress says.

"Two," the man says.

"There's only one left," the waitress says.

"OK, I'll have one then," the man in overalls says. "But why didn't you just tell me that in the first place?"

"I guess I wanted you to think you had a choice how it would be in the end, even if it didn't really matter. It's good for business," the waitress says with a wink. "Now how about some apple pie?"

Thank you for reading.
Please review this book. Reviews help others find
Absolutely Amazing eBooks and inspire us to keep
providing these marvelous tales.
If you would like to be put on our email list to receive
updates on new releases, contests, and promotions, please
go to NewPulpPress.com and sign up.

About the Author

Benjamin Sobieck works for F+W, the parent company of legacy non-fiction magazines, books, TV shows, events and vertical content brands. It's his job to develop these brands into 21st century businesses. He has worked with *Gun Digest, BLADE, Living Ready, Tactical Gear, Deer & Deer Hunting* (and its cable TV shows), *Modern Shooter, Turkey & Turkey Hunting, Trapper & Predator* Caller, *Antique Trader, Goldmine, Sports Collectors Digest, Horticulture, Writer's Digest, Tyrus Books, The Writers Store, Old Cars Weekly,* and *Military Trader,* among others.

He is the author of *Cleansing Eden, 8 Funny Detective Stories with Maynard Soloman, Gal-Damn Detective,* and *The Writer's Guide to Weapons: A Practical Reference for Using Firearms and Knives in Fiction.* His stories have appeared in *Drunk on the Moon 2, Exiles, Four Days of Madness, Crimespree Magazine, Out of the Gutter, Black Heart Magazine; Thrillers, Killers 'n' Chillers,* and other flash fiction 'zines.

Prior to F+W, he was a crime reporter for the Cambridge *Star* in Minnesota.

Ben Sobieck graduated from St. Cloud State University with a major in journalism and a minor in creative writing in 2007. He helps his family run a ranch in North Dakota, where *The Invisible Hand* is set. Much of what is depicted in the novel is based on actual events.

NewPulpPress.com

www.ingramcontent.com/pod-product-compliance
Lightning Source LLC
Chambersburg PA
CBHW070355260626
47161CB00001B/143